signal to noise

gordon bonnet

one

. . .

Dear Professor Vaughan:

I can't TELL YOU how excited I am to finally write to you. I have studied your work EXTENSIVELY and I finally felt like I was ready to take the plunge and contact you. I admire all you've done to bring the field of cryptozoology into its own as a SCIENCE, which is where it SHOULD BE, not relegated to the BASEMENT which is where many unbelievers want to put it. I'm sure that you are aware of the many who criticize you and your efforts, but you should continue to FIGHT THE GOOD FIGHT.

Toward that end, I would like to offer you my assistance. I feel that with my expertise in psychic contact, and your knowledge of zoology and animal behavior, we could team up to track down Bigfoot ONCE AND FOR ALL. I am prepared to come to

Oregon as soon as I receive your HOPEFULLY posi-tive reply...

Tyler Vaughan sighed heavily, dropped the letter into the recycle bin, and opened up the next letter in the stack.

> *Dear Tyler,*
>
> *I hope you don't mind my calling you by your first name, but I feel like I know you already. I saw your interview on Good Morning America, and watching you talking about working in the field, and imagining you out there in the wilderness, sleeping alone in a tent, got me so hot. You are the most gorgeous man I have ever seen, and I can't sleep at night because I'm thinking about what I'd like to do to you. What I'd start with is that I'd unbutton your shirt, and then I'd slowly slip one hand down the front of your...*

He rubbed his eyes, and pinched the bridge of his nose. It was only nine in the morning, and he could already feel a headache coming on. It always happened whenever he started going through correspondence, which he had had to do at least three times a week since the ill-advised interview on *Good Morning America* four months ago. He'd thought that the volume would decrease, but it hadn't—not since a clip of his interview had found its way onto YouTube and had gotten more than 100,000 hits. He received an average of a hundred letters a day, and three times that many emails. It was either go through them one at a time, or else simply trash them all unopened and risk discarding something important—a bill, a letter from his mother, or, god forbid, an opportunity for grant money. He sighed again, and opened the next letter in the stack. There was no salutation—it jumped right in.

You call yourself a scientist. Well your not. Your just a fraud and a phonie. I heard what you said on the Good Morning show about how their could be bigfoots and that kind of thing, and how we evolved from monkies and these bigfoots could be like our cousins and stuff. Well my opinion is if we evolved from monkies why are their still monkies? Can't answer that, can you, Mr. Smart Scientist? And how did the bigfoots and all survive the Flood? I never saw that Noah went and got any bigfoots, their isn't any mention of them in the Bible and that's my science. I'm sending a copy of this letter to my congressman because I know you scientists get you're money from TAX PAYERS LIKE ME and I'm sick of it...

He added this one to the growing pile of letters in the recycle bin.

At the time, it had sounded like a good idea. Even Joe had said so, and Joe DiStefano, the director of the Cascadia Zoological Research Station, was one of the most cautious men he knew. It seemed foolproof. A quick interview on a nationwide television program, an opportunity to get some publicity for his work, which was monitoring mammal populations in logged areas in the Cascades. A chance to highlight the effects of the logging industry on nature, to talk about Minimum Dynamic Areas and Migration Corridors and Keystone Species and How Logging Roads Generate The Edge Effect. A chance to be a combination of Mark Trail and Steve Irwin, with a touch of Jane Goodall thrown in for good measure.

And the whole thing had gone south the moment the interviewer asked him, a smile in her voice, if he'd ever seen Bigfoot while on his long, lonely campouts in the Oregon wilderness.

Tyler smiled. "Not yet."

"You expect to, then?" She raised one stylishly plucked eyebrow.

"I don't know. As a scientist, I can't definitively say that they don't exist. The Cascades represent thousands of square miles of heavily forested land. We can't rule out the possibility that a large, intelligent, presumably wary primate, some evolutionary distant relative of humanity, could be there somewhere, and we might still have no hard evidence. We discover new species every year, after all."

In retrospect, he should have seen what was happening, and diverted the conversation back onto Minimum Dynamic Areas and the rest of it. At the time, though, being in the spotlight was a little like the couple of times in college that he'd tried drugs. It was disorienting, dazzling, and made him feel like he was in complete control while simultaneously causing him to feel like he was hanging on to the steering wheel of an out-of-control car.

She laughed. "That's true, of course. You never know what scientists like yourself are going to come up with next. Well, I'm hoping that if your research ever turns up proof of Bigfoot's existence, you'll come back on *Good Morning America* and tell us about it. But I've seen some of the photographs and video footage people have taken, and I don't think I'd want to camp out there by myself...."

And that was all it took. In under thirty seconds, he had gone from up-and-coming zoologist, out risking life and limb to preserve our wildlife, to a wacko crank who believed in Bigfoot and heaven knew what else.

Of course, it was a forlorn hope that news of his interview wouldn't get to the peer-reviewed world of grant providers. The "grant denied" letters always came with a good justification—the high degree of competition for funds, problems with his proposed budget, the difficulty of supporting a study that had no clearly defined outcome. It all sounded reasonable, but he knew, and his boss Joe knew, that the interview had played its insidious role. For now, Joe was keeping him on at the research station, but Tyler felt that it was only a matter of time before Joe would realize what a liability his name had become, and then it would be off to try to find another job. And with that interview hanging around his neck like a millstone, what lab in the world would hire him?

And as the funds dried up, the letters and emails started to pour in. Within a week after the interview clip had hit YouTube, he already had them mentally sorted into categories. These were:

1) Offers of assistance. Never financial, of course, but usually very earnest.

2) Anecdotal reports of evidence for some combination of: Bigfoot, modern dinosaurs, ghosts, vampires, werewolves. These included the letters, not common but usually very long, from people who believed that they *were* vampires or werewolves. Many of these people had apparently discovered that they were vampires or werewolves after reading *Twilight* and were eager to come to Oregon to be part of Team Tyler.

3) Proposals of marriage and/or sex, the latter usually very explicitly described. He had been excruciatingly single ever since last year, when his last girlfriend had dumped him for "a man who actually has a career and a salary." It also helped that her new lover had a BMW and a posh apartment in downtown Portland. Tyler, by comparison, lived in a rundown trailer in the Three Sisters Wilderness Area, drove an ancient Honda Civic that went through a quart of oil every two weeks, and his only permanent companion was a chronically flatulent dog named Ahab who humped everything that would stand still long enough. In his more realistic moments, he understood why Kelly had left him. In his less realistic moments, the proposals of sex sounded good, but eventually even those sounded as ridiculous as the missives from people who knew they were vampires because their skin sparkled when they stood in the sun.

4) Hate mail. These usually had the worst spelling and grammar, but they still got under his skin. He couldn't help the feeling that despite the catastrophic damage he'd done to his own standing as a scientist, he'd done worse damage to the reputation of science itself. Given the percentage of Americans who believed the Earth was six thousand years old, the last thing scientists needed was Tyler Vaughan making the whole lot of them look like loonies, spouting off about Bigfoot on national television.

He was on the fifth letter when the front door of the research station squeaked open, followed by the clatter of equipment and clipboards hitting the floor. He didn't turn around.

"Still keeping the US Postal Service in business, eh, Tyler?" came a familiar, rather grating voice.

"Still not tired of that joke, eh, Judy?"

Judy Kahn snorted under her breath. "Between all the trees it took to make the paper for the letters, and the gasoline it takes to deliver them all, you're a walking ecological catastrophe, you know that?"

"You've used that one, too."

"How about the one about you being the only zoologist in the world who has groupies?"

"Yup. Sorry."

"Shit." Judy sat down at her desk. "I gotta come up with some new material."

"That's the truth."

"You going out today?"

"Yeah. I think Lardass may have trashed the remote camera up at T-Three. I'm not getting any signal from it, and it was working fine yesterday." Lardass was an enormous, and completely unafraid, black bear who had learned from campers to associate anything that smelled of humans with food. He had claws that could open up the protective steel boxes around the remote sensing cameras as if they were Reynolds Wrap.

"Joe will flay you alive. That's the third one this month."

"What does he expect me to do about it?"

She shrugged, and grinned. "All I know is that when he looks at the budget, and he sees me putting in for little colorful bands for bird legs, and you put in for three new remote cameras, he's gonna wonder why we need an ornithologist *and* a mammalogist on the staff."

He gave a sigh, and rubbed his eyes with the heels of his hands. "Like I don't have enough trouble."

She wheeled her chair over to him, and thumped him on the shoulder. "I was kidding. Joe likes you. You're not in any danger."

"Like hell. I'm a liability. I couldn't pull in a grant if I had a viable proposal to create life. Maybe I should change my name."

"Maybe you should chill. This will blow over."

"It's not blowing over!" he shouted, picking up a letter from the stack. "Listen to this. 'Dear Tyler: This letter is a follow-up to my letter of May 30. I am writing again so soon because I have once again received messages from the Sasquatch family that lives in the woods behind my house. The big male, whose name is Squaa'nuk, has impressed upon me the urgency of the situation. The Alien Overlords will be returning to earth this September, on the Autumn Equinox, and we must spread the message before then so that mankind is ready for the Psychic Convergence when it happens.'"

"Jesus." Her voice was reverent. "Bigfoot, psychics, and aliens in one paragraph. That's a new record." She brightened. "Did you at least get some interesting offers of sex in this batch?"

He glared at her. "You are a pain in the ass."

"Doctor Tyler Vaughan and his lady friend, doin' it Bigfoot style." She grinned. "That was a new one, right?"

"That was a new one. But no. Nothing tempting, anyway."

"Well, if any of 'em send you sexy pics, you can pass 'em along to me."

"Judy, how the hell am I supposed to know what your taste in women is?"

She shrugged, and grinned again. "Send 'em all my way. I'll sift through them."

He gave another sigh. "You going out this morning?"

"Already gone and came back. I had mist nets to check. I couldn't dawdle over coffee and fan mail like some people."

"Just stop."

"All right, all right. But seriously. You really ought to throw all of that shit away without opening it. Every time you sit down and go through it all, you end up depressed for the rest of the day."

"I know. I'll be okay, don't worry about me."

She thumped him on the shoulder again. "I'm not worried about you. I'm worried about *me*. Because if you don't stop whining about getting letters from the woo-woos, I'm gonna shoot you with your own tranq rifle. And then pose you naked for some pictures. And then post 'em on your Facebook."

"You don't know my password." He looked at her in some horror.

"It's 'DieBigfootDie,' isn't it?"

He goggled at her. "I hate you."

She wiggled her eyebrows at him, blew him a kiss, and then got up and left the building.

A half-hour later, Tyler drove up the rutted logging road through alternating patches of old growth Douglas fir forest and clear-cuts. The lab jeep bounced and lurched across potholes that seemed easily adequate for breaking an axle and leaving him with an ignominious eight-mile hike back to the lab.

Judy had christened this particular jeep *The Millennium Pigeon*, and the name had stuck. In fact, six months ago, she had painted *MP* and a dazed-looking cartoon pigeon on the jeep's side, right next to the Cascadia Zoological Research Station logo, much to the annoyance of Joe, the lab director. From the outside, the vehicle looked as if it were held together by baling wire and duct tape, and that a strong breeze would make it lose important parts, but so far it had proven itself to be a dogged survivor. At first, Tyler had been careful to pack large quantities of wilderness survival gear when he took it out, but after three years of working for the lab and driving the thing daily, he had stopped giving it a second thought.

"I want a new life," he mumbled, hanging onto the steering wheel as he hit a gouge in the road that jolted him so hard he nearly smacked his head on the roof. He'd certainly fucked this one up royally. What could he do? Move back to Portland, maybe wait tables for a while. Disappear into the big city where no one knew him.

Wait. Where *everyone* knew him. A hundred thousand people had seen his face on YouTube alone. Did it make sense to go to a place where he was *more* likely to be accosted by nutjobs?

He took a deep breath and tried to return his mind into more a more rational track. Judy was right. It'd all die down sooner or later. And then he could go back to doing his job.

If he still had a job.

Where the hell had that thought come from? His job was safe. Judy had said Joe liked him.

Yeah. right. "I like Tyler" versus "The lab is running out of money because of Tyler." Which would win?

"Shit," he said in a surprised voice. "I'm screwed."

He jammed in the clutch and braked to a stop in a small pull-off near a huge black rock outcropping, a reminder of the fact that however lush the forest was, the Three Sisters were active volcanoes. Deeper into the wilderness area were recent lava flows that looked like moonscapes. This part of the mountain range, however, had been quiet for a while, and the trees grew in dense, damp profusion on the hillsides, attracting wildlife, hikers, ecologists, eco-terrorists, and loggers in equal quantities. He grabbed his backpack, got out of the jeep, slung the pack over his shoulders, and slammed the door shut. The bang of the door was amplified in this quiet wilderness, an incongruous human intrusion into a place where humans shouldn't be. He didn't bother getting out his handheld GPS unit. He knew this area well. He struck off on a narrow trail, hardly visible from the road.

The trail angled sharply to the left and began to go uphill, around dark boulders, through scrubby thickets of salal, vine maple, and salmonberry, and between dark fir trunks he couldn't have reached halfway around. Hiking in this place always made him a little melancholy. Anywhere within the Three Sisters Primitive Area was officially protected from logging, but there was plenty of beautiful forest outside the Primitive Area's official boundaries destined for the chain-saw. He understood that you can't realistically protect every place on earth, and people need wood, but part of him wished they could get their wood from somewhere that wasn't this breathtakingly lovely.

After a steep scramble up a slope, the trail leveled out in a subalpine meadow. He was reaching the end of the Doug firs, the point where they were replaced by silver fir and other trees of the alpine scree. He stopped to catch his breath, adjusted his pack, and struck out to his right, along the edge of the denser parts of the forest. T-Three, the site of the non-functional remote camera, was about an easy half-mile further along, allowing him maybe five more minutes' respite of blissful ignorance before he got the bad news. Maybe it was a minor malfunction. Maybe a falling branch had knocked against the camera housing and jolted something loose. Maybe the camera's electric eye had stopped working, so it was locked in "standby" mode. Maybe...

"Shit," he choked out, as T-Three came into view. He stood there, closed his eyes, and opened them again, hoping what he'd seen would go away.

The camera housing had been ripped right off the tree trunk to which it had been screwed. The metal sides of the housing were sheared through, and the little remote camera, whose small size belied its cost, was in several pieces. He took slow steps toward the spot, torn between swearing, crying, and kicking a tree as hard as he could.

Years of training as a zoologist had taught him you can't blame animals for being animals. It put him in the peculiar position of being livid with rage and having no one to vent it on.

"You..." He swallowed. Then he screamed, "You fucking *bear*, you!" as loud as he could.

And with that, he picked up the forlorn chunks of the camera and housing, and shoved them into his backpack.

As he was doing so, his brain returned to its previous track.

He could be a wilderness trek leader. Lead hikes. Show people around.

Oh, sure. Great idea, Ace. He could be the new guy on *Monster Quest*. That'd be awesome. Then he'd have even more woo-woos knocking on his door than he did now.

Some desperate part of him flailed around, trying to argue. No, no! He'd be the new Bear Grylls. Tough mountain-climber and backcountry hiker! He'd have to fight the women off with a stick!

Right on. "Bigfoot Grylls." That'd make the women want to jump in bed with him. Good luck with that.

"Oh, shut the fuck up." His brain didn't have any ready response to that, so he slung his pack back over his shoulders, and trudged along the forest edge and back toward the trail down to the road.

Tyler bounced and jolted *The Millennium Pigeon* down the logging road toward the lab. On the drive back, he hoped fervently that Judy wouldn't be there when he returned. He liked his coworker fine, but he was not in the mood to endure her inevitable wry commentary on the state of the T-Three remote camera. He'd have prayed, but he had left the church as a teenager and considered himself an agnostic. Praying to a question mark seemed kind of pointless, so he fell back on that weak sister to prayer, hope.

And as he pulled off onto the gravel in front of the Research Station headquarters, he saw that hope, that fickle bitch, had let him down again.

Judy's car, a trim little Toyota Matrix, was parked in front of the building.

The other lab jeep, a marginally more reliable beast with *NSEA Protector* stenciled neatly on the side, was also there, so that put paid to any chance that she'd gone out to finish up her field work for the day. He ground to a halt, opened the door, and hefted his pack out of the back of the jeep. His expression was grim as brought it inside.

She was tapping on her computer as he walked in. She half turned, and gave him a smile. "Yo, Tyler. You know, I want to say, all day I've been feeling guilty for giving you a hard time this morning."

He dropped the pack on his desk. "That must have been an unfamiliar sensation."

"Damn skippy. I don't like it." She nodded toward the pack. "What's the verdict?"

"Lardass really outdid himself this time." He undid the pack and began to remove pieces. "He turned this one into a modern art sculpture."

"Damn." She stood and gave a low whistle. "He really went all out. There's got to be a way to get that bear to leave these things alone. He should have learned by now that there's never food around them."

"Bears are cunning, not smart." He set the main body of the camera, or what was left of it, on his desk. He pushed a button, and there was a little *snick* sound, and a small plastic square popped out of a slot. "The memory card's still intact."

"Memory cards are cheap."

"Yeah, I know. But if I have photographic proof that Lardass is the one responsible, maybe I can talk Joe into seeing if we can design some sturdier housings. Without the pics, it's… I don't know. Like it's my fault."

"Bears aren't your fault."

"I know. The last time it happened, though, Joe looked at me like I was deliberately destroying the cameras myself to cost the lab money."

"Bullshit. Joe's a biologist himself. He knows how it is. And he'd believe you without photographs."

"Maybe. But hard evidence couldn't hurt." He slipped the memory card into a reader plugged into the back of his computer. The monitor came to life. He clicked on a software icon. "Should I check my Facebook to see if you've hacked me?"

"Nah. No need. I'm waiting for the naked pics. That'll be something worth posting. Selling, even."

He snorted, and double-clicked the icon for the memory card. A list of files came up. Judy walked over and leaned on the back of his chair, looking over his shoulder.

"Well, we got some action yesterday." He clicked on the

first file, which was timestamped 09:13 06-16-2015, and got a blurry photograph of the back half of an elk.

She chuckled. "Wow. An elk ass. That's calendar quality."

"They don't have to be beautiful, just identifiable."

The next four, through that day, showed a variety of chipmunks, birds, and mule deer.

She pointed at the screen. "There's a cluster from last night."

The timestamp on the last fifteen files ran from 21:48 to 21:59, and then abruptly stopped.

"So Lardass killed the camera around ten o'clock." He clicked on the first of the files.

The camera was equipped with a low-intensity infrared sensor, and switched over to taking thermal imaging photos after sunset. The first three were mostly dark, with vague green blurs that gave no information.

Number four was more interesting. It showed an orange blob, some distance from the camera, but clearly an animal of some size.

Five through eight were blurred, but showed that Lardass was getting closer. The infrared shots were usually harder to make out anyway, but the bear was moving at a good clip. There was no detail to go by.

Then he clicked on file number nine.

"Holy shit," Judy said, under her breath.

What was approaching the camera was clearly not a bear. It glowed yellow, red, and orange against the black background, but it was up on two legs. Its head was oval, not bullet-shaped, and its arms were too long and thin to be a bear's.

"That's a person," Tyler said.

"Or a Sasquatch." From her breathless tone, he couldn't tell if she was serious or not.

He chose not to respond.

He clicked the next frame with a trembling hand. Ten was poorly resolved, but the creature was closer.

Eleven showed an outline that made it even more certain that whatever had destroyed the camera was not Lardass. The thing in the photograph was elongated, thin, resembling a scarecrow or a stick figure. Tyler was used to the way that infrared photographs distort appearances, but even so, he'd never seen an image of a human that tall. Or thin.

Could it really be… no, he was *not* going to say it.

Twelve through fourteen were blurred red and orange smudges.

He double clicked file number fifteen.

"Jesus *Christ!*" he shouted.

If what was in front of the camera was not a bear, it was not Bigfoot, either. Long, thin arms, impossibly long even though foreshortened by the angle, reached out toward the camera. A narrow torso took up most of the bottom of the field. But at the top, glowing orange in its own warmth, was an oval head, tilted as if it were looking at the camera in mild puzzlement, trying to figure out how best to destroy it.

The face had no features at all. It was a smooth oval, yellow at the edges, orange in the center. No mouth, no nose, no eyes. It was looking into Tyler's face, as if studying him through the monitor screen, but without any of the usual equipment humans would study something *with.*

"Okay." Judy's voice sounded strained, not at all like her usual dry heartiness. "That creeped me right the hell out."

He looked at the photograph, opened his mouth to say something, and then closed it again.

"So." Her voice still sounded airy and thin. "Guy wearing a mask?" It came out halfway between a question and a statement.

"No eyeholes." He swallowed. "Or breathing holes. Look at it. It's completely smooth."

"Could it be a sensor artifact? Not the whole thing, I mean

—but you know the distortion you sometimes get with infrared. Could it lose resolution around the face? Not enough difference in signal to distinguish features?"

"I guess." He moved the mouse—which his hand had been resting on, frozen, since the image came up—and after a few clicks, opened a saved file. Up popped an image of a bear, glowing brightly in the infrared image, but definitely a bear.

"Well, this is a pic I got of Lardass three weeks ago, when he wrecked the camera out at D-Eighteen. There's no doubt of what you're looking at."

Judy didn't respond.

"And look." He pointed at the image of Lardass's face. "See how there are bright oranges and reds around the eyes and nose? Those are the warmest. The fur insulates the rest of his face, so it's cooler, blue to green." He flipped back to the image of the creature that had destroyed T-Three. His chair, which Judy still leaned on, jerked.

"Jesus. I'm sorry, that pic is the freakiest looking thing I've ever seen."

He nodded. "There's no differential radiation." He zoomed in on the tilted oval face, and used the grab tool to move it around. "It's pretty much uniform. If there were eyes, or a nose, or something, or if part of the face had hair, we'd be able to see it. I'm guessing we'd even be able to see the stronger radiation of the eyes, nose, and mouth through a plastic mask, if it was thin enough. The camera is pretty sensitive."

"So whatever this thing is has a face, but no sensory apparatus?"

"Not the usual ones, anyhow."

"What has a face but no sense organs?"

"That sounds like the beginning of a riddle."

"Damn right it is. And a riddle we've got to come up with an answer to."

"We?" He smiled a little. "You don't have to get involved in this."

"Hell, Tyler, you think I'm not concerned about this? If this is what it looks like…" She trailed off.

"What *does* it look like?"

She didn't answer that. "There's something up there on the ridge that can twist up steel like it's taffy, apparently bare-handed. It's less than ten miles from where I'm standing. You think I'm not gonna want to know what it is?"

"I kind of thought this was my problem."

"It'll be *my* problem if this thing starts ripping up my mist nets. It'll be *both* of our problems if it decides to come down the hill and see what we're doing down here. And from the look of the camera housing, I don't think it'll ring the doorbell first."

"Yeah, but what *is* it? You said, 'what it looks like.' What does it look like to you?"

"It looks like an alien."

"An *alien*?"

"Well, shit, Tyler, what did you expect me to say? That it looks like my Uncle Fred? It looks like an alien from a science fiction movie."

"I thought aliens were cute little gray guys with huge eyes."

"There's the lizard monster thing that burst out of the guy's stomach. That one wasn't cute."

"No. But don't you think it's a little premature to be calling this an alien?"

"You *asked*." Her voice regained some of its previous asperity. "I only said that's what it *looks* like. I didn't say it *was* an alien."

"Fair enough." He paused. "Should I show this to Joe?"

"Are you kidding? He'll have a cow."

"So what do I tell him about T-Three?"

"Tell him Lardass did it. Tell him you didn't get any pics.

Tell him you promise it won't happen again, cross your heart and hope to die."

"But how do I know it won't?"

"Lie, Tyler. Lie. Do whatever it takes to make him not focus any attention on this. And while he's in happy middle management la-la land, you and I can spend some time investigating this and seeing if we can figure out what exactly is going on here."

He turned to face Judy. "How will we do that?"

"To start with, we should go up and look around near T-Three. There might be other evidence nearby that you missed because you thought it was a bear that did the damage. When you've already decided on an explanation for something, you miss things."

"That's true."

"It's only a little after twelve. What I need to do this afternoon can wait. We can go up there, snoop around, see what we can find."

"I can go alone, Judy."

She smacked the side of his head. "Don't be a goddamn martyr, Vaughan," she said, not without affection. "You spend entirely too much time feeling sorry for yourself."

"Okay, okay. You win. I need to eat lunch first, though. I'm starving. I won't be much use if I pass out from hunger."

She grinned. "Another opportunity for naked pics. Don't make it too easy for me. The thrill of the chase is what it's all about."

Forty-five minutes later, Tyler was driving the *Pigeon* back up the logging road, with Judy riding shotgun and hanging onto the door handle to avoid being flung about by the potholes.

"Honestly, I think the likeliest thing is that it's some jerk playing a prank." She looked out of the open window at the dark, shadowed trees. "Maybe a logger. Coulda gotten drunk and decided to wreck our equipment. They hate our guts, most of 'em."

"Still doesn't explain the no eyes thing."

She didn't give any indication she'd heard him. "On the other hand, it could be one of those ecoterrorist wackos. They hate us, too. They think we're sellouts, or actually in the pay of the logging companies. And now that I think about it, they'd be more likely than the loggers to wear a disguise. They'd know about cameras and remote sensing equipment and so on."

"No eyes. Ecoterrorist wackos have eyes."

She sighed. "You've been spending too much time reading your fan mail. You're beginning to believe all that woo-woo bullshit. I told you that was going to happen."

"I'm not *believing* anything. I don't think that thing looked human."

"Well, it looked more human than it did anything else. It was upright and bipedal, with an oval head. Thin. Long limbs. There's nothing else that fits."

"That's true."

"So that's the hypothesis we're going to hang on to, until we find evidence to the contrary. I'm sorry I even mentioned the a-word."

"Me, too."

"At least I didn't mention the b-word. Or c-word."

"C-word?"

"Cryptozoology."

He winced. "I hate that word."

"I know."

He pulled the jeep over, set the parking brake, and they got out, slinging backpacks across shoulders. He nodded toward the narrow trailhead, and they hiked up toward the steep slope along the ridge.

An hour later, they came out into the meadow, skirted along the edge of the deeper woods, and walked across the rocky hillside to the site of the T-Three remote camera.

The camera housing had been pulled right over the screw heads that affixed it to the fir tree on which it had been mounted. One of the screws had actually sheared off, and only a bent stub of galvanized steel protruded from the trunk. The rest of the tree showed no signs of damage.

Judy gazed at the ground, scanning the area.

"What are you looking for?" Tyler asked. "I think I got all the pieces of the camera and housing."

"Footprints." She didn't look up.

"Pretty rocky around here."

"You never know. If this was a science fiction movie, there'd be a footprint in the mud. With seven toes. Long, skinny ones."

"Good luck with that."

They searched the area in silence for about fifteen minutes without turning up any further indication of what, or who, had destroyed the camera. Finally she gave up, and sat down on a rock.

"Okay. You were right. There's nothing here to see."

"No alien footprints, eh?"

"I was joking. I don't really think it's an alien."

"I know. But I still don't see this as being a logger or an eco-wacko."

"Don't start with me about the eyes again, Tyler."

"No, that's not what I mean. I mean, if it was a person, an ordinary vandal, why pick T-Three? It's one of the cameras that's the farthest out in the middle of nowhere. We're not near any of the logged areas, not near anything. In fact, we're getting up close to the tree line. Who would even know it was here besides us? And even if they did, why come all the way up here to trash one camera?"

"Didn't want his picture taken?"

"But who…?" He stopped.

"What?"

"Who would be up here to take a picture of?" He frowned. "Unless it already *was* up here and didn't want us to see?"

"Where? Camped out somewhere in the area?"

"I don't know. But maybe we're missing something. Not right here, but around here somewhere." He stared off into the distance, and pointed. "T-Three was aimed that direction. Maybe there's something over there. Something he didn't want us to see a photograph of."

Judy stood, and wordlessly they struck off uphill across the subalpine meadow, only now beginning to show the white and purple blooms of pasqueflower and the creamy tufts of beargrass. The wind hissed through the grass stems, chilly even in June. He shivered and pulled his jacket closer around him.

"There's a lava tube over there." She pointed and headed toward it.

A broken mass of dark rock pushed up through the meadow, looking strangely menacing against the lush green of the June growth. Showing black against the basalt outcropping was the mouth of a narrow cave. These lava tubes, which only a few thousand years ago were the mouths from which poured rivers of molten rock, were often quite deep, and were fairly common in this volcanic area. They provided shelter for bears, and many other smaller denizens of the high peaks.

"Be careful, Judy. Lardass, or another bear, could be in there. Or our faceless friend."

"I wasn't gonna stroll right in." But she kept walking.

Then she stopped, about thirty feet from the cave entrance.

"What?" He caught up with her, and also stopped.

A wave of fear washed over him, and a vibration twanged its way up his spine. Nothing else moved but the wind.

"Um, Tyler?" Her eyes remained fixed on the cave mouth.

"Yeah?"

"I don't know about you, but I have this sudden feeling that we should leave."

"I was thinking the same thing myself."

There was no doubt in his mind that the source of his fear was the cave. It radiated from the black opening in the rock. He had been in caves before, and had no particular apprehension about narrow spots, darkness, or being underground. The crushing terror emanating from this place had nothing to do with claustrophobia. It felt like the distilled essence of every childhood fear he'd ever had—the fear of the unknown, the fear of a monster under the bed, the fear of death, the fear of graveyards, the fear of looking out of the window at night to find someone watching you. Take all of those, boil them down into one concentrated draught of horror. That was what rolled down the slope toward them. Taking one more step forward wouldn't be difficult, it would be impossible.

"Judy?"

"Yeah?"

"Whatever ripped the camera up is in there."

"I know."

"I think it knows we're here."

She swallowed, the sound audible in the stillness. "You know what I said about us being a team, and all?"

"Yeah?"

"If we're not out of sight of that cave mouth in the next three minutes, you're on your own."

"No argument. Let's get out of here." He resisted the impulse to add the phrase, *while we still can.*

They first backed away, then turned and strode off quickly

downhill, but he caught her looking over her shoulder several times. Probably as many times as he did.

The feelings of apprehension diminished as quickly as they had onset. By the time the T-Three site came back into view, they had nearly vanished. He shivered, shucking the last of the fear.

"That may be the creepiest thing I've ever experienced," he said as they struck the trailhead and went back under the trees. The darkness and shadows of the dense forest, far from being frightening, were welcome. They were a shield, stopping them from being seen by… what?

And what if the creature in the photographs was stalking them right now? Or had reached the jeep already, and disabled it, so that they would be trapped on the mountain at night?

He decided not to mention this possibility, but he did notice that Judy gave a little sigh of relief when the *Pigeon* came into view, sitting tranquil and undamaged in the pull-off.

He didn't break the silence until they were halfway back to the lab.

"What do I do now?"

"Beats the hell out of me. It's up to you if you mention this to Joe. But you know the bind, don't you?"

"What do you mean?"

"If you show him the photos, he'll want you to investigate further, which will mean going back up there and checking out that cave. And if you don't mention the photos, he'll want you to replace the camera. Either way, you'll probably have to go back up there."

"No more *we*, eh?"

She looked at him sidelong. "I don't know, Tyler. I think I'm pretty brave under most circumstances. But if I'd had to go any closer to that cave, I'd have regretted not wearing Depends."

"Me too."

She looked back out of the window, at the dark tree trunks slipping past the window of the jeep. It was a few minutes before she spoke. Finally she turned toward him, a determined expression on her face. "I'm not gonna leave you on your own. You're like the little brother I don't have. But I gotta say, if it comes to the two of us being chased through the woods by that faceless whatever-it-is, I'm gonna do my best to trip you."

two

· · ·

R ainey Carrington scanned across the shelves in the little grocery store, and sighed. There was organic peanut butter, but no organic jam. She'd requested the shop owner to get some in at least five times, to no apparent avail.

"What's the point of organic peanut butter and organic bread if the jam is laced with pesticides?" she asked George Colquitt, who stood behind the counter, leaning forward on both hands, watching as she unloaded her groceries.

George snorted, making his copious mustache flutter. "I been eating Smucker's raspberry preserves every day for twenty years." He began to ring up her purchases. "I never come to no harm from it. Anyhow, I told you, I'd get it when I can, but my distributor can't keep it coming in regular. You'll have to check back next Tuesday."

She gave a heartfelt sigh and ran her hand through her untidy red curls. "Well, I'm just *saying*, George." She tried to keep the exasperation out of her voice. Exasperation was bad for your aura. At the last meditation retreat she attended, her guru said that when she got annoyed, she got olive green streaks in the periphery of her aura, which sounded not only unhealthy but unattractive. "I'll make do with honey, then."

George rolled his eyes a little as she paid for her groceries, and muttered under his breath, "Freakin' hippies," as she was leaving.

She heard him, as she was undoubtedly intended to, took a deep breath to flush out any olive green tendencies, and walked out into the mild sunshine of the Oregon summer. The hillsides were dark with Douglas fir forests, and the peaks of the Three Sisters looked down upon the little town of Crooked Creek from forty miles away, starkly imposing even at that distance. Any feelings of olive green annoyance faded into the beauty of the surroundings and vanished.

Crooked Creek was a village of three hundred, lying on both sides of Highway 126 right outside the Three Sisters Wilderness Area. Like most such villages in the Cascades, it was populated equally with families of loggers and aging ex-flower children, who lived in an uneasy truce most of the time. Rainey Carrington, whose given name was Rainbow Peace, was one of the latter.

Her parents had been traveling musicians in the 1960s and had never really reconciled themselves to the fact that the decade was over. They settled there in 1978 and supported themselves quite nicely by selling homemade herbal teas and marijuana. When their daughter was born in 1984, they tried to register her birth certificate with the last name of Moon-Child, but the Oregon Department of Health Statistics balked at her having a surname different from either parent. They reluctantly consented to have her official last name be Carrington, the same as her father. Even so, they referred to her as Rainbow MoonChild at gatherings, and she'd grown up answering to one name at home and a different name at school.

Only as an adult had she developed a faint sense of embarrassment at having such an unusual moniker, and had begun to introduce herself as Rainey Carrington about ten years ago. Everyone called her Rainey now except for Dale

Blodgett, who was the Chief of Police. Dale still called her Rainbow, usually with an exaggeratedly flowery voice. But she had gone to school with Dale, and happened to know his parents hadn't exactly been establishment either. Shortly before his birth, the story went, Dale's parents had been smoking dope and watching *Wallace and Gromit*, and had decided to name their son Wensleydale. No one nowadays dared call him that, but a few of the natives still snickered about it. Knowing the fact made her feel like maybe Rainbow Peace MoonChild wasn't so bad.

She walked down the sidewalk in the sunshine, the breeze fluttering her ankle-length linen dress, and gave a smile and a wave to the two or three people she met whom she knew. At this time of year, there were always a good many visitors, mostly hikers and backpackers, so despite the small size of the town, there were plenty of people she didn't recognize.

She stopped in the post office and stepped into line behind Mrs. Sullivan. Mrs. Sullivan was a sixty-something widow, the owner and operator of the Three Sisters Lodge, and had the demeanor of a duchess.

"I knew it would happen sooner or later," Mrs. Sullivan was saying, a little archly, to Debbie Nordin as she counted out the change for the stamps Mrs. Sullivan had bought.

"It's sad, though," Debbie said.

Mrs. Sullivan sniffed. "No one's fault but his own. That boy's had every opportunity. The Torgesons never took the stern line with him they should have."

"Did something happen to Kevin Torgeson?" Rainey asked, and Mrs. Sullivan pivoted her significant bulk toward her.

"Oh, Rainey, I didn't hear you come in. Yes, he's run away. He went off with his friends yesterday evening, and never came home. He and Rich had a whale of a fight right before, and Kevin told his father that he'd go live with his cousins in California. The cousins are a lot of deadbeats, so Rich implied, and I'm not afraid to say that Kevin is headed down that same road. Druggies and criminals, that's what they are, he and his delinquent friends. I'd wash my hands of him, the way he spoke to his parents."

"He's their son," Rainey said quietly. Behind the counter, Debbie Nordin rolled her eyes, and shook her head slightly, as if to signal her that arguing was futile, but it was too late. The gauntlet had been thrown down, and Maureen Sullivan was not one to let it lie.

"Well, you are entitled to your opinion, of course." From her tone she obviously meant exactly the opposite. "But if my son broke into someone's house at age thirteen, I'd have tanned his hide. The second time, it would be off to reform school. That's how we handled it in my day."

"I didn't think you had children."

"I *don't*." Exasperation showed clearly in Mrs. Sullivan's voice. "I simply disapprove of how parents today coddle children."

"If he and Rich had a fight, I don't think that's really coddling."

"If they'd disciplined him properly when he burglarized the Parchmans' house three years ago, this wouldn't have happened."

"Didn't he have to do community service? And return what he'd taken?"

Mrs. Sullivan gave no impression of having heard. "It all comes from giving children the lead. It's much like dealing with a horse. The parents must have the reins firmly in hand at all times. And not be afraid to lay on with the crop when it's called for."

"Poor Kevin." Rainey chose not to respond directly to what Mrs. Sullivan had said. "I do hope he's okay."

"If he's not, it's his own doing."

"Here's your change, Mrs. Sullivan," Debbie said.

Maureen Sullivan rotated back toward the counter, and Debbie placed the money into her outstretched hand.

"All I'm saying," Mrs. Sullivan declared, without turning back toward Rainey, "is that I certainly will be locking my doors at night as long as that boy is on the loose."

"I thought you said he was with his cousins in California —" She was interrupted by Debbie having a coughing fit and covering most of the lower part of her face with her hand. By the time she was done, Mrs. Sullivan had sailed out of the post office, nose in the air.

"You really shouldn't bother." Debbie chuckled and shook her head. "No one ever wins an argument with her."

"I wasn't *trying* to argue. A book of stamps, please."

"Hardly matters."

"Have the Torgesons called the police?"

"I don't think so, not yet. He hasn't even been missing for twenty-four hours. I only know because Leah Torgeson came in this morning, and had obviously been crying, and being a nosy bitch, I asked her what was wrong." She nodded toward the door through which Maureen Sullivan had exited. "I guess Maureen had it out of Lydia Jewell. She's Leah's best friend."

Rainey handed Debbie a twenty-dollar bill, and Debbie passed over her book of stamps and counted out her change.

"Did his friends come home?"

"Well, yes." Debbie's brow creased slightly. "They did. Kevin's girlfriend Alexis Wilson was out with them, and they came back in her car. Leah told me she called Alexis, and *she* claimed they dropped Kevin off on Pell Hill Road, not too far from your place, at about two this morning. He said he wanted to walk back. Alexis said he was drunk but perfectly capable of getting the rest of the way home on his own." She shook her head. "Leah's beside herself."

"I'm sure. But how is he supposed to have run off to California, if he didn't have a car?"

Debbie made a dismissive motion with one hand. "Don't listen to Maureen Sullivan. She has an ear for gossip, but she embellishes as much as she actually knows. And she never lets little things like facts or logic get in the way of her opinions."

"I hope he's okay."

"Me too. For all that he's trouble, he's a charming kid when he wants to be."

Rainey nodded. "I've always thought so."

Kevin Torgeson didn't come home that night, nor the night after that.

News in Crooked Creek traveled fast, and bad news was the one thing that could create a temporary bridge between the loggers and the hippies—neither side was immune to the temptation of gossip. Two days passed, the police were called. Chief of Police Blodgett organized a search along Pell Hill Road from the place where Kevin's girlfriend had dropped him off to his parents' house two miles away. There was no sign of him. The deadbeat cousins in California were duly called, and they said they hadn't seen or heard from Kevin.

Blodgett didn't act as if he were inclined to put much time into the case. The boy was a troublemaker, and he was in agreement with Maureen Sullivan, not to mention most of the conservative element in Crooked Creek, that Kevin had somehow gone off of his own accord. The Torgesons pushed for him to continue looking, but it simply wasn't a priority, and everyone knew it, even if Blodgett himself gave lip service to wanting to find him.

It was a drizzly morning the following week when Kevin Torgeson reappeared, and it happened that the first person to see him was Rainey Carrington.

She was outside, feeding her chickens, making gentle clucking noises she was convinced put them at their ease, scattering feed around in the front yard, when movement caught her eye. She looked up the road, which curved up the hill to the right, and saw a person limping down toward her. There was something so forlorn about the figure that she stopped, hand still in the feed bucket, and watched as he approached.

He was about a hundred yards away when she recognized him, and her eyes snapped open wide. She dropped the bucket of chicken food, and it hit the ground with a thud, scattering large quantities of cracked corn around, to the delight of the chickens. She hitched up her dress and ran across the wet grass and out into the road.

Kevin looked at her, eyes blank. His chestnut-brown hair was plastered to his scalp. His t-shirt had a great tear across the chest revealing bare skin and a scrape and some blood underneath. He was barefoot, and his jeans were muddy and soaked.

"Good lord, Kevin! Where have you been?"

Kevin looked up at her, and frowned, and then opened his mouth as if to say something. Then he closed it again. Finally he said, in a clear, calm voice, "I don't know. Can I go home now?"

She stared for a moment, then brushed her hair out of her eyes. Something about the boy's lack of emotion was unnerving. But then he was in shock, of course, he'd been out in the woods for four days without food. She shook herself a little, and ventured a smile.

"Why, of course! I don't have a car, but here." She put her hand on his arm. "I'll accompany you home." His skin was icy cold, and he didn't resist her offer of assistance. Part of her was repelled, for no reason she could identify, and it was with an effort that she kept her hand on the back of his arm.

Not normal. No sixteen-year-old boy would want a twenty-seven-year-old woman helping him along. But he said nothing, let her guide him along down the road as the ceaseless drizzle fell around them.

"Are you okay?" she said, as much from trying to break the odd silence as from curiosity.

"I'm fine, Ms. Carrington. But I'm cold. And hungry."

"You must be. You haven't eaten in days." She looked sidelong at him. "Right?"

He didn't answer, only continued to walk, staring at the road, not meeting her eyes.

Ms. Carrington? He'd never called her *Ms. Carrington. No one* called her *Ms. Carrington.* And she had a sudden, peculiar thought—*Is this really Kevin?* But that was such an absurdity she banished it from her mind.

The Torgesons lived only a half-mile downhill from her house, and she saw their neat lawn, with its perfectly landscaped flower beds, from a distance. She tried to feel any response from Kevin from her hand on his arm—a quickening of the pulse, a shudder of anticipation, something. There was no reaction. He kept putting one foot in front of the other.

Leah Torgeson, a thin, angular woman with dark hair going a premature gray, was walking to her car, keys in hand, when she looked up and saw them walking down the road. She froze in place, and the keys hit the driveway with a jingle. Then she was running up to them, and threw her arms around her son, unable to make any sounds but inarticulate sobs.

Rainey stepped back, and watched them, watched Kevin's hands rise, with a strange, fluttery motion, as he returned his mother's hug, looking as if he wasn't sure how to respond.

"Oh, Kevin," Leah finally gasped out, dashing away tears

with the back of her hand, but still not letting him go. "Where were you? We were so worried!"

"I was lost." His voice was flat, uninflected.

"We've looked everywhere. How did you get lost? Alex said she dropped you off only a couple of miles away…."

"Mom, I'm cold, can we talk about this after I've changed my clothes and had something to eat?"

Leah finally let him go, stepped back, and said, a little distractedly, "Oh, of course. I'm sorry, Kevin, I wasn't thinking. You must be starving. And you're soaked to the skin." She looked over at Rainey. "I don't know how to thank you."

She shook her head. "I didn't do anything. I was out feeding my chickens, and he walked up."

"Let's get you inside." Leah turned and propelled Kevin toward the house.

Rainey frowned as she watched them walk toward the door.

There was something wrong here. It looked all right. But it was not what it seemed to be.

As Leah reached out for the front door knob, Rainey shouted, "Leah, don't forget your car keys! You dropped them in the driveway."

Both Leah and Kevin turned around, and only for a flash, Rainey saw Kevin's eyes narrowed to slits, and felt such a laser beam of white-hot anger that she stepped back. The moment hung, suspended. Then it was over. Kevin's face returned to its previous blankness, Leah yelled, "Thanks," and waved, and went to retrieve the keys. Rainey lifted one hand in a weak return of the gesture.

She turned back toward home. There was no noise but the gentle hiss of the drizzle. Even the birds were hushed. She had to resist several times looking over her shoulder as she walked.

Who did she think was following her?

The sight of her little cottage was welcome, sitting in the

midst of its unkempt tangle of flowers and vegetables, all growing together in disorganized profusion. She retrieved her bucket of chicken feed. Empty. The chickens had taken advantage of the bounty with which they had been provided.

Then she went inside.

She considered changing her clothes, then reflected that she wasn't *very* wet, and that she and her clothes were all capable of drying simultaneously. She put a kettle on for tea, and sat down in her favorite armchair. She sat very still, staring at nothing as she thought.

It felt wrong. Nothing specific that he'd said, except for maybe calling her *Ms. Carrington*. But still, it was like watching an actor playing a part, and getting a minor detail wrong, something no one would know except a person who knew the play intimately.

And how on earth could he have gotten lost? He'd lived in Crooked Creek all his life. His father was the foreman of a logging crew. Kevin had been up in the forest since he was a toddler. Put him on any road around here and he could find his way home blindfolded. If Alex had told the truth about dropping him off on Pell Hill Road, there was no way he "got lost."

So there were only two possibilities—Alex lied about dropping him off, or at least about where she dropped him off. Or Kevin was lying about getting lost. But which?

The weird vibe she'd felt from Kevin made her intuitively certain that the latter was the answer.

She had no proof of that, of course. No proof at all. "Kevin was acting odd" was not evidence. And honestly, she didn't know him all that well, so how would she know what "odd" was for him?

Still, she couldn't shake the idea that there was something wrong about him, something that couldn't be explained by his being cold and hungry and scared.

The kettle whistled, and she got up and put a spoonful of

her favorite tea mixture into a little pewter strainer, shaped like a teakettle—the only thing of her maternal grandmother's that she owned. It always reminded her of her childhood, and made her feel a little nostalgic. She dropped it into the cup and poured steaming water over it, and immediately the fragrance of bergamot and lavender and chamomile struck her nostrils. She gave the tea strainer a gentle bob, and then brought the cup back with her and sat down again in her armchair.

She couldn't act on a feeling. People always got impatient with her about that. She acted on feelings. She needed to let it go. Kevin was home with his parents, it all ended happily, she needed to forget about it. Especially, she needed to resist letting her feelings make her do something stupid, like calling up Dale Blodgett and telling him that "Kevin didn't seem like Kevin." What would he say? Probably the same thing he'd said when she'd called him up about seeing lights in the sky in January.

"Stop smokin' that wacky tobaccy, Rainbow," he'd say, in that fruity voice of his. And that would be the end of it.

Even if Kevin was not really Kevin.

She took a sip of her tea, and sighed. Because however much her brain argued against it, her gut knew. There was something wrong.

But she forced the feeling down, and was actually able to make herself let it go, until three days later, when Kathleen Standish disappeared.

three

· · ·

Dale Blodgett took a deep breath before stepping from the bright sunshine of an Oregon summer day into the deep shadow of his mother's house. He couldn't hold his breath forever, but at least it gave him a few moments of fresh oxygen before his nostrils would be assaulted by the combination of patchouli, sandalwood, and marijuana that hung in the air like a pall of smoke.

No matter how bright it was outside, the interior of the house was always dark. Worn tapestries lined the walls, and heavy crimson drapes hung over the windows. A beaded curtain separated the living room from the rest of the house. Piles of books lay scattered everywhere, along with incense burners, bowls of crystals, and decks of Tarot cards. A scale model of Stonehenge sat on the top of an antique bookcase.

"Mom?" The effort of speaking caused a fit of coughing. He took a further step into the room, and looked around. "Mom, you here?"

He walked past her desk, where a book titled *Heal Yourself Through Sex Magick* lay open to a page of illustrations he immediately regretted looking at.

"Jesus," he said under his breath.

At the same time, a screen door at the back of the house slammed, followed by the sound of footsteps. With a swish, Daisy Blodgett came through the bead curtain, threw her chubby hands out. "Wensleydale, honey! I heard your car drive up, but I was out in the back yard working on my Fairy Garden."

Daisy would have been four-foot-eleven in high heels, if she wore them, which she didn't. The last time she had been in anything but an Indian sarong, a Hawaiian muumuu, or tie-dye was when she was coaxed by her date into a formal dress for her senior prom thirty-two years ago, and she'd regretted the decision ever since. At the moment, she was barefoot, draped with about a half-acre of flower-print cloth, and had a necklace of large obsidian beads around her neck. Her graying hair was permed into a wild frenzy of curls.

"Hi, Mom."

"Honey, you should come more often." She stepped back and frowned up at him. "I worry about you."

"I know."

"We live right in the same village." Her voice was reproachful. "And I feel like if you died, I might not know for days."

"C'mon, Mom. I'm not gonna die. It's not like I'm Chief of Police in Portland, or even Eugene. It's Crooked Creek, for cryin' out loud. It's not a hotbed of crime."

"Oh, I'm not worried about the *crime*. I'm worried about the *stress*. Look at how tense you are."

"I'm fine, Mom."

"Look here." She turned and rummaged through a drawer. "I have some essence of lavender. Put a drop or two of that on your pillow at night. It'll do wonders. It balances your energy meridians."

"My energy meridians are fine. Look, I don't want to take up a lot of time, I'm here on official business...."

"Oh, you can't come and visit your mother at other times?

It's been so long since we've had any fun sharing, like we used to."

"I'd love to, but I need to ask you some questions...."

She sighed theatrically. "Fine, of course." She gave a dismissive gesture with one hand. "I'm sure whatever it is is important, dear."

"It's about Kathleen Standish. The girl who disappeared yesterday."

"Oh, well, *that.*"

He stopped, his mouth open. Ever since elementary school, his mother's responses were capable of derailing his brain. Talking with Daisy Blodgett was the conversational equivalent of riding the Tilt-o-Whirl. Nothing ever went in a straight line.

"What does that mean?" His eyes narrowed.

"What does *what* mean, dear?"

"What does 'Oh, well, *that,*' mean?"

"*Nothing,* dear."

"It sounded like you knew something about it."

She reached out and patted his hand. "Why don't you just ask me your little questions, then? I can tell you won't be able to sit still till you do."

He gritted his teeth. Even a five-minute visit with his mother always left him feeling like he was going to wear his teeth down to nubs. He bit back the response that came to his mind, recalling that the last time he'd said, "Stop it with the goddamn patronizing," to his mother, he had been the recipient of a bottle of Flower Essence for Dissipating Anger, delivered right to the police station two days later, much to the amusement of the rest of his staff.

"I'm asking all of the neighbors if they saw anything or heard anything the night she vanished. You live only a quarter mile from her house."

"Well, of course, I *know* that, dear. I live here, after all."

"Kathleen disappeared on Wednesday evening walking up from visiting a friend in the village. She was seen by Jim Smeltzer at a little after eight o'clock, which would have meant she'd have passed your house fifteen minutes or so later. I just thought I'd ask...."

"Of course. I did a Tarot card spread for her last night, you know, and I can tell you that she's still alive. But she's in grave danger. Her cover card was The Nine of Swords. If you can *imagine.*"

"But did you see her?"

"I saw her last week, and she was *distraught,* poor thing, her energy meridians were clogged like a bad drain. I offered to do an energy clearing for her, and she told me to fuck off." She sighed. "If you can *imagine.*"

"But Wednesday night, Mom...?"

"Didn't see her. I was meditating."

"Thanks." His bitter tone missed her altogether.

"Of course, it's important to do what you can to help an investigation," she said breezily. "Can you come to dinner on Saturday?"

"No, Mom, I got a date."

"With who?" Her voice held ill-concealed incredulity.

"*Mom.*" He rolled his eyes. "You don't have to treat me like I'm twelve."

"That's what I thought." She sighed heavily, making her ample bosom heave. "You're trying to avoid having dinner with me."

"Look, I gotta go. I gotta talk with all the other people between here and Kathleen Standish's house."

"That's three houses. And I know Marie Wolverton didn't see anything because I asked her yesterday, so you can skip her house. There's no rush. You could spend some time with your mother."

But he was already backing toward the door, opening it,

and escaping into the sunshine, taking great gulps of fresh air and hoping against hope that the odor didn't cling to his clothes. The last time, he'd made the mistake of sitting down on the couch and smelled like a cross between a lavender sachet and a Willie Nelson concert for the next three days.

She stood in the door, blinking in the bright light and waving. "Come back when you can spend more time, Wensleydale. I miss you." But by that time he was already backing his car down the driveway.

Next on the list was Dean Kress, a retired parks worker who lived alone in a little cottage set back from the road in a cluster of fir trees. After that, his mom's friend Marie Wolverton, who was only marginally less New Age, but at least kept her windows open and didn't burn six pounds of incense a week. Then there was the mobile home housing the Garton family, and finally the neat little ranch house where Darla Standish lived with her daughter Kathleen.

Lived. As in past tense. Of course, Kevin Torgeson came back. Maybe Kathleen Standish would, too. Then he began to consider the implications of that, and found he didn't like where it was leading.

It was all too easy to believe Kevin Torgeson had gotten stoned, become lost on the way home, and spent a couple of days wandering around the Three Sisters. Kevin was a pothead and troublemaker. Kathleen Standish, on the other hand, was a straight arrow—an honor student at McKenzie High School, a talented clarinetist in the school orchestra, a star forward on the varsity soccer team. There was no way that she had "gotten lost."

But if her disappearance wasn't because of being a druggy, then Kevin's wasn't, either. How could two teenagers disappear within a week of each other, and the two not be connected?

With that not particularly reassuring thought, he pulled into Dean Kress's driveway, shut off the engine, and got out.

An hour later, Dale was heading back into the village. Visits to all three of the households between his mom's place and the Standishes left him with no further information to go on. On the other hand, he did end up with a jar of blueberry jam from Marie Wolverton that had been delivered with an adjuration to "Visit your mother more often. She worries."

He was worried himself, but not about his relationship with his mother. His mom should be able to look after herself by this point. Not only that, it wasn't like he didn't do anything for her. He was conscientious about gifts on birthdays and Christmas, even though his mother had long since abandoned celebrating Christmas in favor of having a gathering on the Winter Solstice. But mostly what Dale thought about was the fact that he turned a blind eye to Daisy's herb garden, which featured a thriving stand of herbs that could have landed her in jail.

What he was worried about was this case. This was a problem. He'd wanted the job of chief of police in Crooked Creek precisely because he didn't want to have to worry about cases. He didn't want to deal with all of the big time nastiness he'd face in a big city. There was a wide streak of laziness in his character. He'd have been perfectly happy to lope through life as a village cop till he retired, and never come across anything more serious than parking tickets, drunk teenage boys pissing off of bridges, and the occasional fight in Dorrie's Bar and Grill. This kind of stuff—he hadn't planned for that. And if the state police got involved, it would make more work, more trouble, more time away from relaxing at home.

It wasn't that he didn't care about Kathleen Standish. It wasn't, honestly, that he hadn't cared about Kevin Torgeson. It was more that part of him really resented their intrusion on his routine. The thinking part of his brain knew it was ridiculous to be annoyed with them for disappearing, but on some level, that's exactly what he felt.

He pulled into a parking place next to the police station, got out of the car, and walked inside. Sheila Clarke, his secretary, looked up momentarily from her computer.

"Bob called in." Her normally placid voice sounded strained. "Logger up near the end of Stark Road, almost to the edge of the wilderness area—he found a shoe. Looks like a girl's. Thinks it might be Kathleen's."

"Shit. All the way up there?"

"Yeah. Doesn't sound good, does it?"

"No."

"Let's hope that it was dropped by a hiker or something. She's a nice kid. If her shoe was up there… she didn't get up there by herself, you know what I mean?"

"I know. Is Bob coming back in?"

"He was on his way back when I talked to him."

"Good." He heaved a sigh. "Nobody along North Fork Road saw her after Jim Smeltzer. It should have taken her a half-hour, tops, to get home after he saw her walk by when he was out mowing his lawn. He said she smiled and waved, seemed fine."

"So between there and home…" Sheila stopped.

"Somebody must have picked her up."

"It might not be her shoe."

"I have a feeling it is." He rubbed his forehead with one hand. "I just have this feeling."

Dale's feeling was correct. When Bob McCloskey, the officer who had been called out, came back, he had in his hand a white and pink sneaker. On the back of it someone had neatly lettered the initials *KS*, probably for gym class. It didn't leave much doubt.

"Shit," Dale said again.

"Who's gonna tell Darla?" Bob looked like he'd have shouted out "not it" if he'd dared to.

Darla Standish was a tall, outgoing, athletic blonde, a PE teacher at McKenzie High School. She was a compulsive runner, a largely self-taught carpenter who had renovated most of her house single-handed, and a forthright and tough single mom. She was well-respected by nearly everyone in Crooked Creek's sometimes divisive citizenry.

Now, as she opened the door, Dale had to repress an urge to gawk at how the disappearance of her daughter had changed her. She seemed on the verge of collapse, and looked like she'd lost twenty pounds in the last three days. Her expression was blank, her face colorless except for the red rims around her eyes. When he asked her to identify the shoe, her eyes brimmed over, but she sat still and silent, as if even crying hard was physically beyond her capabilities.

"It's Kathleen's, then?" He hated to force her to respond to a question whose answer he already knew.

She nodded. "Where was it found?" Her voice was nearly a whisper.

"Up near the end of Stark Road."

"How..." She swallowed. "How could she have gotten up there?"

"We don't know. We're trying to find that out. We think it might be connected to Kevin Torgeson's disappearance. Did Kevin and Kathleen know each other?"

"Of course." She looked up at him. "All the kids know each other. But Kathleen was…" She stopped, hitched a sob, and started over. "Kathleen just graduated. Kevin's a sophomore. They didn't have classes together. They didn't socialize with the same kids." She cleared her throat. "Kathleen's friends are all good kids, Dale. This isn't some kind of thing, you know… involving drugs or alcohol. None of them are into that stuff." She didn't add, *Like Kevin Torgeson's friends are*, but the implication was obvious.

"I know that." He tried to keep his voice reassuring. "But it's too much of a coincidence to believe that the two disappearances are unconnected. When was the last time we had any kind of thing like this happen in Crooked Creek?"

"I've only lived here six years. But I'm guessing never."

He shrugged and shook his head. "Never in my experience. We have the usual stuff—some drugs, petty thefts, that sort of thing, especially during the summer—but nothing like this. I'm working on the assumption that the two are related somehow."

"Kevin came back."

"Yes."

"So, it's possible…" She left the question hanging.

"It's always possible." He also did not complete the thought—*until we find the body.*

Two mornings later, George Colquitt, owner of Crooked Creek Food and Sundries, was heading down to open up at 6:30 AM. It was a raw, damp sort of day, with fog flowing down off the ridge and twining through the streets, although the weather forecast predicted sun for later in the day. George parked his car in back of the store, and let himself in, climbing the stairs up into the stockroom and then out through the pocket door into the store itself. He flipped the light switch, and there was the buzz and flicker that preceded the fluorescents coming on. Humming tunelessly to himself through his thick mustache, he tossed his lunch bag on the counter, and went to the front to unlock.

He threw the deadbolt, and twisted the handle to release the lock in the doorknob.

The door opened inward, and with a thud, a person slithered backwards and landed across his feet.

George stepped backwards, and bumped a display of apples, which shuddered and cascaded to the floor. He looked down, and for a moment as the panic skittered through his brain, didn't recognize who it was. Then he did, and it took him almost a full minute to regain his voice.

"Kathleen? Are you okay?"

Kathleen's eyes were open, staring. Only a small twitch of her eyelid convinced him she was alive. Finally, without getting up, she slowly rotated her head toward him, and lay for a moment, looking up at him from her position lying on her back on the floor of the grocery store.

Then she said, in a level voice, "I'm cold. Can I go home now?"

That evening, Dale Blodgett sat in Dorrie's Bar and Grill, drooping morosely over his pint of Olympia, chatting with Dorrie Keene, the owner and bartender. Dorrie was a many-tattooed peroxide blonde with a cheerful smile and a right hook that could fell a musk ox. Dale liked her, mostly because she was capable of taking care of her own problems, seldom called for his services, and would top off his pint for free if he kept her engaged in conversation.

"So, she's back? And she's okay?" She wiped a grimy pint glass with a cloth, to no apparent effect.

"She was a little spacey. But otherwise all right, yeah."

"Not..." She swallowed, seeming reluctant to say the word. "Not raped, was she?"

"No. Darla took her right to the doctor, and they checked her over from stem to stern. No sign that anyone hurt her. A couple of little cuts and scrapes, and her feet were pretty sore. She lost both shoes somehow, up in the Sisters, and looks like she walked all the way back. We found one shoe way up at the end of Stark Road. That's how we knew she'd been up the ridge."

She whistled under her breath. "But safe and sound?"

"Yeah. No violence of any kind." He took a sip of his beer. "I'm glad, you know, but it makes it even weirder."

"And she's not telling what happened to her?"

"Says she doesn't remember. Exactly like Kevin Torgeson. She says the last thing she remembers is walking home from her friend's house. Then she wakes up flat on her back in the store, with George Colquitt standing there."

She raised one eyebrow. "You don't think that... that George coulda had anything to do with it?"

"Nah." He gave a little gesture of dismissal with one hand. "He claims he opened the front door of the store from the inside, and she kinda fell in, like she'd been leaning on it. His wife corroborates his story. He left at six as usual, nothing amiss. He called nine-one-one right when he found her. And he was nowhere near where the Torgeson kid was found. Rainey Carrington's the one who saw him first, walking right down the road in front of her house."

Dorrie leaned on the bar. "You think the kids might be lying? You know how kids are."

"Don't know why they would. It's not like anything happened that they'd have a motive to lie about—you know, a break-in, anything reported missing or vandalized. And they're apparently not friends or anything. The two of them hardly know each other. I can't think of two kids who'd be less likely to be in cahoots with each other." He took a deep drink from his pint. "I don't like it. It's a mystery. I hate mysteries."

"You're in the wrong profession, honey." Dorrie grinned.

He gave her a sardonic look. "I didn't count on running into mysteries in Crooked Creek."

four

. . .

Tyler Vaughan took a sip of his coffee and gave a squinty-eyed look at the stack of letters sitting on his desk. So far, he'd had three reports of Bigfoots—Pittsburgh, south Florida, and some pissant little town named Trumansburg, New York that he'd never even heard of, a seven-page letter about something called Mothman supposedly going on the rampage in West Virginia, a letter from a chick in England claiming that her hometown in Devonshire was being plagued by a humming noise that no one could pinpoint a source for but was giving her headaches, and a fairly detailed offer by a young lady who wanted to be Tyler's scientific assistant and secret love slave.

Then he picked up a letter neatly addressed to *Tyler Vaughan, Zoologist*, in care of the Cascadia Zoological Research Station. The return address was Crooked Creek, Oregon. His eyebrows rose. Crooked Creek was only ten miles down the road, and in fact was where he went for food, access to post office and bank, an occasional visit to a bar, and other such amenities. One of the woo-woos was only ten miles away?

"They start showing up on my doorstep, and I'm outta here," he muttered under his breath.

He opened it, and pulled out a letter in the same precise handwriting that was on the envelope.

The letter read:

Dear Mr. Vaughan:

I know it is very presumptuous of me to contact you. Someone as famous as you are probably gets a lot of letters from admirers.

Tyler snorted loudly.

But I'm hoping that you'll give this one some attention, because we're in a really serious situation here, and I know you live in the area and I thought you might help us. I know that you are a world-renowned expert on paranormal phenomena—

Another snort of derision.

—because I saw a clip on YouTube from your interview on Good Morning America, and you certainly sounded like you had a lot of experience in the field.

Two weeks ago, a boy from our village disappeared suddenly, while walking home at night. He mysteriously showed up three days later, and as luck would have it I was the first one to see him. Then, a girl disappeared, and she also reappeared three days later. Neither of them remembered anything about what happened while they were missing. And now, just yesterday evening, a ten-year-old boy vanished from his front yard while he was playing with his puppy.

There is nothing to connect the three of them. The little boy who vanished didn't even know the other two kids—his family moved here from Eugene last year. We're all hoping that he'll come back like the other two did, but it's got the whole village scared.

Neither of the two children who came back were harmed in any way, or at least in any way that is obvious. Both of them seem fine —the first day they were a little disoriented, but I guess that's not surprising, considering.

I know it may be weird for me to contact you. I've been trying to think of people who might help us. Our local chief of police, Dale Blodgett, means well, I guess, but he kind of has the attitude that if the kids came back unharmed, the case is closed. And he's figuring that Phil Collette—the little boy who disappeared—will show up eventually, too, so he's not really looking too hard. I'm really worried, Mr. Vaughan. There's something going on here, and I don't have the scientific training to figure it all out. So I sat down last night and did a Google search for "paranormal expert Oregon," and your name came up, and then I remembered seeing the video clip, and I thought of writing to you.

You may not have time to help us, which I totally understand given your other duties, but I thought it couldn't hurt to try. I thought that maybe because you're so close by, you might be able to lend us your expertise. Or maybe if you know of something paranormal happening in the area that might explain this, you could at least write back and tell me, and I could take it from there. I tried not to jump to a paranormal explanation, but at this point I really do think this isn't something that can be explained in a more conventional way.

Thanks for at least reading this, and I hope you'll respond. My address and phone number are below.

Namasté,

Rainey Carrington

He sat back, and sighed again. He'd actually been believing it until the *Namasté* part.

He chucked the letter and envelope into the recycle bin, picked up the next one, and opened it. This one was from a very earnest-sounding man in Texas who had been having trouble with El Chupacabra killing his sheep, and wanted Tyler to head a team to come and investigate.

The door of the lab opened, and Judy Kahn walked in, tossed her backpack on her desk, and sat down.

"Morning." She poured herself a cup of coffee from a thermos. "You need anything down in Eugene? I'm heading down there in a little."

"Don't think so. That's right, you have that presentation thing today, don't you?"

"Yeah. Program for teenagers. Part of some kind of summer assignment for an AP Biology class. Lecture on bird banding. Because we all know how vitally interested high schoolers are in birds, right?"

"You'll do fine, Judy."

"Oh, I'm not worried. I've got a PowerPoint with some pretty pictures, and I'll slip in a couple of references to bird sex. They'll listen."

"Ornithological porn." He chuckled. "Keep it clean, or they won't invite you back."

"An added benefit. How's today's fan mail?"

"The usual assortment of weirdos. One of them from right down the road. Some chick in Crooked Creek wrote to me."

"Bigfoot?"

"Nope. Something about kids disappearing."

Her eyebrows rose, and she leaned forward in her chair. "Yeah, I heard about that. Made the newspaper. Two teenagers were missing for a couple of days. I guess they got lost up in the Sisters. The newspaper turned it into a 'Make sure you bring along survival gear, the forest is big' sort of story."

"Seriously? It's real?"

"Well, the part about the kids being missing for a couple of days was. What did she tell you about it?"

"I dunno. Like I read the letters carefully. All I remember is that she thought it wasn't just kids getting lost in the woods." He leaned over and rummaged around in the recycle bin. He pulled out a sheet of paper, and passed it to her.

She sat for a time, reading the letter with a frown on her face.

"Sounds like it's three kids, now," she said without looking up.

"I don't know what she expects me to do about it."

"I'm not sure she does, either. She reminds me of Princess Leia. 'Help me, Obi-Wan. You're our only hope.'"

Tyler snorted. "Sorry, my ability to use The Force isn't what it used to be. I don't know why she thinks it's some kind of paranormal phenomenon. Sounds to me like they should be looking for some skeevy pedophile type. She should contact the police."

"Apparently she did."

"Well, okay, then. It's their problem, not mine."

She grinned. "You're a heartless bastard, you know that? Some damsel in distress contacts you, and you chuck her letter in the garbage? You should rush to her rescue. Maybe she'd be so grateful that you'd finally get laid. It's been what, a year and a half? You gotta be getting antsy."

He gave her a sour look. "Har de very har har." He snatched the letter out of her hand, and threw it back into the recycle bin.

She took a sip of her coffee. "What are you planning for the day?"

"I got images from T-Seven and T-Nine to go through. I think the elk are still moving to higher ground. We got some serious hits last night."

"No more cameras wrecked?"

"Nope. I got Joe to agree to replace T-Three, though. The new camera should be in early next week. Maybe put it in a titanium housing riveted to a steel pipe sunk in concrete."

Her face suddenly grew serious. "You show Joe those photos?"

"You kidding? I took your advice and told him some vandal wrecked the camera, but the images weren't clear enough to see who it was."

"Those pics gave me nightmares."

"You're the one who kept saying it was some eco-nut in a hockey mask."

"You remember the cave?"

He didn't respond for a moment. "Yeah, I remember."

"Look, Ty, when you get the new camera let me know, okay? We'll go up there together."

"Twist my arm. Ow ow ow, stop. Okay." He looked at her solemnly. "That place scared the living hell out of me."

"You and me both, brother." She leaned back in her chair. "You don't…" She stopped.

"I don't what?"

"You don't think whatever killed your camera could have anything to do with those kids disappearing?"

"Why would it?"

"I dunno. It was only a thought."

"I'd think that from the way that steel camera housing was ripped apart, those kids wouldn't have come back—they'd be finding body parts strewn from here to Mount Hood."

"You're probably right. You thought any more about who that was? The faceless guy in the photo?"

He shrugged. "No idea. But yeah, I've thought about it. A lot."

"And your answer is?"

"I don't know. That's my answer." He gestured angrily at the recycle bin. "You want me to start sounding like these people? Finding a strand of hair caught on a barbed-wire fence, and turning it into the Abominable Snowman?"

She patted the air with both hands. "Calm down, sport. I wasn't trying to pick."

He took a deep breath, let it out slowly. "I know. But what do we have? One photo that's actually clear enough to see with any detail, and when you look at it, there's no detail to see. I don't believe that whoever it was had no facial features. I've gone over this every which way from Sunday, and it has to be some kind of equipment failure. Maybe when the camera was damaged."

"Damage to the camera selectively erased the guy's face, and left the rest of the image unscathed?"

"I don't know." The anger rose in his voice again. "But there's got to be a sensible, natural explanation. Up at that lava tube we got spooked because we were already primed to see ghosts. Normal human fear of dark places, plus being out in the middle of the wilderness, plus seeing what had happened to the camera, plus seeing the creepy photograph. We let our primitive fear centers run away with us."

"Yeah." She didn't sound convinced.

"Don't tell me you're going all woo-woo on me."

"No. But here's the problem. Suppose that in all of this morass of bullshit, there was one legitimate sighting of… of something. Something that science hasn't explained yet. You're disbelieving it all, because the signal-to-noise ratio is so low. But if you'd already decided to discount it wholesale, you'd ignore the actual, legitimate data point when you saw it."

"I don't know how to compensate for that."

"Me either."

"It'd help if all of the wingnuts out there would shut the hell up."

"That's not going to happen. But promise me one thing. Don't go up to T-Three alone, okay?"

"Agreed."

Tyler got home a little after five o'clock, after a trip down into Crooked Creek for groceries. "Home" was a trailer he rented from the lab, situated in a small clearing halfway between the lab and the village. It was in reasonably good repair, trim and clean on the outside, but the inside was a chaotic, disorganized clutter of books, scientific journals, printouts of his own research data, and the required single-guy number of empty beer bottles and dirty socks.

His sole companion, a dog named Ahab, didn't help in the cleanliness department. Ahab was a large, wiry-haired mutt who looked like the product of an unholy union between an Airedale terrier and a woolly mammoth. Tyler had picked him up out in the Sisters two winters ago, a little lost puppy shivering in the snow, and repeated advertisements, with photographs, brought no one out to claim him.

Since then the dog had increased in height by a factor of five, in weight by a factor of twenty, and in sheer exuberance by a factor of about a thousand. His genial disposition toward everyone was somewhat offset by the fact that he had also developed an unfortunate intestinal condition that caused him to produce toxic flatulence. Ahab could, when properly primed, clear a room in thirty seconds flat. The result was that no matter what Tyler did, his trailer always smelled like a combination of air freshener and dog farts.

He opened the front door gingerly, pushing it open with one foot while balancing two bags of groceries in his arms. There was a crash as Ahab barreled his way past, slamming the screen door back on its hinges. Tyler teetered on the edge of the porch, and nearly went over backwards, groceries and all, but an excellent innate sense of balance kept him from disaster.

"Goddammit, Ahab, will you watch where you're going?" he shouted.

Ahab, completely unperturbed, gamboled ponderously about in the front yard, and then went over and peed on the mailbox post for what seemed like a minute and a half.

"C'mon, hound." Tyler held open the door with his foot. "Get in here."

Wagging happily, Ahab bounded across the yard and up the steps, and capered about in the living room as Tyler unpacked groceries into the fridge and cabinets.

There was a sliding noise, followed by a crash. Tyler ignored it. From long experience, he could tell by the sound that it was a pile of magazines and an empty coffee cup, swept from the end table by Ahab's tail. Filing it in the category of *I'll deal with that later* he put a pot of water on the stove, turned the heat on "High," and got out a package of spaghetti noodles and a bottle of pasta sauce for that night's dinner.

Kids disappearing from Crooked Creek. He suppressed a shudder. Judy had suggested a connection between the abductions and the photos of the mysterious person who had destroyed the T-Three camera, and he'd scoffed at her—but truthfully, part of his reaction was because the same thought had already occurred to him.

He didn't like it.

Signal to noise. He recalled a statistics professor he'd had, describing what it's like to try to find a pattern in data with a lot of scatter. "You have to pull a net through the bullshit and try to catch a pearl." It was an unusually apt metaphor.

But was this letter the pearl? Or more bovine waste? How could you tell?

The water was boiling. He pulled out a handful of noodles, cracked them in half, and dropped them into the pot. Then he walked over to the bin of dog food. Ahab, using the canine telepathy that all dogs have when it comes to dinner time, came skidding into the kitchen and collided with him, nearly sending him sprawling a second time. Then ensued a frenzy of leaping about. Each time his 120 pounds of weight thudded to the floor, there was an echoing jingle as dishes rattled in the cabinet.

"Sit, beast."

Ahab sat in response to his stern voice, entire body quivering, whining with excitement as Tyler poured a large scoop of food into his bowl.

"Okay."

Ahab, evidently not wanting to take the chance that his master might change his mind about its being dinner time, instantly fell upon his food.

Twelve seconds later, when Ahab was finished inhaling dinner, he retired to his dog bed with a satisfied belch, and Tyler gave his own meal a stir.

How in the hell had the person in the photograph masked his face? He had to admit that the explanation he'd mentioned to Judy—that the damage to the camera had somehow erased the vandal's facial features—was pretty ridiculous.

Other explanations, though, were just as wildly far-fetched. Those thermal imaging cameras were extraordinarily sensitive. They had to be, or otherwise any warm-blooded animal would come out as nothing more than a colorful blur. That afternoon, he had gone to the camera manufacturer's website, and had found a false-color photograph of a shirtless man. Every feature of the man's face and upper body was discernible. You could even trace where the large blood vessels in the man's chest were because their larger heat signal made them glow orange against the yellow background of his skin.

That was no mask. That was something that had no face.

Meaning not human.

"Shit. That is not possible. Not. Possible." He put a

strainer into the sink, then picked up the pot and dumped the spaghetti into the strainer.

Five minutes later, he was sitting at his computer, balancing a full bowl of spaghetti in his lap, typing *monster humanoid faceless* into a Google search.

The first ten hits all had to do with video games and Japanese animé. He changed the search parameters to *skinny faceless human.*

The first hit was on a paranormal site, an entry entitled "Encounter With a Faceless Man in Black." He clicked the link.

The poster, who called himself Ryan B., told a story about a "friend of his," usually "completely reliable and rational," who knew "a kid" who had a frightening encounter on a country road in New Mexico one night. The story concluded:

He then noticed a black figure walking on the right-hand shoulder of the road about two or three minutes ahead of him. Nothing unusual. Everyone is accustomed to seeing hitchhikers, runners, and sometimes kids running, playing, or walking beside the highway. But as he neared this individual, it became apparent that this was no ordinary person.

First off, he was very skinny and very tall. This by itself was strange enough to notice. As he got closer, he saw that this individual was wearing clothes that were entirely black. Well, it was nothing to be frightened about, he told himself, and he even contemplated picking up the person. He slowed his truck down and peered out to see the guy as he passed. At this point, the individual dressed entirely in black had halted, but was still facing forward.

Finally, as the vehicle gradually moved forward, he noticed with horrific realization that the man dressed in black had no face! No eyes, no mouth, no nose structure at all. Nothing! The kid was shocked, so he hit the accelerator, and eventually went over a rise and out of sight of the black-clothed faceless man. Finally collecting his wits enough to think, he turned around and drove back toward the point where he first saw the man with no face.

Even as he started back, he saw that there was no one there any longer. He passed the point where he had seen the man, and stopped again and turned around once again in the direction he was headed originally. He drove up to where the man was standing only moments before... and all he saw was footprints in the sand.

Tyler sighed. He'd heard these anecdotal reports, coming from "a friend of mine whose cousin's best friend's great aunt's gardener swears that it happened," all too often. All you needed was to add a tag line that when the kid got home, he found a piece of an alien tentacle hanging from the car's door handle, and you'd have the nucleus of every urban legend ever told. He returned to Google, and typed in, *faceless man children abduction.*

The first hit was on a link called "Cryptic Fiction." The bit of it below the link listing read, "... a **faceless** being called Slender **Man**......police investigating the **abductions** of **children**..."

"Fiction," he murmured, but clicked the link anyway.

The opening paragraph of the story read:

After you read this, you may not want to believe it. No one does. They call it fiction. They make up stories about how the whole thing is invented, how all of it started because of a contest to see who could create the best Photoshop image of a monster. The winner submitted an image of a faceless being called Slender Man. The creator, when his image was awarded first prize, went to great lengths to laugh it off, to say that he'd made the whole thing up. He was afraid to let the truth be known.

Slender Man is no myth.

His faceless, spider-like presence has been seen, and

captured on film, more than once, and wherever he is seen, children disappear. They come back, yes. In days or weeks, they come back. But they come back different. They look the same, their voices are the same, but the ones who know them best know that there is something changed about them. The psychologists call it abduction trauma, but I know better.

I can't even get this story published by anyone who will treat it as fact. I'm left with the option of posting it as fiction, and hoping that someone will understand, someone will recognize that what I'm saying is true. Someone will, like me, start going through photographs taken by police investigating the abductions of children, and look in the background, and see the faceless man in black looking back at them.

"Jesus." He closed the window.

Ahab sidled up to him, and nudged his leg.

Tyler jumped, and then looked down.

Ahab was staring meaningfully at the barely-touched spaghetti in the bowl, as if to say, *Hey, dude, if you're not gonna eat that, I can take care of it for you.*

Tyler scowled, and said, "Buzz off, mutt," not without affection, and leaned back in his chair and took a bite. Ahab watched him chew and swallow the mouthful, gave a sigh of disappointment, and went back to his dog bed. A moment later, the rich smell of canine flatulence wafted through the air. Tyler was so used to it, he hardly noticed.

"Slender Man," he said thoughtfully, and took another bite of his spaghetti.

The next morning, Tyler drove in to work, blinking sleepily, concentrating on not nodding off during the ten-minute drive to the lab.

He'd stayed up until one in the morning, reading story after story about Slender Man. The second piece he'd read, that referred to a Photoshop contest, seemed to be accurate at least in that regard. He found a complete account of the creation of the first Slender Man photos, along with the back-story and the connection to abductions. The photos made his skin crawl. Except for the fact that they were black-and-white, and not false color thermal photographs, the creature was the same one that had appeared in the last shots taken by the T-Three remote camera. He had to keep telling himself, *Not real. It's all fictional. A guy named Victor Surge admits that he made the whole thing up back in 2009.*

Even so, the story had caught people's imagination, and a whole mythology had arisen about the creature. People wrote stories, created more photographs, did artwork. One rock band had even mentioned him in a song.

There were, of course, the usual loonies who took it all seriously. He thought about the images from T-Three. Was he one of them? Maybe Judy was right. Maybe he did spend too much time poring over his fan mail.

"I'm losing my marbles," he said under his breath.

Still, when he arrived at the lab, the first thing he did was to look into the recycle bin by his desk.

It was empty.

When Judy arrived at the lab twenty minutes later, Tyler didn't even say hello. He said, trying not to sound frantic, "What did you do with the recycling?"

"Good morning, sunshine." She set down her backpack. "I took it out last night before I left. This morning's the trash and recycle pickup. Why? Change your mind about taking one of your fans up on an offer? I hope it's a good one. Maybe you won't be so twitchy afterwards."

He didn't reply, but stood up and walked out of the building.

He was back less than a minute later. "They already picked it up. Dammit."

"What did you lose?"

"I wanted to reread that letter I got yesterday. The one that talked about the kids disappearing in Crooked Creek."

"Really? Why?"

He looked at her, a little hesitant. "I only wanted to read it again, that's all."

She gave him a sly grin. "You're a lousy liar, Tyler. What did you find out last night?"

"Find out? Nothing."

She shook her head. "C'mon. What do you think I am, stupid? Out with it."

He sighed. "I did a couple of searches. I was thinking about what you said, that maybe our mystery man who killed the camera might be connected."

"Okay. And…?"

He took a deep breath. "You ever heard of Slender Man?"

"I've heard of plenty of slender men. You're no heavyweight, yourself."

"No, not plural. Slender Man, singular. It's a faceless thing, skinny, bipedal. Connected with abductions, particularly of children."

She gawked at him. "You're shitting me."

"Nope."

He had a momentary twinge that he'd left out the part about the whole thing being fictional, but decided not to go there unless asked.

"You think…" She stopped.

"You see why I want to see the letter again?"

"Yeah. Sorry. I wish I'd known. The recycling could have waited till next week."

"It's not your fault. Do you remember the name of the woman who wrote it?"

She frowned for a moment. "No. She had kind of a weird name, I remember that, but I can't recall what it was."

"I think her last name was something like Harrington or Barrington. That's not quite right. I can't come up with her first name to save my neck."

"Did you look in the phone directory?"

"Yup. No Harringtons or Barringtons."

"Well, still, that should be enough. Go down to the store in Crooked Creek and ask if there's a chick named Harrington or Barrington who lives in the area. Town that small, someone will know who you're talking about."

"You're probably right."

She looked at him thoughtfully. "Tyler, you sure you want to get involved with this? This is exactly the kind of thing you hate. Some mysterious sighting of some mysterious creature, and a chick you've never met wants Tyler the Handsome Zoologist to come in and save the day. If you want to repair what's left of your reputation as a scientist..." She didn't finish the sentence, just looked at him and shrugged.

"I know. I can't explain it. It feels like..." He stopped, and his gaze met hers. "It feels like this might be the pearl."

"The pearl? What does that mean?"

He shook his head. "Nothing. Never mind. I'm heading down to Crooked Creek. If I'm right, I'll explain it when I get back."

five

. . .

"Yo, Rainey," George Colquitt said from behind the counter. "I got your organic jam. I held onto a case here, I figured you'd be in."

Rainey turned away from looking at a bin full of tomatoes, and her face lit up in a glowing smile. "George, that was really sweet of you!" She went up to the counter, and as George thumped the case of jam onto the countertop, she reached out and gave his shoulder a squeeze.

George blushed crimson. "How many of 'em you want?"

"Let's see, it's twelve jars?" She leaned over and looked at the label. "Raspberry, lovely! I'll take them all. The jam will keep, and I've got room in my pantry. I've got a few other things to pick up." Her face suddenly clouded over. "However will I get it home? It won't fit into my panniers, and I don't think I'll be able to balance it on my bicycle."

He shrugged. For George, this clearly fell into the "Not My Problem" department.

She sighed. She'd figure it out somehow. If the universe got her a dozen jars of jam, the universe would provide a way to get it home. But there was no one else in the store except for Maureen Sullivan, the owner of the Three Sisters Lodge, who had told her about Kevin Torgeson's disappearance in the Crooked Creek Post Office two weeks earlier. Maureen was picking over summer squash with a pinched, disapproving expression on her face.

Probably no sense even asking Maureen. Not a pleasant person. Besides, Rainey had the sense Maureen didn't like her much. She'd acted even more unfriendly than usual lately.

Rainey had returned to selecting tomatoes when the bell over the door jingled, and she turned her head. A tall, well-built young man with dark brown eyes and tousled chestnut-brown hair was walking up to the counter. He looked somehow familiar, but he wasn't a townie. She knew all of the townies on sight, and he wasn't one of them. Also, something about the way he moved put her on alert. He acted ill-at-ease, tense as a skittish horse.

"Um, excuse me?" he said tentatively.

George made a muffled noise of response through his mustache.

"I'm trying to contact someone who lives in Crooked Creek. All I know is that her last name sounds like Harrington, or Barrington, or something like that."

George looked at him in silence for a moment, and then gave a gesture of his head toward the vegetable aisle. "Hey, Rainey." His voice was deadpan. "Guy here wants to talk to you."

The man looked stunned for a moment, then turned and stared at her, looking even more stunned, for some reason.

I know who that is! It's Tyler Vaughan, the Bigfoot expert! Wow, he's a lot handsomer than I remember.

The Tyler Vaughan she remembered from the YouTube clip was relaxed, self-possessed, authoritative. That had some attraction, true, but this Tyler Vaughan seemed vulnerable, unsure of himself, and that brought out her naturally powerful instinct to help and protect the entire world. He had to be at least thirty years old, but there was something a little awkward about him, like he still hadn't quite outgrown his teenage boy coltishness. She found herself wanting to take both of his hands and tell him, *Don't worry, it's going to be okay.*

"Hi. I'm Tyler Vaughan."

"I know. I'm Rainey Carrington."

"I didn't think finding you would be this easy." He gave her a crooked grin.

"I put my address, phone number, and email in the letter."

"I lost it. So I had to rely on my memory. It's quite a coincidence that I happened to run into you here."

"There are no coincidences." She shifted her shopping basket to the other hand. "No snowflake ever falls in the wrong place."

"That's a nice saying. Yours?"

"No, it's a Zen Buddhist maxim." She smiled again. "Did you drive here?"

He frowned a little at the *non sequitur.* "Yes. I was trying to find you, because I think that…" He paused. "I need to talk to you about… You know. What you wrote to me about."

Maureen Sullivan looked up from a bin of tomatoes she was picking over and gave her a questioning stare. She would love to know what they were talking about, that much was obvious. Well, she wouldn't get the satisfaction. No sense giving Maureen an opportunity to discuss her with people at the post office.

"And I need someone to help me get my jam home," she said to Tyler, pointedly not making eye contact with Maureen. "So it all works out." She walked over to the counter and unloaded her groceries.

George silently rang up her purchases.

"Jam?" Tyler said.

George jerked a thumb at the case of raspberry jam, and rolled his eyes a little.

"Oh."

Groceries paid for, she perched her grocery bag on top of her jam, and picked it up, leaning backwards to counterbalance the weight.

"Can I help?" Tyler said.

"Nope," she answered cheerfully. "Strong like bull, that's me. You can get the door, though. Which car is yours?"

She went out as Tyler held the door, and he pointed. "The blue Civic. It's kind of a crappy car, and the inside's dirty. Mostly because of my dog. Sorry."

"No problem."

He opened the trunk of the car, and she put her groceries into it.

"I'll have to leave my bicycle. Maybe after we talk, you can drop me back off here and I'll ride home?"

"Sure. Wish I had a bike rack and could save you the trip. Are you sure your bike will be okay, leaving it here?"

She smiled. "Nobody will bother it."

They climbed into the car, and he turned the key. The engine coughed into life, idled uncertainly for about a minute, and then resigned itself to running for a little while longer.

"Where to?"

"Up at the top of Pell Hill Road."

"That's a steep ride on a bike." He pulled out into the road.

"It's not bad. It can be a little uncomfortable in the rain, but my clothes are wash-and-wear drip-dry, and so am I, so it's all good."

He looked at her, and she immediately saw the worried, uncertain look return to his eyes. "Has anything more happened about… you know, about the kids? The ones who disappeared?"

"Phil Collette returned. The little boy who vanished. A logger found him wandering around on a trail up in the

Sisters. He was almost to the road, heading down toward the village."

"On his way home."

"Seems that way."

"It sounded like..." He stopped. "In your letter, it sounded like you weren't telling me everything you were thinking."

"Is that ever a good idea?"

"Why wouldn't it be?"

She stifled a smile. Most people thought she was naïve and trusting, but even in their short acquaintance she could tell this guy had her beat by a mile. It was kind of sweet, but it meant he probably had been kicked in the ass a lot.

"So, you're asking me what I think is going on? Not only the facts of it, but the explanation?"

"Yes."

"Well, I don't know. I'm sure that a scientist like yourself scoffs at the idea of intuition, but I feel like most of what I know isn't about thinking, it's about feeling. It's hard to explain, but I *feel* that something is wrong here. When I found Kevin Torgeson walking down the road... well, I was thrilled to see him alive, of course, but something about it *felt* wrong. One of those moments in which my brain was saying, 'You should be happy,' but my heart was having the screaming meemies."

"Kevin's the first kid who disappeared?"

"Yes. He's a troubled sort. Smokes a lot of dope with his friends, and got caught breaking into someone's house a couple of years ago. But basically a good kid."

"That sounds like an odd definition of 'a good kid.'"

"There's a difference between who someone is and what he does. Kevin's got a good heart. His parents are hyper-controlling types, and Kevin has had some fierce arguments with his dad. Rich Torgeson has a hard edge. He wanted a kid who was a B student, captain of the football team, a yes-sir no-ma'am type. He got Kevin." She stopped, thought for a moment. "But even so, given a few years of growing up, Kevin would have been fine."

"Would have been?"

She looked over at Tyler. Okay, time to take a chance. See if she was right about him. "The boy who is now staying with the Torgesons isn't Kevin anymore."

His foot jerked, and the Civic lurched a little bit.

"I know it sounds odd." She looked at him, but he was staring straight forward, hanging onto the steering wheel like grim death.

He didn't answer.

She took a deep breath and decided to plunge on ahead. In for a penny, in for a pound. "It's true for all three of them. It's subtle. They act the same, sound the same, look the same. I don't know Kathleen Standish as well as I do Kevin Torgeson, and I barely know Phil Collette at all. But I've seen all three of them since they came back… and there's a difference. It's something about the eyes." She pointed. "My house is the next one on the right."

Tyler, still silent, pulled into her driveway, and turned off the engine.

"I get it if you don't believe me. It sounds crazy."

"That's the problem. It sounds crazy, and I *do* believe you."

She looked over at him. He still faced forward, and that vulnerability she had noticed in him appeared to have morphed into actual fear.

"I'm guessing that you haven't told me everything you know, either."

"No."

"Let's go inside. I think this is going to be a 'discuss this over tea' thing, and not a 'tell me about it while we sit in the car' thing, am I right?"

"You'll probably think this is a 'Jesus Christ, are you a

freaking lunatic?' thing," But he got out of the car, and went around to help her with her groceries. This time she didn't object, and he followed her up to the house, carrying the case of jam.

"Watch out for my cat," she said as she opened the door. "His name is Bonkers, and he has an uncanny ability to sense when you're carrying something, and pick that moment to twine between your legs."

He set the jam down on one of the only bits of kitchen counter unoccupied by bundles of herbs, trays of small bottles, and an assortment of potted plants, teacups, and a pair of garden hand-clippers. He looked at her with a questioning smile.

"I am the owner and only employee of Cascade Tea Company. I make herbal teas."

"For a living?" He sounded a little incredulous.

She smiled. "I raise all of the plants organically, cut and dry them myself. People order them. They're good."

He returned her smile, and his face relaxed a little. "It makes the house smell wonderful."

She put a pot of water on the stove, turned on the heat, and then turned and leaned on the counter and looked at him. She said, a little reluctantly, "You were about to tell me something else you knew. About the disappearances."

"Well, I don't know that I'd say it's something I *know*. It's more something that I suspect is connected." And he told her about the destruction of the T-Three camera, the images he and Judy had seen, the experience at the cave. Then, seeming slightly embarrassed, he added what he'd found out about Slender Man.

"A faceless entity," she said, thoughtfully. "You have to wonder how he senses anything."

"I…" He stopped.

"What?"

His forehead scrunched up, and suddenly he looked very young. "I'm not supposed to believe in any of this stuff. I *don't* believe any of this stuff. Or didn't. I don't know." He stopped, pinched the bridge of his nose, and closed his eyes for a moment. "You should know. I'm not a Bigfoot researcher. I'm only a zoologist. I mostly research elk. The Bigfoot thing happened kind of by accident, and now everyone thinks I believe in all that stuff. I'm actually a skeptic about the paranormal."

She raised one eyebrow. "So?"

He looked at her in complete incomprehension. "What do you mean, so?"

"You saw the photographs, right? They're real."

"Yeah."

"Well, then."

He frowned. "Well, what?" He sounded exasperated.

She kept her voice level and calm. "As far as I can tell, there's no normal and paranormal, there's no natural and supernatural. There's only normal and natural, and some parts of it we don't know about. It might be that your Slender Man exists and he's the one who abducted Kevin and Kathleen and Phil. Or maybe there's another explanation. But it's all one thing, really. I think what you're doing is drawing an imaginary line on the ground and then fretting about which side of the imaginary line something falls."

He looked taken aback for a moment. "But..." he began, and then stopped.

"But what?" She smiled.

"I don't know. I'd never really thought of it like that. But the problem is... I'm a scientist. I can be all open-minded and everything, but the grant funding agencies aren't. If I don't reestablish myself as a researcher soon, I'm gonna be out on the street."

"Oh, *practical* stuff." She gave a dismissive little motion of her hand. "That stuff *always* works out. It's the existential things that are the problem. Once you've got those into line, all of the logistics seem to happen. Like my jam, for instance."

The teakettle whistled, and she put scoops of tea into tea-strainers, dropped them into two mugs, and poured hot water over them.

"Your jam?"

"Yes. When I found out that George had set aside a case of jam for me, I figured that somehow, I'd be able to get it home even though there's no way I could have gotten it home on my bicycle. And lo, you showed up."

"I'd have showed up even if you hadn't bought jam today. And vice versa."

Her smiled widened into a grin. "And even given two ways the universe had to screw me over, it didn't."

"So, you're saying that I shouldn't worry about the fact that I might get fired if I investigate this?"

She shrugged. "I'm not exactly saying 'don't worry about it.' I'm more saying that worrying about things is not a good way to determine what the right action is."

She picked up her mug, walked into the living room, and sat down in a recliner. Almost immediately, a large, lean black cat appeared out of nowhere, jumped into her lap, and curled up, then looked up at Tyler with sleepy yellow eyes as he followed her in and sat down in an armchair.

"In any case, we should decide how to approach this situation. I'm afraid, Tyler. Whoever, or whatever, is behind this isn't working from good intentions. I wish you could have seen the look Kevin Torgeson gave me, right before he turned to follow his mother inside, the day he came back. I'd heard the expression 'if looks could kill' before, but now I think I know what it means."

"Why? Why would he have been angry with you? You were trying to help him."

"I don't know. It felt like… it's hard to explain, but it felt like he recognized me. No, that's wrong, because Kevin knows me, of course, so obviously he recognized me. It was like he had suddenly recognized that I was a threat to him. Like he had this realization that I knew who he was, that I had recognized that he wasn't really Kevin." She shook her head. "I'm explaining it badly. But if you'd seen that look—it was sharp as a razor. He wanted me gone. He wanted me erased."

"But you don't know anything definite, right?"

She took a sip of her tea. "No. But all the same, I *did* know. I knew immediately. I think he realizes that."

"Interesting that his parents didn't see a difference."

"They weren't looking for one. All they saw was someone who looked exactly like their son walking up, wet and bedraggled, and they instantly labeled the situation 'Kevin is back.' They're the sort of people that if they can put a label on something, they think they understand it, and then they can dismiss it. For example, my label is 'the hippie girl up the road who makes herbal tea and raises chickens.' They'd never see the need to know anything more about me." A little pang of sadness struck her. "It absolves them of the hard work of thinking."

"I've known people like that."

"They're awfully common."

He nodded. "But it remains to be seen what we can do about this. All three kids are safely back home. From what you've said, the police aren't all that concerned."

She shook her head. "Dale is so used to taking the easy way. We might be able to get him going, but it wouldn't be simple. He wouldn't see the need."

"The first thing to do is to talk to the kids. That might not be easy, though. They'd certainly be suspicious of me. I'm a total stranger. Maybe you could try? I think it's worthwhile finding out what we can about them, and seeing if your sense that they're different bears out. Maybe it *is* post-abduction trauma."

"Maybe." She could hear the lack of conviction in her own voice. "I could probably find a way to talk to Kevin. He lives right down the road, and I know him fairly well. Kathleen and Phil would be harder. I'd have to invent some kind of reason to talk to them."

"The other thing we need to figure out is if this really does have anything to do with the destruction of the remote camera, and what happened to Judy and me at that cave."

Her forehead creased with concern. "That's a really hard idea for you to consider, isn't it?"

He looked at her in silence for a moment. "Yeah. It is."

"Why?"

"Because if there really is some faceless humanoid thing in a cave up there, and that thing killed my camera and has been abducting children... well, it tells me that I know fuck-all about the way the universe works." He looked down. "Pardon my language."

She leaned forward, and said, earnestly, "But that's it, isn't it? We actually know fuck-all about *everything*. You scientists are trying to fix some of that, which is why I love science, even though I could never be a scientist. But because you're the ones who have some of the answers, it's easy to become convinced that if you don't have *all* of the answers, you're a failure."

He looked up, and she smiled at him.

"It's okay not to know. It's okay to be whistling in the dark, every once in a while. It keeps you humble."

He smiled back, a little tentatively. "I still don't like this situation."

"Neither do I. Whether or not Slender Man has anything to do with it, it's pretty awful. Which is why I feel like I can't sit back. It's why I wrote you the letter."

He nodded. "Same reason as why I came down to

Crooked Creek to look for you. I felt like I couldn't let it drop, not without knowing more."

"So what do we do?"

He considered. "I think we can break it down to three possibilities. First possibility—the kids' disappearance has nothing to do with the camera, and photographs, and Slender Man. The kids are being kidnapped by some kook up in the Sisters, and are suffering from post-abduction amnesia, and it's a job for the police."

"Okay."

He took a deep breath. "Second possibility—there's something weird going on. I'll use the word 'paranormal' for convenience, acknowledging your objections to the label"— and here she smiled a little—"but this paranormal *something* is unconnected to the camera and the cave. The kids are being abducted, for reasons unknown, and are being returned changed, once again for reasons unknown. Perhaps replaced."

"Yes."

"Third possibility—the abductions and reappearances, and the changes in the kids' behavior, are connected to, and perhaps perpetrated by, the person we caught an image of on the camera."

She nodded. "Slender Man."

"For want of a better name."

"I agree. Those seem like the only possibilities."

"Next, though, we need some sort of game plan."

"I like your suggestion of talking to the kids first. I'm sure I can find a way to talk to Kevin, and possibly Kathleen or Phil."

He nodded. "And Judy and I are going to go back up to T-Three to reinstall the camera in a couple of days. We'll bring flashlights and check out the cave, creeping horrors be damned."

She took a sip of her tea. "Could you email me the photograph that your camera took? I'd like to see what we're up against. Assuming that theory number three is correct."

"You have email?"

She smiled at the surprise in his voice. "Of course I have email. Just because I choose not to have a car doesn't mean I'm *backward*."

He grinned. "Sorry. My bad."

"My email is teawoman12@gmail.com." She picked up a scrap of paper and a pen from the coffee table, and put it on top of Bonkers the cat, who still was sprawled on her lap, snoozing peacefully. "What's yours?"

"Mine's much more prosaic," Tyler said. "It's tvaughan@czrs.edu. Let me know what you find out."

"Same." She jotted down the address.

He finished his tea, and set the mug on the end table. "Okay, I think we have a plan. And I should get back to work. You still want a lift back down to the village?"

"Yup." She set down her own mug, and then gently pushed Bonkers, who got the hint only after repeated urging. He jumped down to the floor, gave his owner a reproachful look, and proceeded to wash himself in such a way as to show that his dignity was undamaged.

"Hey, Rainey?" He gave her an embarrassed look as they walked toward the door.

"Yes?"

"I'm glad we're working on this together."

She smiled. "Me, too."

Tyler brought Rainey back down into Crooked Creek, and the rest of the conversation revolved around reassuringly everyday topics—the beauty of the Cascades, a mutual love of alternative rock, a discovery that they'd both visited England as teenagers. She got out of the car in front of George

Colquitt's store, and then bent over and peered into the interior.

"Remember. Email me the photo. And let me know if you find out anything else. Let's make sure we share information, okay?"

"Definitely."

"Thanks for finding me. And thanks for helping me to get my jam home."

Tyler smiled at her. "No problem."

She watched him drive away, and then walked over to the bike rack in front of the grocery store, extracted her bicycle, and rode off toward home.

So she had to find a way to talk to all three of the kids. Which meant coming up with some kind of story. She could probably fake running into Kevin, but for the other two, she'd have to come up with something plausible.

She gave a hand signal and turned left out of the main road through the village onto Dailey Road. The Standishes lived in a neat little house not too far from there, and when she saw the road sign for North Fork Road up on the left side, she made a sudden, impulsive decision, and pedaled her way up a steep hill.

What could she say to her? "I'm here to see how you're doing?" It's not like she even knew Kathleen well. Plus, she was not a very good liar. Maybe the direct approach was called for. But what if Darla answered the door? She didn't want to have to explain herself to Darla, and what possible reason would she have for wanting to talk to her daughter?

She passed Daisy Blodgett's house, the back yard and its thriving crop of illicit herbs shielded from view and unauthorized sampling by a tall cedar fence. Not too much farther along was Darla Standish's trim ranch house with its nicely maintained flower gardens. And there was Kathleen, kneeling on the grass, pulling weeds, and layering bark mulch around thriving clumps of perennials.

She should have known to follow her intuition. It never led her astray.

Kathleen looked up as she coasted to a stop in front of the house.

"Hi, Kathleen!" she called out.

"Hi," Kathleen responded, a little tentatively. She stood, brushing the dirt off her hands, and walked toward Rainey. Kathleen was a tall, athletic girl, blonde like her mother, with a sprinkling of freckles across the bridge of her nose. To all appearances, she hadn't changed at all, but still, there was *something*. And whatever that unspecified something was gave Rainey the creeps.

Rainey's eyes narrowed a little, and she had to suppress an urge to turn her bike and pedal like mad back down the hill, but she concentrated on keeping her smile steady.

"I was biking around. I heard about how you got lost, and I thought I'd stop by and see how you were doing."

"I'm fine. Thanks for asking."

"It must have been terrifying, getting lost like that."

"I managed. There were wild berries around. I was hungry but didn't starve."

She swallowed. Time either to ask her or else say goodbye and get the hell out of there. The moment stretched out, Rainey looking at the girl, Kathleen staring back at her, watchful, wary, her eyes intent and cold.

"Do you know if the reason you got lost… if it might not be the same reason that Kevin Torgeson got lost? And Phil Collette?"

Kathleen's left eyebrow twitched upwards a little. "Why would it be?"

"I think that was what I was asking *you*."

A trace of a smile appeared on her face. "I hardly know Kevin or Phil."

"And that still doesn't answer the question."

The smile vanished. "Then, no. No, there's no connection. Does that answer the question?"

"Yes, it does. I'm glad you're back safe and sound."

"Thanks."

Rainey picked up her bicycle, pointed it back downhill, and pushed off. As she gathered speed, she turned and looked over her shoulder. Kathleen was still standing there, watching her, a speculative and not particularly friendly expression on her face.

Kathleen was lying. She tried to evade, and when that didn't work, she lied outright.

Rainey zoomed down the hill and shot back out onto Dailey Road, took a left, and pedaled up the slope toward her house.

That wasn't like the Kathleen Standish she knew. A shudder vibrated its way up her spine. Kathleen always seemed like a nice girl. Straightforward, a little blunt some-times, but she wasn't cold and suspicious like that. Something fundamental had changed in her. But what? No one else saw any difference.

She turned right on Pell Hill Road, pushing ahead up the steep slope toward her house. She passed Kevin Torgeson's house on the left, with its swath of neatly manicured lawn, but her luck failed her there. No one was outside, and the carport was empty. Maybe Kevin was there, in the house by himself, but after the experience with Kathleen, she couldn't bring herself to go up to the front door and knock.

They'd changed. They'd all changed. But what did that mean? Either something happened while they were missing that was making them act different, or they'd been... replaced.

She shuddered again, and turned her bicycle into her drive-way. This was not simply post-abduction trauma. There was no doubt in her mind. So that left her with two possibilities—

either someone, or something, was making them act different, controlling them, working through them, like what people said about demon possession. Or else the Kathleen, Kevin, and Phil now living in Crooked Creek were identical duplicates.

And if that was true, what had happened to the real children?

six

. . .

Dale Blodgett was just getting out of the shower when his phone rang. He swore loudly, wrapped a bath towel around his waist, and padded off, dripping, into his living room.

"Hello?" he growled into the phone.

"Hi, Dale, it's Sheila," said an apologetic voice. "I'm sorry to call you at home, but I thought you might want to know before you drove in. Something apparently happened last night up at the research station in the Sisters. A break-in of some kind. I thought you might want to drive straight up there before coming in to the station."

He sighed loudly. "Jesus. What's with this place? We have about one crime a year around here, and in the last two weeks we have three abductions and a break-in."

"Sorry, Dale." If she expected him to say, *Don't apologize, Sheila, it's not your fault,* she was doomed to disappointment. He tended to blame inconveniences on whoever happened to be nearest, and if no one was around, on any handy inanimate objects.

"I'll go up there directly. I'll be in the office after I'm done out there." He hung up.

It didn't help that he had woken up in a foul mood. His visit to his mother the previous week had resulted in a series of phone calls, and ultimately being shamed into going over for dinner. The vegan enchiladas were palatable, and open windows took care of the worst of the house's smell, but even so it always took several days after a visit for the feelings of annoyance to dissipate. The topics of conversation were predictable—Dale's lack of a Nice Female Friend, Daisy's thriving business of supplying pot to Crooked Creek's chapter of the Recreational Drug Enthusiasts' Association, Dale's high blood pressure, Daisy's embracing of the latest bizarre ideas from the crystals, pyramids, and magic spells set. Neither of them ever budged a bit themselves, but both lived in the continual hope of changing the other's mind.

So he was predisposed to snarl at everyone today, and it would be at least three days before he was inclined to be civil. The call about the break-in at the research station did nothing to improve his mood, and as he dressed, ate breakfast, and a half-hour later, drove up into the Sisters, he wore a persistent glower and at intervals muttered profanity-filled imprecations under his breath.

A little after nine o'clock, he pulled up in front of the squat, blocky bulk of the Cascadia Zoological Research Station. He got out of his car, looked around for any signs of vandalism—there weren't any—and then went into the building through the front door, which stood open.

Three people turned to look at him when he entered. There was a young guy, maybe twenty-eight or so, with a skittish, wary expression. Next to him was a thirty-something woman, solid, no-nonsense, dressed in a plaid shirt and jeans, with an unflattering bowl haircut and rather incongruous large green earrings. In the back of the room was a tall, stooped man with short salt-and-pepper hair, gold wire-framed glasses, and a harassed look.

The older man stepped forward, and extended a hand. "Chief of Police Blodgett?"

He shook his hand. "Yes."

"I'm Joseph DiStefano, the research station director. I don't think we've met before."

Dale grunted.

"This is Doctor Judy Kahn, and Doctor Tyler Vaughan, who form the station's permanent zoological staff. Thank you for coming up so promptly."

Joe's deference tempered a bit of Dale's irritability. "No problem. You had a break-in?"

Joe nodded. "Most unfortunate. But I'll let Tyler tell you about it. He's the one who discovered it this morning when he came in to work."

Dale looked over at the nervous younger man, who flashed a glance at the other two and then stepped forward.

Jittery type. Nervous as a young colt. Something had got him really shook.

"When I got here this morning," he began, but Dale interrupted him.

"When?"

"About seven-thirty. I got here and found the door unlocked. I thought that was weird because we're always really careful about locking up. We've got a lot of expensive equipment that someone might want to steal. Plus, being up here and isolated, there's always the possibility of vandalism."

Dale nodded.

"So, I came inside, and flipped on the light. One of the trash cans was knocked over. I know you're not supposed to touch anything at a crime scene, but I wasn't thinking, so I set it upright. That's when I noticed my computer was gone." He pointed at his desk, which now had a large empty spot where his computer had been.

"Anything else missing?"

"Yes." Tyler's glance met Judy's for a fraction of a second.

Dale, for all of his basic laziness, had gone into police work largely because he possessed one outstanding skill—he was extraordinarily good at noticing subtleties. As unsubtle as he was as a person, he was keenly aware of minute changes in tone of voice, posture, and body language in the people around him. As soon as Tyler flashed a glance at his coworker, it was plain that the next thing he said would be an evasion, if not an outright lie.

"The only other thing missing is some pieces from a broken camera."

"A *broken* camera?"

Tyler swallowed, and nodded. "Yes. I have remote cameras set up all over the Sisters. I study the migration patterns of mammals. They're expensive pieces of equipment. They take visible light photographs during the day, and switch over to color-enhanced thermal imaging at night."

Again, there was that nervous microseconds-long glance at Judy.

"And this one was broken?"

Tyler nodded again. "It was knocked out of its housing and smashed a little less than two weeks ago. We think by a bear. I brought the pieces down here, to see if anything could be salvaged from it. It was sitting on my desk, next to the computer. It's gone."

"Were the pieces valuable? Could it have been repaired and sold?"

"I don't think so. It was pretty far gone."

"Do you have any idea why anyone would steal the pieces of a broken camera?"

"No. None whatsoever."

Okay, that was a lie. No question about it.

"Any thoughts about why the thief took your computer, and left that one behind?" He pointed to Judy's computer, still sitting in its place on her desk.

"No clue."

Dale put on his best "Look, mister, I'm the law around here, and you don't mess with the law" expression, and said, "Doctor Vaughan, I think you're not telling me the whole truth."

Tyler's eyes widened a little. "I'm telling you the truth. Of course I'm telling you the truth. Why would I lie?"

"I didn't say you lied, just that you're not telling me everything you know."

The tough-looking woman in the plaid shirt—what had the old dude said her name was? Cohen? Kane? Something like that—took a step forward.

"Look, officer, a lot of our research is scrutinized pretty carefully around here. We're under the microscope of logging interests, environmental interests, and community interests, not to mention a variety of eco-wackos and other such scary folks. We've got to tread a very narrow line to stay in business. Tyler and I want to avoid publicity, so we're not trying to make a big deal about the vandalism to the camera. These things happen. But we're concerned about the break-in here because it's a threat to our research, and could mean a threat to our personal safety."

Very clever. She'd neatly deflected his question from her high-strung friend, and made it look like pushing his buttons about what he knew was jeopardizing the progress of science. He looked at Tyler. The fretful expression had relaxed somewhat. If she hadn't stepped in, he might have gotten Tyler to crack. But she gave him time to think through an answer, so pressing him further probably wouldn't work. However, it did mean that whatever Tyler knew, she was in on it.

"I understand that, Ms…" Dale hesitated.

"Kahn. *Doctor* Judy Kahn."

He scowled. "Right Doctor Kahn. And understand that I got no beef with you folks being up here. Far as I'm concerned, as long as the loggers, scientists, hikers, and econuts, and even the plain old ordinary citizens of Crooked Creek, mind their business and don't break the law, I got no problem with any of 'em. Let me remind you, though, that *you* folks are the ones that called *me* in here, and I'm not going to get along very fast at tracking down the culprits, and maybe getting your computer back, if you don't tell me whatever you know that might be relevant."

Judy nodded. "I understand that."

"Good." He studied the room. "Are you sure nothing else is missing?"

"Nothing that we know of," Tyler said. "We checked pretty carefully. Nothing else looks like it's been touched."

"Were there any windows left open? Have you checked any other entrances?"

"There's only one other entrance, at the back of the lab. It's locked. And all the windows were shut and locked as well."

Dale went over to the front door. "I expect all of you have handled the doorknob. Probably too late for fingerprints, but we could give it a shot." He knelt, studied the knob, and frowned. "It doesn't look like it was forced. Who has a key to this place?"

"Only myself, Doctor Vaughan, and Doctor Kahn," Joe said, a little stiffly. "We have a set of duplicate keys that are used by temporary research staff when there is a project going on, but the last such project ended three weeks ago, and we don't have another scheduled until the end of July. I keep the duplicate keys in my office, and I can assure you that they are all accounted for."

Dale didn't respond, but looked at the bolt, and frowned. He then took a handkerchief out of his pocket, draped it over his hand, and turned the doorknob gently. It turned, but made a faint grating noise as it did so.

"What is it, officer?" Joe said.

Dale pointed at the bolt. "Look here, where the bolt comes out of the door. Scorch marks."

Joe peered nearsightedly over his shoulder. "What does that signify?"

Dale shrugged. "No idea. You have a screwdriver? Phillips."

"I have one in my desk." Tyler went to retrieve it.

Dale reached out for the screwdriver without turning his head, and then quickly undid the screws that held the doorknob on. Still holding the knob carefully with his handkerchief, he pulled it, and with a creak it slid off the shaft. He peered into the hole.

"Huh." He tried to keep the surprise out of his tone, but his mental voice shouted, *Jesus Christ, it's completely melted!* He gave a come-here motion with his left hand. "Come over and take a look at this."

Joe, Judy, and Tyler came forward and peered into the hole left by the removal of the doorknob.

Dale pointed. "The lock mechanism is pretty much gone. It looks like it's been melted. Or burned away. The knob still turns, but the inner workings of the lock are toast."

He stood up, still holding the doorknob, and looked at the three members of the lab staff. Joe, looking mystified. Judy, defiant but scared. Tyler, frightened to the point of bolting from the room.

Dale stuck the melted doorknob under Tyler's nose. "Any idea what could do something like that? You have an idea, don't you, Doctor Vaughan?"

For a third time, that lightning-fast glance toward Judy Kahn. Dale observed, with satisfaction, that Judy gave a tiny little frown, and an almost invisible shake of her head at him.

"No. I have no idea at all. I certainly can't think of anything that could burn a lock mechanism without destroying the door at the same time."

"And you really have no idea why anyone would want your computer—*only* yours, and not Doctor Kahn's—and the apparently worthless pieces of a broken camera?"

"No."

Dale nodded. "Okay. I'll file a report on this, and we'll send someone up to take fingerprints. Doctor Vaughan, you should probably stay out of your desk until it's been dusted. Will there be someone here, so we can leave the door open until we check it, as well?"

"Of course, officer," Joe said.

"We'll try to get someone here this afternoon. After that, you can feel free to replace the lockset. I'd imagine you would want to do that quickly, so that it's as secure as it can be tonight."

"If whoever broke in has a way of destroying locks," Joe observed, "I don't know that it will do us much good."

"You might consider a deadbolt. That way, even if the interior of the doorknob lock gets fried again, the door will still be secure."

"That's a good idea." Joe shook his head. "We've never had a break-in before, so we've been able to get along without thinking about such things. It's a shame."

Dale nodded. "I'll be in touch."

He returned to his car and sat for a few moments making notes on a sheaf of paper attached to a clipboard. Then he started up his engine, and pulled out onto the road.

Vaughan and Kahn knew more than they were saying, that was clear. And they were covering for each other. Vaughan was the weak link, but as soon as Dale had pressed him, Kahn came for him like an attack dog and gave Vaughan time to regroup. But covering up what? Vaughan didn't seem like the type who'd steal his own computer, maybe to sell, and then fake a break-in. And there was the camera thing. Why take pieces of a hopelessly broken camera? Almost certainly Vaughan and Kahn could both have answered that question.

Peculiar business. The whole place had been peculiar lately. And then a strange thought came, unbidden, to his mind. Could this have had anything to do with those kids disappearing? It seemed like such a *non sequitur* that he dismissed it, but it kept pulling at his brain. But how on earth could they be connected?

Then he remembered what he'd said to Sheila when she'd called in the burglary at the research station—*We have about one crime a year around here, and in the last two weeks we have three abductions and a break-in.* There was no logical reason to connect the two, and yet he was left with the nagging feeling that the sudden crime wave in Crooked Creek couldn't be an odd set of coincidences.

Dale's feelings of unease gradually diminished during the day, as he was able to put aside both the mystery of the break-in at the research station and the memory of last night's dinner with his mother. He'd get someone out to dust the lab, probably find nothing other than prints belonging to the lab staff, and be able to file the theft of the computer under "cases that will probably never be solved, and which I honestly don't give a rat's ass about anyhow." He considered that, on the maternal annoyance front, at least he'd gotten dinner with Daisy over with, and couldn't be reasonably expected to dine with her again for another month or so. This cheered him considerably.

Five o'clock rolled around, and he headed home, an easy ten-minute walk from the station. He usually drove anyway, even in good weather. Dinner—a couple of hamburgers and a bottle of Olympia—was consumed, and he proceeded on to his nightly ritual, which was watching random television shows until he fell asleep in his recliner.

The phone shrilled at eleven o'clock, jolting him out of a dream involving Scarlett Johansson and a clothing-optional beach, and he stumbled across the room, swearing incoherently, and picked it up on the fourth ring.

"Hello?" he said thickly.

A hysterical voice came out of the telephone's speaker like an auditory ice pick.

"Dale! Dale! You've got to come over here! Someone's tried to kidnap Hannah!"

"Hannah?" He squeezed his eyes shut in an attempt to clear the mental fog. "Who is this?"

"It's Abby! Abby Cleary! I thought of calling nine-one-one, but it would take too long! You've got to get over here!"

He blinked a couple of times. "I'll be right over." Then he hung up the phone and said, "Fuck."

Abby and Mason Cleary lived in a beautiful log cabin only a quarter of a mile from Dale's house. Mason was a decent enough guy. He owned the Crooked Creek Hardware Store. Dale sometimes ran into him at Dorrie's Bar and Grill, and they usually passed a pleasant time talking about the Seattle Seahawks.

Abby, however, was another story. She was a chronic complainer who was allergic to damn near everything, sometimes wore a surgical mask while walking out to get the mail, and allegedly had an entire pharmacy's worth of pills in her medicine cabinet. Dale often wondered how a regular fellow like Mason Cleary had ever hooked up with a head case like Abby, but they seemed to get along great. This reinforced Dale's determination to keep out of romantic entanglements. They rotted out the logic centers of the brain.

Abby and Mason had one daughter, Hannah, a thirteen-year-old who seemed destined to follow in her mother's footsteps. She was in seventh grade but apparently spent more time in the nurse's office than she did in class, and was notorious around the village for spinning tall tales. Dale was already primed to disbelieve everything she said, but he dutifully drove down to the Clearys' house, although still muttering imprecations under his breath about missing the end of the dream about Scarlett, which had been looking pretty promising.

As soon as his footsteps clunked their way across the front porch, the door was flung open by Abby, who was still weeping. She managed to choke out, "Dale, thank you, come in, thank god you're here," and stood aside to let him in.

Mason Cleary sat on the couch in the living room, and damned if the guy didn't look concerned himself. Dale frowned. If Mason was taking this seriously, maybe there was something in it. Nobody who loved the Seattle Seahawks could be discounted *entirely.* Seated next to Mason, and leaning on him, also crying, was Hannah.

Hannah Cleary shared more than her mother's personality —she looked like a little clone, compact, round-faced, olive-skinned, with a mass of dark curly hair. Nothing of Mason Cleary's tall, red-haired, freckled DNA had had any apparent effect on her makeup. Hannah looked up at Dale, and burst into a histrionic series of sobs.

Mason hugged her closer. "Dale, what the hell is happening around here? Someone tried to snatch Hannah right off the street."

Dale sat down in a rocking chair near the couch. "Hannah, can you tell me what happened?"

Hannah was seemingly able to turn the tears on and off like an internal faucet, and looked up at him with watery eyes. "I was... I was... going out to bring out the trash to the curb. My parents said... said I had to."

"She'd forgotten to do it earlier." Mason looked embarrassed, as if he was ashamed at having had to make such outrageous demands on his daughter. "It's one of her weekly chores. So I told her to quick do it before she went to bed."

"So… so I got the trash together, and put it in the trash can, and went outside. I was so scared, because it was *all dark*, and *so scary.*"

Hannah waited for some sign of commiseration from Dale, but none was forthcoming, so she continued.

"So I brought the trash out, and I'm like thinking, *anything could jump out and grab me*, and I'm like thinking, *all those other kids disappeared exactly like this, out on the street all alone*, and I had just put the trash can at the curb when there was a noise in the bushes along the driveway, and *omigod something grabbed my arm!*"

There ensued another three-minute bout of tears, interspersed with noises of sympathy from both of the Cleary parents.

Dale waited until there was a lull. "So, what was it?"

"Well," Hannah said, obviously relishing the drama of the situation and determined to drag it out as long as she could, "I screamed. And tried to get away! I like struggled and struggled! But it was so strong! And it was trying to pull me off into the bushes!"

"It?"

"Well, I didn't *know* who it was." Hannah was clearly exasperated at this interruption of her story. "I wasn't looking! I was all, like, *omigod, I'm gonna disappear like those other kids! And I'll never be seen again!*"

Another three-minute intermission for hysterical sobbing.

"Yes, and what happened then?" He tried to keep his voice gentle, but his actual desire was to grab the little brat himself and shake her until her teeth rattled.

"Well, I finally pulled so hard my t-shirt ripped!" She pointed at her sleeve, which was missing a chunk of cloth. "And I fell down. And they were on me in a second. But I got to my feet, and ran, and they ran after me a little way, but then gave up. I ran up the stairs on to the front porch, and *then*"—she paused, to accentuate the dramatic climax of the story—"*then* I looked back to see if they were still there."

"Were they?"

"Oh, *yes*. Standing there, staring at me. Then they just turned and walked off."

"Did you recognize them?"

Hannah looked at him as if he'd lost his mind. "Of course! Haven't you been listening to like anything I've *said*?"

"So, who was it?"

"It was them. Two of the kids."

There was a sudden drop in the pit of Dale's stomach, like the sensation of rising in a fast elevator. "Kids?"

"You *know*." Her tone of voice sounded like she was talking to a very young, and unintelligent, child. "Kevin Torgeson and Kathleen Standish."

seven

. . .

"Belize," Tyler said. "I hear that Belize is really nice."

"Will you get a grip?" Judy said.

"Tropical. Warm water. Snorkeling. Shirt-optional weather year round. Lots of scantily-clad women bringing you drinks with little umbrellas."

"Tyler!" Judy shouted. "You can't run away!"

"The hell I can't."

"Look, yesterday, you were the gallant young knight rushing in to help out his fair maiden. Today you're being a chickenshit."

"*Scorch* marks." He gestured to the recently-repaired door. "The inside of the doorknob was fried. Metal, Judy. This thing can melt *metal*."

"Yes, I know, but…"

"My computer stolen. Police guys fingerprinting my fucking *desk*. Kids disappearing right and left. At this point, I'd take a job doing rectal exams on warthogs, as long as it wasn't anywhere near Crooked Creek."

"What happened to wanting to figure this out?"

"Oh, I think that evaporated when I found out that Slender Man knows I'm on to him."

"Okay, I get that. But Tyler. We can't let this drop. You said that yourself."

"I know. But what can I do? Evil Superpowerful Alien Who Can Melt Metal versus Tyler the Chickenshit Zoologist. Who will win, I wonder?"

"I think we have to try."

"Allow me to remind you that *you* were the one who was cautioning *me* about getting involved. My Reputation As A Scientist, remember?"

"I know. But you know, now that the lab's been broken into..." She gave him a crooked smile. "It's like Bugs Bunny always used to say. 'Of course you know, *this* means war.'"

"Great. Now you're getting your inspiration from *Looney Tunes*."

"Yeah, well, Bugs always wins. I think he's a damned good role model."

"I'm more of a Daffy Duck type." He couldn't keep the mournful tone out of his voice. "'I don't like pain. It hurts.'"

She patted him on the shoulder. "Time to grow a pair, buddy."

He sighed. "So I can't run away?"

"No. I'm perfectly capable of finding you and dragging your sorry ass back here. You know that."

He sighed again, more deeply this time. "Belize would be nice."

"Save it for vacation."

"Man, you're tough."

"Yup. And think about your red-haired sweetie down in Crooked Creek, waiting for you to save the day. You were drooling yesterday when you described her to me, remember?"

He glared at her. "Was not."

"Were *too*. So here's the game plan. You promised her you'd update her with new developments, right?"

"Yeah."

"Okay, so you email her from my computer to let her know what happened. Then we go up to replace the camera at T-Three. The new one's ready to go, right?"

"Yes. I unpacked it yesterday afternoon. I have a spare camera housing waiting. But I don't know what's to stop Slender Man from waltzing up and smashing this one, too."

"Consider it an experiment. See what he does next."

"It's an expensive experiment."

"Hey, *you* don't have to pay for the camera."

"Don't say that in front of Joe."

She grinned. "I won't mention it if you don't."

A half hour and two cups of coffee later, Tyler had the following email composed.

Hi Rainey,

I wanted to contact you this morning because there's been a new development out here. The lab was broken into last night and my computer was stolen, along with the broken pieces of the remote camera. I got to meet your friend, Chief of Police Blodgett, and he's as charming as you described. I think he suspects me of having staged the break-in to accomplish who-knows-what, but for the time being I got away without telling him about the photographs and the whole cave incident.

We're going up to the ridge this morning to replace the camera. I don't know if it'll do any good, or what's to stop it from getting smashed again, but it's either that or tell my boss that I don't want to replace it, and that would involve doing a lot more explaining than I'm comfortable doing right now.

So please hang on to the jpg of the creature I sent you—now that my computer and the camera memory card have been stolen, it's the only copy left of the photograph. If I do have to explain at some point, I want to have at least that much in the way of evidence.

In any case, I'll still be able to use Judy's computer to check my email, so that's the best way to get a hold of me. I should be back in the lab my mid-afternoon and I'll check then. Maybe we could get together for dinner tonight and compare notes, if you're free?

cheers,

Tyler V.

Judy read it while peering over Tyler's shoulder, a frown on her face.

"What do you think?" he said.

"Only one criticism. You didn't sign off 'love and kisses.' But other than that."

He gave her a sardonic look. "Be serious."

"All right, all right. But no worries, it looks fine."

He maneuvered the cursor to the *Send* button, and then hesitated. "Judy, do you think…" He stopped, frowning.

"Do I think what?"

"Do you think that sending this could put Rainey in danger?"

"Why would it?"

"Think about it. Slender Man knew to take the camera, which is not surprising, but he also knew to take *my* computer, which was the one that the images had been downloaded to. He didn't touch yours."

"The camera was on your desk."

"True. But what if he somehow has access to my contacts, and connects Rainey to me?"

"You think Slender Man has *email*?" She snorted laughter. "Next thing, you'll be saying he's on TikTok and Facebook, too."

"He probably is. Some kind of highly technological alien species, who knows what he can do?"

"I doubt, somehow, that he has to resort to hacking our emails."

"You never know." He clicked *Send*, and the email to Rainey went off with a little whooshing noise.

"Okay, let's do this," she said. "You got your pack together? We dawdle much longer and I'm gonna go get some of my own work done, and leave you to go put that camera up by yourself."

"No, I'm ready. And you promised to come with me."

"Yeah, yeah, I'll hold your hand. No worries. Let's get at it. You got your flashlight, right?"

He looked at her in silence for a moment. "You serious about wanting to go into that lava tube?"

"Yeah. Once I get there, you may have to drag me in, crying like a little baby, but I think we should give it a look." She gave him a crooked smile. "Don't you want to check it out?"

"Yes." But there was something in there that could rip steel up like taffy, and fry a lockset. In situations like that there was a big difference between "we should" and "I want to."

The *Millennium Pigeon* bumped along the road toward the trailhead, with Tyler driving and Judy riding shotgun.

"So, how do you think that Slender Man connected the camera to the lab?" he asked.

"Who else puts cameras out in the woods? It sure as hell isn't the loggers."

"Yeah, but how would *he* know that? I mean, think about it. You're some alien dude, really smart and everything, but you don't come preloaded with knowledge about what humans do. You see a camera pointed at the cave where you've set up housekeeping, you go and kill the camera. It doesn't take much of a stretch to figure that some smart, technologically advanced species would be able to infer what the function of a camera is by looking at it. But then somehow, you look at the pieces of the camera, using your Spidey-senses because you don't have eyes, and somehow you think, 'Hey, I know where this came from! It's those two biologists who work in that brick box down the road!' It doesn't make any sense."

Judy didn't answer for a moment. "I don't know."

"That's why I'm worried about Rainey."

She grinned at him. "Not so worried about *me*, I notice."

Heat rose in his cheeks. "I don't mean that. I figure, you're getting involved in this because you're choosing to."

"So is she, as far as I can tell."

"Yeah, but you're a scientist. Taking risks to discover stuff is what we do. She's… hell, Judy, she makes herbal tea for a living. And she could be in danger."

She looked at him and shook her head. "You've got it *bad.*"

He pulled over, and shut off the engine. He hefted his pack, heavier than usual from the weight of the camera and housing, onto his back with a grunt, adjusted the straps a little, and trudged off up the trail.

"You scared?" she said, after they had hiked in a little way.

"Terrified. You?"

"I haven't pissed myself yet. I consider that an accomplishment."

The meadow at the edge of the forest rustled peacefully in the breeze, the pasqueflowers still shimmering like purple velvet in the sun. They came to the site where the ill-fated camera had been attached, silently shucked their packs, and looked around. He tugged at his t-shirt where it was glued to his back with sweat, and ran his hands through his hair, making it stand on end.

"I used to love this hike." He opened his pack and pulled

out the camera, housing, a box of screws, and a cordless drill. "Should I point it in the same direction? Or is that asking for trouble?"

"Of course it's asking for trouble. But that's kind of the point, isn't it? There's something in that direction that Slender Man doesn't want you to see."

"I'm just as happy not seeing it," he grumbled. "I'd be thrilled with nothing more than lots of images of elk roaming around."

Ten minutes later, a new galvanized steel housing was in place, hanging from the fir tree right above the broken screw shafts that marked the location of the old one. He gently picked up the camera, opened a panel in the side, and pressed a few buttons. There was a beep as the camera activated.

He aimed it at Judy. "Say cheese."

She made a face at the camera.

He pressed a button, and looked at the little digital display screen. "Okay, we're in business." He snapped the panel shut, slid the camera into the housing, then closed the lid over it and stuck in a metal pin to hold it shut.

"Now for the fun part." She rummaged around in her pack and pulled out a large, heavy-duty flashlight. "No need for the packs?"

"Can't see why we'd need them, given that we're going to die." He pulled out his own flashlight.

"I love an optimist." She walked off uphill toward the lava tube.

Even though he was ready for it this time, the feeling of apprehension flowing down the hill toward him still came as a shock. It was like a chilly blanket, dimming the sun, making the odd shapes of the lava outcroppings look like hunched, malign monsters. The apprehension grew to a clawing, desperate fear by the time he neared the cave mouth, and just as happened last time, both of them stopped, nearly simultaneously.

"Okay," she said. "This sucks."

"It's hard for me to even think about taking another step. My brain is screaming, 'Run away! Fast! Don't look back!' And then it wants to crawl into bed, pull up the blankets, and have a nice long cry."

"Wussie."

"I don't notice you storming the gates."

She took a step forward, and with an effort, he followed. Gradually, as if their feet were mired in thick mud, they approached the cave mouth, and switched on their flashlights.

The mouth of the lava tube was a little over six feet high. He only barely missed having to duck. They moved into the cool shade within, flashlight beams sweeping the floor, walls, ceiling, looking for any sign of... anything. The rock was rough and black, with a burned appearance, like broken charcoal.

The feelings of terror didn't abate, once they were in the cave, not that he expected them to, but at least they didn't grow stronger. Fortunately, or he'd have been reduced to a whimpering heap in the corner, and Judy'd have to radio for someone to come up and bring him back on a stretcher. But still, the unaccountable feeling of creeping horror surrounded him, and he felt a sense almost like a physical pressure pushing him away, out of the cave.

The floor was fairly smooth, and sloped downward ahead of them for about twenty feet before disappearing into gloom. The ceiling dropped until finally both of them were stooping, the daylight left behind, the flashlight beams illuminating an oval of dark wall or floor ahead.

Suddenly they came to a wall.

He swept the beam of the flashlight across it. The cave clearly ended in a blind wall. There was no opening in the ragged lava face.

"End of the road." His voice sounded breathless even in his own ears.

"This doesn't make any sense. There's got to be something more here." She peered into the corners and crevices of the cave, but all the light illuminated was bits of broken rock fallen from the walls and ceiling, and fragments of plant debris blown in by the wind.

"No footprints except our own. Nothing. It doesn't look like anything lives in here."

"That by itself is odd. Nice dry cave on a mountainside? There should be someone in here, or at least a trace of somebody. Bear, pika, marmot, something. Nice real estate like this doesn't go unoccupied for long."

"Maybe the animals are as afraid of it as we are."

Her brow creased. "I was sure we'd find something. I was sure."

"What were you expecting? Alien suitcases? A sign saying 'Slender Man is IN'?"

"Something. Some trace. Some clue or another."

"He's not going to leave my computer sitting on a rock ledge for me to find."

"I know. But there's still something wrong about this."

"Yeah?"

"Okay, so we've figured that Slender Man was somehow using his amazing superpowers to make us too scared to come in here. Right?"

"I guess."

"And he kills your camera because it's pointed at the cave mouth."

"Yeah."

"And he goes to all of that effort to keep us out of a bare lava tube that we never would have gone into in the first place if it hadn't been for his calling attention to it?"

He shrugged.

"Look, I don't buy that he's that stupid."

"Or maybe we're missing something. There's more here than we can see."

She nodded. "That's exactly it. There's more here than we can see." She went up to the rock wall at the end of the cave and shone her flashlight on it. She reached out and touched it, ran her hand over the jagged rock surface. "Feels real."

"What's that supposed to mean? There's such a thing as an unreal rock?"

"Of course. You can fake anything." She pushed tentatively on the rock outcropping.

Nothing happened.

"What, are you expecting that there will be a switch, like in the old horror movies where if you pulled out one particular book, the bookcase swiveled around?"

She shrugged. "I have a feeling. This wall is way too convenient."

He bumped it with his fist. "Even if you're right, I don't think we're going to get through it without high explosives."

She nodded. "And I think if I have to stand here calmly discussing this much longer, I'm going to start running around in circles screaming. Let's get out of here."

"No argument." Much faster than they had entered, they retreated up into the welcoming daylight.

As before, the feelings of dread diminished in direct proportion to their distance from the cave mouth, and by the time they had reached the T-Three site, they had vanished entirely. He tossed his flashlight into his pack and pulled the toggle to cinch it closed. He gave a rueful glance at the camera, its shiny black glass eye looking out at him through a circular hole in the housing.

"Good luck, buddy." He shouldered his pack, and he and Judy trudged off downhill toward the woods.

"You really think there was something behind that wall?" he said, as the tree trunks closed in around them and cut off the bright sunlight of the meadow.

"It's only a hunch. I don't have any evidence at all."

A few minutes of silence passed.

"Hey," he said. "We didn't die."

"Yeah. There's that."

"I wonder how long the new camera is going to last?"

She shrugged. "I give it a couple of days."

"Maybe we'll get a better image this time. More to go on."

"I wonder. He must have realized you got a good image of him. Why else steal the old camera and your computer? I doubt that we'd be that lucky again."

A few more moments passed in silence, and then suddenly he grabbed Judy's arm.

"What?" she yelled, and whirled around. "God, Tyler, don't do that. I'm not completely recovered from my cave-o-phobia yet. I managed not to wet my pants so far, but I'm not sure how much longer my luck will hold."

"Judy. Why did Slender Man break in and steal the camera?"

"Probably so you wouldn't have photographic evidence of his existence."

"Yeah, but how did he know? If he'd thought there'd be photographs, why wouldn't he have taken away the pieces of the camera after he wrecked it? Or destroyed it to the point that there was nothing functional left? He fried the doorknob lock, he could have melted the memory card, and then we wouldn't have had jack."

"Okay."

"So he had to know some other way besides the fact that we had the pieces of the camera. He stole the camera *and* the computer."

"Oh." Her eyes widened a little.

"Jesus. You were joking when you said he couldn't have hacked my email. But that's the only way he could have known about the photograph. When I sent the jpeg to Rainey."

"How… how could he have done that?"

"I have no idea. But otherwise, how could he have known?"

"Somehow he accessed your computer memory via the lab server?"

"No, that doesn't make sense. The server is in Eugene. How could he have access to it?"

"It makes better sense that he hacked your email from a cave in the Sisters?"

"Email and so on, all that stuff, is transmitted wireless these days. I don't pretend to understand computers that well. My uncle is a computer geek, though, and I remember him telling me that the weakest point in information security is *always* when you transmit something. When it's just sitting there on your computer, it's much harder to get at."

"So, that means…" She stopped, and glanced over at him.

"Yeah." His voice was grim. "Rainey."

Tyler drove the *Pigeon* down the rutted logging road at an alarming speed, hitting potholes that sent the little jeep airborne more than once.

"Christ almighty, Tyler." Judy had a death grip on the dashboard. "You're not going to do her any good if we end up piling into a tree."

He slowed down—a little—and they made it back to the lab intact. He jumped out of the jeep and ran up to the door, unlocked it, and landed in Judy's desk chair hard enough that it spun around on the tile floor.

"Come on, come on," he hissed at the monitor as the computer booted up, and he watched intently, fingers drumming on the table, as the spinning timer sat there, waiting for his login credentials to be accepted. By this time, Judy had come up behind him, and was watching the screen.

"You Have Two New Emails," came a message. He ignored the first one, which was from a zoologist from Cornell who was going to be heading out to the Sisters to do field work in three weeks, and clicked on the second, which was from teawoman12@gmail.com. It had been sent about an hour and a half earlier.

He closed his eyes for a minute, and let out a long, held breath. Then he started reading.

Hi Tyler!

That's really scary about the break-in. I hope you and your friend Judy are taking precautions. Your safety is more important than the camera or computer.

We've had some new developments here, too. Unfortunately. A girl who lives right in the village, Hannah Cleary, was the victim of an attempted abduction last night. I heard about it from Maureen Sullivan, who is the owner of the Three Sisters Lodge and is the commander-in-chief of the Crooked Creek gossip network. The problem is that Hannah is kind of notorious for stretching the truth, so it's hard to tell where the truth ends and the embellishment begins. But she said that she was outside after dark, bringing out the trash, and she narrowly escaped being kidnapped… by Kevin Torgeson and Kathleen Standish!

You met Dale, so you can imagine how he reacted. I guess he went right over and questioned Kathleen and Kevin, and they readily admitted being out together. Kathleen apparently said, "We were walking and talking over our experiences of being lost in the forest," as if that was the most natural thing in the world, which it isn't because if you knew those two kids you'd look far to find two people who would be less likely to want to socialize with each other. But Kevin corroborated her story, and they claimed that they were walking along, and heard Hannah scream, and ran up in time to see her sprinting up the sidewalk. They told Dale that they saw a shadowy figure disappear around the back of the house, but didn't have any idea who it was. They were going to follow Hannah up the sidewalk and try to help her, ask her what had happened, but she screamed and ran inside and slammed the door, so they went home.

It's all wrong, Tyler. I feel it more strongly than ever. It's calm, rational, plausible, and wrong. I'm trying not to freak out, but it's difficult. I haven't talked to Kevin yet—my talk with Kathleen was enough to give me nightmares for a week, and the crazy thing is, nothing happened. There's nothing she said or did that wasn't completely innocent-sounding. But I have a bad case of the heebie-jeebies. Silly of me, but there it is.

I'd love to have dinner. However, if we're going to discuss all this, let's not go out. At this point, I don't know who I should worry about overhearing. So I can make us dinner here. I make a killer spinach quiche, if that sounds good. Shall we say six?

Namasté,

Rainey

Tyler read the email twice, then looked up at Judy.

"This is getting freakier and freakier."

She nodded. "You ought to warn her."

"I will."

Tyler typed out a quick email in response.

Hi Rainey,

That is creepy as hell. I want you to be careful. I have reason to believe that Slender Man, or whoever is doing all this, broke into the lab because he somehow picked up on the fact that I'd sent you that image. If you have a flash drive, put the image on the flash drive and then hide it somewhere, and delete it off your computer. Stay inside and keep your doors locked.

I'll be there at six sharp. I'll blow the horn a couple of times so you know it's me. If anyone else knocks on your door, pretend you're not home.

cheers,

Tyler

p.s. Quiche sounds awesome.

. . .

"You write her a note cautioning her to lock herself inside her house, and fear for her life, and you sign off 'cheers'?" Judy said.

He shrugged. "Trying to stay upbeat, here." He sent the message.

Tyler arrived at Rainey's house at a little before six, after a quick stop at home to let Ahab out and give him his dinner. The cottage, in its exuberant tangle of garden, was peaceful and quiet. He gave a couple of quick beeps on the Civic's horn, and relief washed over him when Rainey pushed aside the curtains and gave him a smile and a little wave.

"Hi." She unlocked the door and let him in, and shut and relocked the door behind him.

"Hi. I guess you weren't lying that you're freaked out. You took my advice about locking the doors."

She nodded. "I've had the shudders all day. This thing with Kevin and Kathleen trying to abduct Hannah Cleary… well, it's like a nightmare. And the problem is, who could I go to? Dale wouldn't believe me. He figures that someone probably came up to her in the dark, and she freaked out, and the rest is Hannah making up a story. And heaven knows she does that. But this time it's true, and no one believes her. Except maybe her mother, who believes everything she says." She paused, and looked at him. "And me."

"And me. I believe her. And I believe you."

Rainey gave him a smile, and reached out and took his hand and squeezed it. "That helps. It really does."

Bonkers the cat appeared from nowhere, and rubbed on his leg. He hunkered down and skritched the cat's ears. "I gotta tell you what happened up on the ridge today."

"Would you like a glass of wine? I've got some chardonnay chilled."

"That'd be awesome."

She went into the kitchen, and there was the clink of glasses. "So, what happened? Did you put out the new camera?"

"Yeah." He stood and walked into the kitchen, where she handed him a glass of wine. "Cheers." They touched glasses as Bonkers came up to him with a disconsolate meow and rubbed against his leg again.

She gave the cat a little frown of disapproval. "Just ignore him. He can be a total pest."

"Wait'll you meet my dog."

She took a sip of her wine. "Did you go into the cave?"

He nodded. "Not something I'm anxious to do again, any time soon."

"What happened?"

"Nothing. Exactly nothing. It's like how you described your conversation with Kathleen. It'd make the world's most boring horror movie. 'And they went into the cave… with their flashlights… and… *there was nothing there.*'"

She regarded him solemnly. "But you *felt* it again, right?"

"Oh, yeah. It was terrifying. Like all of your experiences of thinking something was under the bed, thinking you were being watched, and thinking that a monster was stalking you, all rolled into one. Even Judy, who is one of the most practical, down-to-earth people I know, was shaking in her boots."

"I know exactly what you mean." She leaned against the counter. "I know I should go talk to Kevin Torgeson and Phil Collette, but I'm scared to death to actually do it."

"If you can believe this, Judy was convinced that the back wall of the cave was fake."

"Fake?"

He nodded. "She had this impression that there was something behind it. Like I said, Judy is not prone to flights of fancy, so when she says something like this, I tend to listen. I mean, maybe it was the fear acting on her, or maybe it was because we were so convinced there'd be something in the cave, and there was nothing. Not a trace of anything. Not a footprint, nothing. No signs of habitation, even by animals, and that's odd in and of itself." He paused. "Did you put the jpeg I sent you on a flash drive?"

She nodded. "That was a good idea. I hid the flash drive inside a mug on the top shelf of that cabinet"—she pointed—"and I can't imagine that anyone would think of looking there."

"Good. I hope I'm wrong that the email may have connected you to me and the camera incident."

She shrugged. "We'd have been connected sooner or later anyhow. All anyone would have had to do is follow you when you left work today, and I'm involved."

"I hadn't thought of that."

"I wouldn't worry about it," she said lightly. "When will you start getting images from the camera?"

"I should be already. It's motion-activated, and I tested it before I put it out. It should be working now."

"Are you going to go back to the lab tonight and see what you've got?"

"Out of curiosity?" He grinned. "Not if it means cutting our visit short."

She gave him a smile. "Let's eat, shall we? I think the quiche is ready."

For a while, Tyler tried consciously to steer the conversation away from the bizarre occurrences of the previous week, and as they chatted about trivia—his research, her tea business— he thought, *Is this a date? It's either that or a strategic planning meeting. I like the idea of "date" better.* Certainly she acted as if she were interested in him, but it was hard to tell if it was only because they were allies.

Spinach quiche and a nice bottle of wine sort of made it clear, though. You can plan strategy over tortilla chips and cheese dip. Nah, this was clearly a date.

Of course, maybe she was like this with everyone. She did seem like the type who would offer an IRS auditor tea and homemade biscuits.

She looked across the table at him. "Lost in thought?"

His cheeks warmed, and he hoped it wasn't obvious in the dim light. "Just trying to figure out what to do next."

"I think in your case, the ball is in Slender Man's court. We'll see if he takes the bait. As far as me, I have to cinch up my courage and go talk to Phil and Kevin. I'll do it tomorrow morning. But I'll have to dream up some reason for why I want to talk to them, especially with Phil."

"I wonder if you'll get any more out of them than you did out of Kathleen."

She shrugged. "Honestly, I doubt it, but you never know. In any case, we have to cover all bases. Then, I think we sit back and wait for something to happen. It's not the best plan in the world, but we don't exactly have a lot of leads to follow up."

He looked over the top of his wine glass at her for a moment. "Please be careful."

She smiled a little. "I will be. I will be stealthy and cunning. I'm very good at acting like a scatterbrained nitwit when I want to. I don't think I'll be in any danger, if they think that it's the crazy tea lady making sure that their cosmic vibrations are in harmony. You need to be careful, too, you and Judy both. You're the ones whose workplace got broken into, remember?"

"I know. I'm not used to thinking about that, you know? I mean, I've worked with animals for years, and you always know that animals can hurt you. But this is different. You're working with something that is intelligent, and has its own motives, has an ability to deceive."

"Like people."

He nodded. "That's part of why I became a zoologist. You never have to worry about an animal lying to you, or manipulating you. If they want something, they try to get it. If they're afraid or angry, they react. It's simple and straightforward."

"But they can't love as deeply, either. Dogs and cats may come close. They're the ones that are the most like us, I think."

"My dog is pretty attached to me, I guess, but I think that's mostly because I feed him and play with him. Honestly, Ahab has about three working brain cells. I don't think he ponders much."

"I wonder if you're right about that. I'll bet they think more than you realize. Who knows what they'd tell us if they could talk?"

He laughed, but then his smile died away, and he looked down. "Rainey, I had this thought. It's kind of a downer."

"What is it?"

"It occurred to me that maybe I could die. You know, trying to stop Slender Man, trying to stop the kids getting abducted and all. I saw what he did to the lock and the camera housing. I guess he could kill me if he wanted to." He looked up. "I wondered… if something does happen to me, could you look after Ahab? I mean, he's kind of a big oaf, but I love him." He took a quick sip of wine, and looked down again.

She put her hand on his. "Of course. I'd have done it even without your needing to ask. But of course." She smiled a little. "I'm not going to admit that as a possibility, though. All shall be well."

"I hope so."

He stayed to help wash the dishes, had a cup of tea while playing with Bonkers with a piece of string, and had a tour of part of Rainey's three acres of herb gardens in the last of the daylight. Finally, and reluctantly, he said, "It's getting late. I'd better go."

She nodded. "Yes. Tomorrow will be a busy day. I've got some scary children to interview, and you have to see what happened with the camera overnight. Email me when you know something, okay?"

"I will. You too."

"I will." She came up to him, and stood on tiptoes and gave him a quick kiss on the mouth. "I had fun tonight. Let's do it again."

He grinned as a little shiver of pleasure vibrated down his backbone. "Me too. I'll cook next time. I can't make quiche, but I'll see if I can come up with something edible."

She smiled at him. "It'll be fine, whatever it is."

eight

. . .

Rainey lay awake in bed, with Bonkers curled up against her, a deep purr rumbling his chest. She ordinarily had no difficulty sleeping, especially with her cat pressed up close, purring contentedly, but sleep was evasive tonight.

Should she be more worried? Tyler actually thought that they might try to kill him. That honestly had never occurred to her. He was worried enough to ask her to take his dog if he ended up dying.

Of course, he seemed like the worried type. She smiled. The kind who can't help but think about the worst-case scenario. At the same time, he was not very careful himself. He gave the impression of being the type who worried about vague possibilities, and then in the here and now went ahead and trusted everyone, and got taken advantage of.

Rainey, on the other hand, worried about specifics. She was honestly scared of Kevin and Kathleen and Phil. There was something dangerous about Kathleen. Wary. Like a predator, sizing you up, trying to figure out if you're worth killing.

She shuddered. No sense getting herself all freaked out.

Tonight was still tonight, and tomorrow wasn't here yet, and she'd deal with that when the time came. For now, let it be.

It was still another hour before she slept.

Tomorrow came with cool fog rolling down from the ridge, and a clear drop of water on the tip of each leaf. Not uncommon in the Cascades, but still a little ominous. Holding a mug of steaming lavender tea, Rainey looked out her window toward the woods across Pell Hill Road. The tree trunks were mere shadows, indistinct even at this distance.

Fog hides everything. It makes the world surreal. Somehow, it blankets not only sight but sound, wrapping the whole world in a shifting, curling gauze that takes familiar objects and turns them dreamlike. It made her want to walk quietly, for fear of attracting the attention of whatever was just out of sight.

She went through her morning rituals—feeding Bonkers, feeding the chickens, getting a light breakfast, giving a cursory look to the newspaper—all the while fighting down a nauseating sense of panic. It reminded her of when, as a teenager, she'd had to have surgery to repair torn cartilage in her knee, the result of a fall while climbing a tree. She woke on the morning of the surgery feeling terrified, as if she couldn't possibly face walking calmly into the hospital in Eugene under her own power, and lying down on a gurney so they could cut her open. It seemed impossible.

Then, the thought had occurred to her: *At some point, this will be over. There will come a time when all of this will be in the past.* At that, the panic subsided. It had become a thing already accomplished. No need to be afraid—there would be a time when she had, in fact, done this thing. It seemed more like a story in a book, where after the scary part there comes a page that says, *And they lived together happily, ever after.*

So, there would be a point when the conversations with Kevin and Phil would be in the past. She took a sip of her tea. Somehow, that made it better. It was all a trick of her mind, she knew that, but it made it better nonetheless.

The fog had lifted a little by the time Rainey mounted her bicycle and coasted off downhill toward South Fork Road, where Phil Collette lived. She figured Kevin Torgeson, like most teenagers, wouldn't be awake yet, so she'd tackle Phil first. She'd even come up with a plausible story. At least, it sounded plausible to her, and she hoped it would to Phil's parents, and to Phil himself.

The Collettes lived in a two-story log cabin on the south edge of the village, about a ten-minute ride from her house. She pedaled her bike up the long driveway, braked to a stop, and got off, leaning it against a tall fir tree in the front yard. Shaking a little, but her face set and determined, she strode up the sidewalk and to the front door.

Her knock was answered by a heavy-set balding man, who smiled at her a little questioningly. "Hi?"

"Hi. I don't think we've actually met, but I've seen you around the village. I'm Rainey Carrington."

He reached out and shook her hand. "Dave Collette."

"I was wondering if I could speak with your son for a moment. I have an herbal tea business, and now's a busy time, cutting, drying, and so on. I could use a hand, and your son was recommended to me as a hard worker. I thought maybe he might want a summer job."

Dave Collette smiled. "He's a good kid. I'll get him."

A few moments later, a small, slender boy came out from the interior of the house. He had a narrow face, gray eyes, and hair of a rather nondescript shade of brown. A perfectly ordinary little boy.

So why did he give her the shudders?

"Hi, Phil?" She tried to keep her voice steady, and mostly succeeded. "My name's Rainey. I wonder if you might like to have a summer job. Only a few hours a week."

"Doing what?"

"Cutting and drying herbs. I make tea."

"Oh." His eyes never left hers. "Why do you need my help?"

"I… could use some help, that's all."

"Oh. I don't know. I'd have to ride up there on my bicycle. It's kind of a long way."

"It's not so far." She hoped her tone was encouraging.

Phil shrugged. "I'll have to talk to my mom and dad about it."

"Okay. You can call me. My phone number is in the telephone book. My last name is Carrington."

"Okay."

"By the way, I hope you're recovered from your adventure? That must have been scary, being lost in the woods."

Phil's eyes narrowed for a moment, and when he spoke, his voice was still level and uninterested. "Yeah. It was."

"I'm glad you're back, safe and sound."

"Me, too."

"Bye."

"Later."

She walked off down the sidewalk, and as she was getting on her bicycle, the front door snicked closed behind her. She gave a quick glance over her shoulder, and caught a swift glimpse of Phil's pale face looking at her through the living room window. But as soon as their eyes met, he retreated back into the gloom of the house's interior and vanished from view.

Rainey pedaled toward home, the fog twisting and swirling around her, opening in front of her and closing behind.

Not right. What was it about them? Everything they said was normal. To any observer, it would just be a kid talking to some adult he didn't know. But it was all wrong, and she couldn't figure out what was wrong about it.

She strained her way up the steep slope of Pell Hill Road. As she came around the corner, Maureen Sullivan was pulling her powder-blue Mercury Grand Marquis out of the Torgesons' driveway. So Maureen was keeping tabs on Kevin, too, most likely to feed her appetite for gossip. Rainey couldn't recall hearing that she was a friend of the Torgesons until Kevin disappeared. She tried, unsuccessfully, to keep her mental voice from adding, *I really dislike that woman,* as Maureen swept past in her hulking car, giving her a curious look, and then vanished downhill toward town.

Rainey pedaled the rest of the way up the slope and turned off into the driveway of the Torgesons' house, with its immaculate lawn and carefully maintained garden. Rich Torgeson, Kevin's father, would already be off to work, but Leah, who taught fourth grade and was off in the summer, would probably be there. She coasted to a stop and laid her bicycle down on the edge of the driveway. The lawn was manicured to the point that she didn't dare ride onto it, or even set her bicycle down on it. She went up to the front door, and rang the bell.

Leah answered the door, and gave her a curious little smile. "Why, Rainey? Hello," she said, as if the last thing she expected was a visit from her neighbor. And indeed, Rainey and the Torgesons had so little in common that she couldn't remember a time they'd ever chatted for more than five minutes together.

"I was wondering if Kevin is here."

"I think he's still inside." Leah turned and called, "Kevin?"

There was a voice that called, "Coming," and a sound of footsteps, and Kevin came into view, barefoot, wearing jeans and an old t-shirt and looking completely unremarkable.

"Hi, Rainey," he said.

"Hi, Kevin. I was wondering if you wanted a summer job?"

He gave her a little smile. Cunning smile? Knowing smile? Just a smile? Heaven help her, she was beginning to see evil omens in everything.

"What made you think of me?"

"You live so close. Plus, I didn't think you were working."

"Keep me out of trouble, right?" The faint smile still played around his lips.

"Sure. It's cutting and drying herbs."

Kevin chuckled. "Oh, so that's why you thought of me. That, I can do."

"I figured." She smiled at him. "I won't be able to pay you that much, but I thought you might be interested."

"Definitely."

"So, can you start soon?"

"Any time. Tomorrow morning, maybe?"

"That sounds great. Maybe a couple of good hours tomorrow, and see if you like the work? It's not the most exciting thing in the world."

"I'm sure it'll be fine. And maybe if I get busy, there are a couple of other kids in the area that I could share the work with."

Her smile faltered a little. *Don't let him see that you're rattled. Keep talking.* "Sure, that'd be no problem, as long as they are good workers."

"They are. No worries in that regard."

She studied Kevin. He still looked vaguely amused, but there was no sign that the comment had meant anything other than the obvious. "That'd be fine with me. So, who are these other kids you're thinking of, who might be willing to work, too?"

"Just some friends. I'll mention to them that we talked. But I don't want to push them on you. It's your business. Maybe I'll tell them that they should come by your house and talk to you themselves about it."

She stood there, staring at him, unable to think of anything to say. She felt like she had been punched in the stomach. Kevin didn't react to her silence. He simply continued to look at her, a little smile on his face.

Finally, she managed to get out some words. "I... I better get back home. I've got a lot to do today."

"Okay. So, see you tomorrow morning? Maybe about nine o'clock?"

"Sure. Nine would be great."

She walked back down the driveway to her bicycle, got on, and forced herself not to look back as she pedaled the short distance back to her house.

But when she got home and went inside, she locked the door behind her.

Rainey considered emailing Tyler, but what would she tell him? That both of the kids had acted completely normal? That was news of a sort, but she didn't want him thinking she was jumping at shadows.

You are, came an answer in her mind, but she frowned it away. Why else would she have reacted like that to what they said? Nobody said anything, or did anything, in the least out of the ordinary.

But still, there was something. There was some little thing, some comment that had slipped by almost too fast to notice, but she couldn't put her finger on it. She couldn't even remember which of the kids had said it, or what it had been about. It had been a fleeting phrase, something that didn't quite fit. Deciding that it would come if she let it go, she went out to work in her herb garden for a couple of hours. Afterwards she'd get some lunch, and if it still hadn't come to her, she'd check her email to see if Tyler had had any success with the new camera.

She wandered up and down the rows of bergamot, lavender, chamomile, and mint, cutting and weeding. She spent a good half-hour pulling mint out of the path—she loved the plant but it had a tendency to take over. Then there was washing the cut stems and tying them into bundles, and hanging them from racks in the drying shed. She reached up and gave a tentative feel to a bundle of borage she'd harvested two weeks earlier, but the hairy leaves still felt soft and pliable. Not quite dry enough yet.

Everything dried out so slowly up here on the ridge. But the dampness was why the plants grew so well. Something about her land was perfect for gardening. It was the right spot for growing herbs, even if it was a bit of a haul from the village.

And suddenly she stopped, hand still in the air, brushing the borage leaves. Her eyes grew wide, but they weren't seeing what was around her.

Of course. That's it. It was Phil.

She thought back to that morning, with her standing on his front step in the fog, and Phil's flat, uninterested voice saying, *I don't know. I'd have to ride up there on my bicycle. It's kind of a long way.*

How on earth had Phil known where she lived? His dad didn't even recognize her when he answered the door. The Collettes had only lived in Crooked Creek for a little over a year. She'd seen the family around, but had never spoken to them before today. She hadn't mentioned where her house was, she was sure of it. Why would a ten-year-old boy who she hardly knew have any idea where she lived?

She tossed her hand clippers on a table in the drying shed, and walked back inside, once again locking the door behind her.

There was an email from Tyler waiting for her. Evidently he didn't mind contacting her to deliver the news that there was no news.

Hi Rainey,

I downloaded the photographs from the new camera, and there's nothing much that's very interesting. One of them has a little blob in the distance, something moving that doesn't look like an elk or a bear but is too large to be most of the other animals you'd find up there, but the resolution is crappy and there's no way to tell what it is. Anyway, nothing much to report here, which I suppose is good news.

Email me when you get this, okay? I'm still kind of worried that I may have put you in danger by sending you that photograph. I know it's probably silly, but I can't help it.

Dinner last night was awesome. The quiche was wonderful. So was the company.

cheers,

Tyler

She smiled a little, then clicked "Reply," and hastily typed out a message.

Hi Tyler,

I was able to talk to both Phil and Kevin this morning. It was just like with Kathleen—everything was completely ordinary, but there was this sense that something was wrong. There's still an underlying current of spookiness about all three kids that I sense every time I'm around them. If you read a transcript of our conversation, it would seem like the most boring thing. Nothing they said was weird, but it still isn't right.

There was one thing in my conversation with Phil, though. I decided to use the pretense of offering him a summer job helping me out with harvesting herbs, and he made a comment about how it would be a long ride on his bicycle to come out to my place. The thing is, I'm pretty sure that he has no way of knowing where I live —I don't even know his parents at all. It was an odd thing to say. It's giving me the shivers, just thinking about it, but that's probably because I'm already kind of in a creeped-out mental state.

So, that's my news. Not much concrete. Not sure if that's a good thing or a bad.

I had fun at dinner, too. Let's do it again, soon.

Namasté,

Rainey

She clicked *Send*, and then sat at her computer, staring at the screen in silence for a few moments.

To what extent had she and Tyler tipped their hand to Slender Man by their investigations? It was too late for Tyler and Judy to investigate covertly. The break-in was enough to show their interest in Slender Man's activities had not gone unnoticed. But had Rainey given away her knowledge of what was going on by talking to all three of the children who had been abducted? She remembered Kevin's comment—it now seemed sly and deliberate—about there being "a couple of other kids" who would be interested in working for her. Kevin had known perfectly well what she had been trying to do, and that she'd talked to the other two.

The whole thing was disquieting.

She spent the afternoon trying to distract herself by getting involved with her chores. She had three orders to fill, and did the work in a vague, abstracted sort of way, and kept having to start over because she'd forgotten what tea ingredient she had just weighed out.

Finally, she decided to spend some time weeding. At least that was a job that left your mind free to wander. But kneeling in the rows of the herb garden, with no sounds but the wind, birds, and the very occasional noise of a car on the road in front of her house, she became increasingly aware of how alone she was, up here on the ridge. Hers was the last house before the road narrowed and wound its way up into the forest. Her three acres of cultivated land, surrounded by seven more acres of woods, was a lovely spot, but didn't contribute much when what you really wanted was the security of being around people. The nearest house was the Torgesons', and that was a half-mile away. And the fact that Kevin lived there didn't exactly make it a safe haven in any case.

The sun was getting low, and her stomach was growling, so she brushed the dirt from her hands and went inside. She hung her sun hat on a peg inside the door, and turned and locked the door behind her. Bonkers immediately appeared out of nowhere, twisting around her ankles and meowing to be fed, so she made some soothing noises at him and put a scoop of kitty chow in his bowl. He gave a little *brrrrt* of contentment and started eating.

Rainey, despite being hungry herself, went first to her computer to check for emails. She smiled at her own eagerness.

"Rainey Carrington," she said, "you're acting like a high schooler, checking every time you pass the computer to see if your crush has written back to you." Still, it was with a wash of relief mixed with pleasure that she saw that there was a message from tvaughan@czrs.edu.

Hi Rainey,

Are you sure that Phil wouldn't know where you live for any other reason? You didn't sell tea to his parents, or something? No reason his folks might have pointed out your house to him? If not, then that's really scary.

I'm now seriously worried about you being alone. Would you like me to come down to your place tonight & spend the night?

That's not a proposition, I'd be fine on the couch or in a sleeping bag on the floor or whatever. It might be best for you not to be all alone, esp. now that you've talked to all three of them. If they are in cahoots (which seems likely since you said that two of them were seen together the night that girl almost got kidnapped) then they probably will talk to each other and figure out that you've been going around talking to them all. After that, it wouldn't be hard for them to put two and two together.

I'll be in the lab till about five or so, I've got a ton of photographs to analyze (not only from T-Three, and none of them of anything creepier than elk, marmots, and an occasional fluffy bunny). But you can call me, 228-7088, if you get this after I leave. I can be at your place in ten minutes flat.

I can also check my work email from home. Just let me know how you are, okay?

In any case, please be careful.

cheers,

Tyler

She looked at the clock on the wall. It stood at six-thirty. Tyler would certainly be home by now, and probably worried sick. But something in her was reluctant about calling him and asking him to come over. She didn't want to be perceived as needing protection. Maybe she should go over to his house?

And I might not want to sleep on the couch, either.

That thought made her blush, and laugh out loud.

Rainey had been on her own for a long time. Her mother had run off with the bassist in her father's band when she was twelve, and her father had died of a heart attack, brought on by years of poor diet and drug and alcohol use, when she was nineteen. She was an only child, and had inherited her parents' property—ten acres of land, much of it devoted to marijuana, and a house in significant ill-repair—and had set herself to the task of renovating both the house and the reputation of her family name.

Eight years later, she was largely self-sufficient, and her expenses were low. The mortgage was paid off from the proceeds of her grandmother's estate, and she did almost all of the house repairs herself using very little more than her muscles, a few tools, and a book called *Make Your House Into Your Dream Home*. The marijuana thickets were replaced by sweet-smelling, and legal, herbs. She had nothing in particular against marijuana in moderation, but to her it represented one of the factors that had destroyed her parents' lives, and she felt like she simply had no need for it.

Twice, as her dinner was cooking, she found herself moving toward the telephone, ready to call Tyler and take him up on his offer, and maybe even on the proposition. Both times, she stopped herself. They were equal players in this game, and she needed to show him that she was capable of taking care of herself. She didn't think that his worry was motivated by any kind of myth of the weaker sex, but even so, her pride rebelled at even giving the appearance of needing his protection.

Besides, he was more at risk than she was. The only scary thing that had happened to her was a couple of weird conversations, whereas he'd gone up to that cave, twice, and had his camera and computer stolen. If anyone should be helping anyone, she should be going over to his place.

She gave a quick look at the oven timer. Six minutes till her stuffed eggplant would be done. She went over to the computer, opened her email browser, and clicked *Reply* to Tyler's last email.

Hi Tyler,

Thanks for offering to come over—it's not that it's not tempting in a variety of ways, but I'll be fine here tonight. I don't want you feeling like you have to drop everything you're doing to come take care of me if I get a bad case of the shivers. Let's see what happens.

In any case, I think you're the one in more danger. After all, the lab got broken into, and your computer stolen. So you be careful yourself, okay?

I'll email first thing in the morning to let you know I'm okay. Sleep tight and don't worry about me, okay? Like I said before: All shall be well.

Namasté,

Rainey

She clicked *Send* just as the oven timer went off.

After dinner, Rainey checked her email again, once more laughing at herself for constantly being drawn back. This time there was no email. She had a momentary pang of worry that maybe she'd sounded too dismissive, that perhaps she had come across as not liking him or having been insulted by his offer. But she finally told herself, *He's a big boy, I don't need to walk on eggshells.* She picked up the book she was reading—an Agatha Christie murder mystery she'd found in a used book store on her last trip into Eugene, called *A Murder is Announced*—and spent an agreeable hour or so trying to work her way through an entirely different set of hints and clues as the daylight slowly faded and night fell.

At about nine-thirty, she set down her book, and looked around. The only light in the room came from the reading lamp next to her rocking chair. Bonkers was sound asleep on her lap. She gave a little shudder. Something had distracted her, some soft noise, some movement, but she couldn't identify it.

She listened. Nothing. The night was still.

She had been sitting with her legs curled up to the side,

and she stretched them out and put her feet on the floor. Bonkers roused, arched his back, looked up at her with disapproval in his golden eyes, and jumped to the floor. She stood, went to her front window, and pushed aside the curtains.

The light was dim enough inside that she could see the front yard, the vague dark shapes of the shrubs and trees silhouetted in the faint gleam of a half-moon. It was a clear night, a little chilly, and there was already dew on the grass. She went to the front door, switched on the front porch light, and returned to the window.

The front yard was empty.

Another shiver rippled its way up her backbone. She had the queer feeling that she was not alone. She turned and looked into the shadows of her living room, but it was empty except for her cat, who had returned to the rocking chair and curled up in the blanket she had left draped over the seat.

She went out of the living room, back toward the kitchen. The light was off, and when she looked out of the window over the sink, she could faintly see the first rows of her herb garden, the even, well-maintained plantings disappearing backwards into the darkness. She went over to the back door, leaned forward, cupped her hands around her eyes, and put her face to the window.

Just on the edge of the shadowed garden, something moved.

She jumped backwards, heart pounding. After a moment, though, she willed herself to unclench hands she'd balled into fists. It was just an animal. They got bears down here sometimes, and there were always rabbits and deer. She forced herself to go back to the window again, but now there was nothing there.

Again she felt the urge to call Tyler. He'd said he could be there in ten minutes.

But she stopped herself. If he rushed up there and found that she'd gotten all freaked out because there was a mule deer munching on her lemon balm plants, she'd look like a frightened child.

She flipped the outdoor light switch on and the back flood light—installed so she could work after dark in the short days of late fall and early spring—washed over the back yard. She peered out again.

Then Phil Collette stepped out of the shadows and stood there, staring at her.

She gave a little yelp and stepped back.

He didn't move toward the house. He remained completely motionless, gaze focused on her, his pale, narrow, little boy's face wearing an intent, and thoroughly adult, expression of concentration. A moment later, Kevin Torgeson stepped out from the other direction and joined him, and then Kathleen Standish came from the direction of the drying shed.

The three of them stood in a row, all watching her.

Her hands felt cold, and she tried to fight down a sense of panic. She walked over to her kitchen sink, and slid open the window above it, only a crack.

"What do you want?" she said, in a loud voice.

Kevin spoke in response. "We need to talk to you, Rainey."

"Why?"

"I think you know why."

"Why don't you tell me anyway?"

Kevin gave a quick look at Kathleen. Kathleen's face looked hostile, suspicious, almost angry, but Kevin gave a faint smile, just as he had that morning when Rainey had talked to him on the front step of his parents' house.

"Rainey, we need to find out what you know about us."

"Why should I tell you that?"

"It would be in your best interest."

"Really? Is that a threat?"

"Not unless you want to take it that way."

"That's what I thought."

"We were hoping you'd be reasonable."

She smiled grimly. "Implying that if I do tell you, you'll leave me alone? I doubt that. You show up here, all three of you together, and basically corroborate any idea I have that you're all up to something, and I'm supposed to believe that if I tell you what I know, then we can all be friends?"

Kathleen said, in a harsh voice, "I told you there was no point in talking to her."

Kevin gave Kathleen a stern glance, and she subsided.

"If we promise not to harm you?" he said.

"Where are the real Kevin, Phil, and Kathleen?"

"What makes you think we aren't them?" Phil asked.

"Stop playing games."

"They're safe," Kevin said. "That's all you need to know."

Could she get to the phone? At least give Tyler a warning? No, if they saw her pick up the phone, they'd break the door down to stop her. Plus, even if she could get a call through to him, he'd come charging over trying to save the day, and he'd get caught, too. How could she get a message to him without alerting them?

She said, leaning forward toward the crack in the window, "And what do you intend to do with me? I'm not going to walk out there for a happy little chat." As she did so, she picked up a pencil off the counter, and the only handy paper —her spinach quiche recipe, left out since the previous night —and wrote on the margin, *"PKK here I'm in trouble will contact you if I can BE CAREFUL."*

Kevin said, "You know we can come inside if we want to."

"Yes."

"So, you may as well save the unpleasantness, and the door repair, by coming outside. We won't hurt you. You have my word."

"I think you're lying about that." She turned and dashed out of the kitchen, and through the living room. She fumbled with the front door lock, swearing under her breath, but finally the door was open, and she pelted down the front step and away down the walk, toward where her bicycle leaned against the front porch rail.

She jumped over the seat, and gave a hard push against the pedal. She felt the bicycle start to move beneath her, and the cool night air brushing her face, when a pair of hands clamped onto her arm like a vise. She screamed and struggled, then two more hands grabbed her, and then two more, and she was pulled off the bicycle and drawn back toward the house, kicking and fighting with more ferocity than she thought she was capable of. Then there was a sudden rush of lightheadedness, and the black night sky washed over with silver, and the world was swallowed up along with her awareness.

nine

. . .

"Oh, Dale," Scarlett said, "you shouldn't lie out in the sun like this, with no shirt on, without sunscreen! You'll get a terrible sunburn on your beautiful muscular shoulders and chest."

Dale looked up at her. She was silhouetted against the sun, and her cool shadow fell across his face. "You wanna put some on me?" He gave her a rakish, crooked smile.

"I would love to rrrrub some *all* over you," she said, rolling her r's seductively. She leaned over, and he felt her cool hands on his chest, and through his half-closed eyes, he watched the seagulls wheeling overhead, trilling like bells.

"I wish those damn birds would shut up."

"Oh, Dale, don't worry about the birds." Scarlett leaned closer, her mouth moving toward his. "The birds don't matter."

"But they're making an ungodly racket."

"Just kiss me. We can talk about birds… afterwards."

He closed his eyes, waiting to feel the press of her lips against his. It never came. He lay there, mouth slightly open, for a few moments. Then he opened his eyes, and said, in a plaintive voice, "Scarlett?"

Scarlett was gone. He was in his bed, his clock alarm ringing. "Dammit," he grumbled as he hit the *Off* button on the clock with rather more than the necessary force, and dragged himself out of bed.

Forty-five minutes later, he was showered, shaved, and sitting at his table eating a quick breakfast of toast and eggs over easy. The coffee was brewing, and his feelings of frustration over the *smoochus interruptus* he had experienced with Scarlett Johansson fading. He looked over the newspaper. It was the usual. Republicans criticizing the president, the Democrats defending him, unrest in the Middle East, more depressing economic news. Yup, life as usual. But Crooked Creek had gone six days without a kid disappearing, so that was good. He tried to smile a little. After all, there was always tonight for another chance with Scarlett.

He finished his breakfast, poured out a cup of coffee into a travel mug, and picked up his car keys.

Just an ordinary, easy day. That's what I want. Not too much to ask for.

Ten minutes later, Dale walked into the station. Sheila was on the phone with someone.

"Look, sir," she was saying. "We can send an officer out right away, but you need to tell me..."

There was a pause.

"If it's an emergency, sir, you should have dialed nine-one-one. It's not..."

Another pause. Sheila looked up at Dale, who was watching her questioningly. She shrugged and gave an angry little shake of her head.

"Hang on, sir." She said to Dale, "Guy on the phone here, says there's some kind of emergency, but he won't say what it is. He says he'll only talk to you."

He rolled his eyes. "Great. Who is it?"

"He won't tell me. He sounds like a nut."

He sighed, and then winced, as a pang of indigestion jabbed him in the solar plexus. "All right. I'll take it in my office."

He stomped off into his office, slammed the door, plopped down into his chair, and picked up his phone on the first ring.

"Chief of Police Blodgett."

"Okay," said a male voice, with no preamble. "We've got a situation, here."

He didn't answer for a moment. The caller sounded wound tightly, to the point of having his mainspring snap. He didn't like dealing with people who sounded like that. They had a tendency to act unpredictably, which was his least favorite thing of all, if you didn't count having to deal with the aftereffects of not having sex with Scarlett Johansson.

"Who is this?" He tried to make his voice calm and non-threatening. To his surprise, the caller answered his question immediately.

"Tyler Vaughan. The biologist up at the zoological research station. The one who had his computer stolen."

"Oh, it's *you.*" The heartburn poked at him again, and he shifted in his chair. "What now?"

"Rainey has vanished."

He frowned in complete incomprehension. "Rainey *Carrington*? What the hell does she have to do with it?"

"Everything. I put her in danger by sending her a photograph, and now she's disappeared."

He shook his head to clear away the confusion, and found that it didn't help. "Look, Doctor Vaughan, why don't you tell me what's happened? From the beginning."

"Okay." Tyler took a deep breath. "There's this thing, Slender Man, living up on the ridge, in a cave. It's what's been abducting the kids and replacing them with duplicates. I accidentally took a picture of it with my remote camera, and so it broke my camera. When I got the pieces, I found out that the memory card was intact, and I downloaded the image and sent it to Rainey. She'd contacted me because she saw the interview I did about Bigfoot. Slender Man broke into the lab and stole my computer and the pieces of the camera. But then Rainey went and talked to the duplicates of the abducted kids yesterday, and they kidnapped her. You've got to help!"

There was about fifteen seconds of dead silence. Finally Tyler said, "Hello?"

Dale blinked a couple of times. "Okay. You want to try that again? A little slower this time?"

"Look, Officer Blodgett, I think you need to come down here."

"Where is 'here'?"

"Rainey's place."

He squeezed his eyes shut and tilted his head back. There went any hope of it being a quiet day. "Yeah. Okay. I'll be up there in ten minutes."

"Thanks."

He hung up without responding.

As he was leaving the station, Sheila said to him, "What was with that guy?"

"Damned if I know," he replied without turning around.

Dale pulled into Rainey's driveway. A battered, dirty blue Honda Civic was parked next to the house, and he recognized it as the same car that had been at the lab two days before. He put his car in park and got out. Tyler Vaughan sat on the front step of the house, his chin in his hands, looking strangely lost. Whatever that guy had to do with all this, he wasn't in the role of Head Villain. He looked like a scared little kid.

Tyler stood and walked over to him, and reached out and gave Dale's hand a firm shake.

"So," Dale said. "What brought you down here? How did you figure out Rainey was missing?"

"We'd talked yesterday. Well, via email, anyway. And she said she'd contact me first thing in the morning to let me know she was okay. She didn't, so I came down to see if she was okay. She's missing."

"And why did you suspect she wouldn't be okay?"

Tyler looked at him, and shook his head. "Look, it's complicated."

"I gathered that during our phone conversation," he said dryly. "Can you give me the tl;dr version?"

"I can try." Tyler swallowed. "Okay. There's this thing up on the ridge. That's what's been abducting the children."

"Skinny Man."

"Slender Man. And anyway, Rainey had contacted me because she thought I might know something about it."

"How did *she* know about it?"

"She didn't."

"I thought this was going to be the easy version."

"Look. Rainey was concerned when the kids started disappearing and was looking for someone nearby who might be able to help her figure out what was going on. She picked me because I have a reputation as a Bigfoot expert, which I'm not, but she saw this YouTube video—"

"*That's* where I saw you!" He couldn't keep the triumphant tone from his voice. "I *knew* you looked familiar. You're the dude who was on *Good Morning America*!"

Tyler winced. "Yeah. That was me. But anyway, that's why Rainey thought of me. That and the fact that I was nearby. And it turned out, when I got her letter, that I'd just gotten some photos of something up on the ridge, something that we later identified as Slender Man. At least, we think."

"And Slender Man is...? And if you say 'slender,' I'm not gonna be happy with you."

"We don't really know, but there are reports from all over

the United States that there's this faceless creature that is associated with abductions, especially of children. He's been photographed a few times."

"And you got a picture?"

"Yes." Tyler reached into his pocket and pulled out a red flash drive. "It's on here."

He nodded. "Okay, so anyway. Slender Man is involved in the abductions. You got a picture. What next?" He held up his hand. "Wait, I got it. Slender Man broke into the research station and stole your computer and the camera with the pictures. But you got 'em on a flash drive. Smart guy."

"Yes. Actually, it's Rainey's flash drive. She downloaded the photograph onto it, and then hid it. I went and retrieved it this morning."

"Okay."

"The problem is, I thought sending a copy of the best of the photos to Rainey would be a good idea, so she could hang on to it in case something happened to my copy. I didn't realize it might be putting her in danger until after I sent it."

"So that's why she was kidnapped, you think."

"That, and also because she decided that she wanted to investigate the kids a little, so she went and talked to them. None of them said anything suspicious, except for one thing that the kid said, the little boy…"

"Phil. Phil Collette."

"Yes. Apparently he said something to Rainey that led her to believe he knew where she lived. And she said that was pretty unlikely."

Dale gave a noncommittal shrug. "That's probably true. The Collettes haven't lived here very long."

"So evidently they thought she was onto them, and now they've abducted her."

"You're sure she was abducted? She's not, like, away on vacation or something?"

Tyler scowled. "C'mon, you think she's going to ride off to Cozumel on her bicycle?"

"Okay, you have a point."

"And there's this." Tyler motioned for him to come into Rainey's house, and went up to the front door. "The door was unlocked when I got here. I'd advised Rainey to lock her doors, and the back one *was* locked, but the front one wasn't. And when I got here, and knocked, and she wasn't there, I let myself in. I was worried that she might be hurt, or..." He stopped.

"Dead."

"Yes."

Tyler opened the door, and they went into Rainey's living room. "Nothing was disturbed. Everything looked just as it did when I was here a couple of nights ago."

Dale's eyebrows rose a little, but he didn't say anything. The note, *Boyfriend?* went into his mental card file.

"Then I went into the kitchen and found this." Tyler picked up the spinach quiche recipe, and handed it to him.

"PKK," Dale said.

"Phil, Kevin, Kathleen."

He nodded. "'I'm in trouble.'"

"They must have come last night. I got an email from her last night that was timestamped a little after six-thirty. She said she was fine, I shouldn't worry, everything was okay, she'd talk to me in the morning."

"And she didn't."

Tyler swallowed. "Yes. That's why I called you. I'm sorry I stonewalled you when you came out to the lab. But I thought you wouldn't believe me, and anyway, telling you everything wouldn't have helped to get the computer back. Nothing would have, if I'm right about who took it."

"So why did you call us out at all?"

"If I hadn't, my boss, Joe DiStefano, would have

wondered why. Joe doesn't know about Slender Man, or the missing kids."

He nodded again. "But now…?"

Tyler shook his head. "No. Not until I have to. I'm not anxious to tell him. Joe's a nice guy, but he wouldn't believe me. No way would he want to get involved in this." He paused. "He's not… not imaginative."

"And you think I am?"

"Look, Officer Blodgett…"

"Dale. I'm okay with Dale."

"Dale. I feel like I got Rainey involved with this. Even though she's the one who contacted me, I feel responsible. If I hadn't answered her letter, or had advised her not to get involved… or whatever. Plus…" He stopped.

"Plus what?"

"Plus, I like her. I mean, she's not my girlfriend or anything. We've only known each other a few days. But I really like her."

"You'd like her to be your girlfriend."

Tyler blushed crimson. "Yeah. I would. And I want to try and find her. And I don't know how to do that alone." He paused. "I don't know of anyone else around here who can help me."

Dale didn't answer for a moment. "Okay, assuming I do believe your story—which takes a shitload of believing, allow me to point out—where do you think she might be?"

"I don't know. But there's a cave up in the Sisters where we think Slender Man is. It's about a three-mile hike, off a logging road that comes off of Stark Road. Judy—Judy Kahn, who you met when you came out to the lab—she and I went up there. We brought flashlights, and went down into the cave. It was completely empty."

"You just walked up and went into a cave where you think this thing lives?"

"Yes."

Dale's eyebrows went up. The guy had balls, had to give him that.

"And no sign of anyone there?"

"No. Nothing."

"So what makes you think that's where he lives, then?"

"That's what the camera was pointed at. The camera that got destroyed, the one that captured the images of him."

"Ah."

"We still haven't figured out about the cave yet. So we don't know where he's holding Rainey, but I'm guessing that it's somewhere up in the Sisters."

"If she's still alive."

A flash of anger showed in Tyler's eyes. "You and I both know that's a possibility. You don't need to tell me that."

"Sorry."

Huh. There was more to this guy than he'd thought at first.

"I'm working under the hypothesis that Slender Man, evidently acting through the three kids, has kidnapped Rainey and is holding her somewhere up on the ridge. I can handle going back up to the cave to see if there are any traces up there, but I suspect that's going to turn up nothing, just as it did last time. I need you to handle talking to the kids."

"You want me to go question the three kids?"

"Yes, of course."

"On what grounds?"

"The note. The fact that Rainey talked to two of them the day she disappeared."

Dale sighed. "Given the questions you want me to ask, I think their parents might have some objections."

Again, the momentary flash of anger. "Tough shit. It's your job."

He looked at Tyler with pursed lips, and said, after a moment, "You know how all of this sounds."

"Yeah. Like some kind of crazy science fiction thing."

"Pretty much." He gave Tyler a raised eyebrow. "Can you show me the photograph?"

Tyler shrugged. "Sure. I don't see why not. I'm not sure where Rainey's computer is, but if I can get onto it without needing a password, I can show it to you right now. Otherwise, you'll have to come to my house or up to the lab."

They found Rainey's computer in a neat, well-lit little study in the back of the house. There was a vase of fresh flowers on the desk, and a small embroidered wall hanging that said *Be Here Now*. On a bookshelf was a framed photograph of Rainey's parents, both dressed in tie-dye, her mom grinning at the camera and giving the photographer a peace sign.

Duncan and Gillie Carrington had been two of Dale's mother's best friends. Just seeing their picture brought him back years, to a time when he'd felt like he was living in a strange, upside-down world, the parents running around with the wrong kind of crowd and smoking weed and getting into trouble, and the kids, Dale and his sister Carmen, being responsible and conservative and holding down jobs.

Carmen had gotten out of Crooked Creek as soon as she could, and now was a nurse practitioner in Tacoma. Dale had stayed behind long enough to watch the whole thing fall apart. The "wrong kind of crowd" had eventually all died or run off or settled down to become respectable citizens, leaving only Daisy Blodgett and a couple of others still living in the past, their influence dwindling without their being aware of it. The thought made him a little sad.

Tyler said, "I'm on," as the computer booted up, making rumbling noises deep within its electronic guts. A desktop background of Rainey's herb fields in full bloom popped into view.

Tyler plugged the flash drive in, and clicked on the icon that came up. He looked up at Dale. "A warning. This photograph is pretty creepy."

Dale nodded, and Tyler clicked on the file.

Dale wasn't sure what he expected to see. Whatever it was, the image on the screen wasn't it. He took an involuntary step backwards. The featureless face, tilted in a quizzical way, looked out through the monitor glass at them, contemplating the two men like a predator trying to decide which helpless prey to dispatch first.

Looked like he wouldn't be dreaming about Scarlett tonight, after all.

His heart pounded.

"Okay," he said, a little thinly. "I get it now. Thanks."

Tyler turned and gave him a grim smile. "I warned you."

He nodded, and then looked at Tyler and frowned. "Look. I know what the answer to this is, but I gotta ask. Is this some kind of hoax? An elaborate practical joke? I know Rainey doesn't like me much, and I guess it's deserved. I have a thing about hippies."

Tyler scowled, and started to say something, but Dale held up his hand.

"And Rainey's a sweet woman. I got nothing against her personally. She's never broken the law that I know of. I just got history, you know? So if Rainey wanted to rattle my cage a little, all I'm saying is that I probably deserve it. But I gotta know, right now, if that's what this is. If it is, hell, I'm a good sport, I'll have a nice fat laugh about it, and pat you on the back for one fine joke at my expense, and that'll be that." He looked at Tyler steadily. "But I have a feeling that's not true, is it?"

Tyler shook his head. "I wish it was."

"So everything you've told me—God's honest truth, or scout's honor, or whatever you like to swear by—it's all true, far as you know."

"Far as I know, everything I've said is the literal, factual truth."

Dale scowled. "Shit. I was afraid you'd say that."

"I think you need to go talk to those kids."

"Yeah." He shifted his weight to the other foot. "I guess."

"You got another approach you can think of?"

"Not really."

Tyler closed the image, ejected the flash drive, pulled it out of the socket, and put it in his pocket. "I only have one other piece of advice."

"Yeah?"

"If Rainey shows back up in a day or two, don't trust a word she says."

Dale drove back toward Crooked Creek feeling dizzy and a little sick. He had the sensation of teetering on the edge of a cliff, and the cliff was called "The World As Dale Blodgett Knows It." Before today, he'd believed Tyler Vaughan was a scared, weak person, a bookish scientist who had clumsily arranged for his computer to be stolen, for some as-yet-undetermined reason, and was a poor liar, to boot. Everything about him, when Dale went out to the lab to investigate, cried out *Liar!*

Now… now, he still seemed scared, but it was pretty clear that a coward, he wasn't. He was ready to risk his own life to help Rainey, and he had no problem with maneuvering Dale into doing the same.

And after looking at that photo, he had to admit Tyler had a reason to be afraid. That blank face, that eyeless oval that still clearly somehow could *see*, was one of the flat-out scariest-looking things he had ever seen.

He was, in his own way, a much more thoroughgoing skeptic than Tyler was. He had a remarkably simple view of the world. The world was what you saw in front of your face. Period, end of story. He didn't actively disbelieve in the paranormal—in fact, he didn't think about it at all. He ignored it into oblivion. His only contact with it was watching *Monster Quest* on the History Channel, which he'd always considered to be comedy. The dawning realization that there was something out there, something terrifying and beyond his understanding, had come as a profound shock. The story Tyler told was like some sort of nightmare come to life. And the problem was, Dale was perceptive enough to know when he was being lied to, and unlike the interview at the lab, he was convinced that here, Tyler was telling the truth.

Which meant Dale was in serious peril of going right off the cliff.

It also, unfortunately, meant that questioning those kids was essential. This was very likely to be dangerous. He had stayed in Crooked Creek in part because it was one of the only places you could be a policeman and be almost certain of never taking any risks at all. Now, that assessment looked like it was about to be proven untrue.

He considered driving back to the station, having a third cup of coffee, doing some paperwork, and giving himself time to think about it. "Thinking about it" was one of his favorite strategies. Many problems, he found, would simply work themselves out if you gave them time by "thinking about it." Often, this entailed someone else coming in and taking care of things, but he had no problem with that.

Here, though… these weren't problems that would simply go away. No one else would step in. He could wait and see what happened, but what if Rainey *did* come back? He recalled with a shudder Tyler's last comment—that if Rainey came back, she shouldn't be trusted, the implication being that she wouldn't actually be Rainey anymore.

He remembered seeing *The Invasion of the Body Snatchers* when he was in middle school, and he hadn't admitted at the time how much the concept had creeped him out, mostly because he'd been trying to impress Kirsten Larson, his girlfriend at the time, and he didn't want to let on that he didn't want to walk home from the theater alone. But he'd looked at everyone askance for a few days afterwards, the thought skittering through his mind, *I wonder if he is one of... the Pods?*

It was experiences like that which had cemented him into a completely pragmatic worldview. It was the only possible option other than being afraid all the time. But now, apparently, there were three people in Crooked Creek who were, in fact... *the Pods*. And it was his duty to go and question *the Pods*, which would clue *the Pods* in to the fact that he knew. That, apparently, was how Rainey had been caught. Would he be next?

One difference, though, was that Rainey wasn't armed. He put his hand on his gun, felt its comforting weight in its holster clipped to his belt, and turned into Kevin Torgeson's driveway.

He got out of his car, and walked down the sidewalk to the front door, trying to slow down his own pulse. He worked his face into what he hoped was convincing impassivity, and knocked on the door.

"Dale," said Leah, opening the door and drying her hands on a dish towel. "What brings you out here?"

"I was wondering where Kevin was yesterday evening."

A look of frustration and anguish swept over Leah's thin, angular face. "Oh, no, what is it this time?"

"I'm not certain yet. And I don't know for sure if Kevin was involved. I just need to know if he was home last night."

"Rich and I went out to dinner last night. We didn't get home until a little after nine. I didn't see Kevin when we got home, but I figured he was in his bedroom. He came out to get a snack right before I went to bed. I think it was about ten-thirty. I have no reason to suspect he wasn't home the whole time."

"Nor any way to know if he wasn't."

Leah's lips tightened. "No."

"Is Kevin here now? Can I speak with him?"

"Dale, what's this about? I think you should tell me."

"I don't object to telling you. But I'd rather Kevin was here when I do, if you don't mind."

Leah looked at him for a moment, worry furrowing her brow, and then turned and called, "Kevin?"

Kevin came out from a hallway just a little too quickly. He'd heard everything Dale and Leah had said. Oh, well, nothing he could do about it now.

"Hi, Kevin."

"Hi, Officer Blodgett."

"Kevin, I'm wondering if you would mind telling me where you were yesterday evening."

Kevin's face looked slightly puzzled and completely innocent. "Sure. My folks went out to dinner. So I made myself a couple of hotdogs, and then watched TV for a while. Then I got bored, so I called a couple of my friends to see if they wanted to hang out. They were all busy or not at home, so I went out for a walk. Then I came home, listened to music for a while, then went to bed."

"About what time did you get home from your walk?"

"About eight, I think. It was getting dark."

Dale nodded. "And that's all? Nothing else happened?"

Kevin shook his head. "No. Why? What happened?"

Keeping his eyes on Kevin's face, Dale said, "Rainey Carrington disappeared last night."

Kevin's eyes grew wide. "Someone kidnapped *Rainey*?"

Leah said, "Oh, my god, Dale, what is going on here?"

"That's what I'd like to find out."

"Why did you want to talk to Kevin?"

"For one thing, I understand that Rainey talked to Kevin yesterday morning. He may have been one of the last people to see her before she vanished. I was wondering what she said to you, Kevin. If anything struck you as odd, or significant."

Kevin looked upwards for a moment, thinking. "No. It

was ordinary stuff. You know. She wondered if I might want a summer job, helping her out with her herb gardens. I said sure, that sounded great, I could start any time." He shook his head. "That was it. She acted totally normal."

Dale nodded. "And nothing you saw last night on your walk... you didn't see anything strange? Did you pass her house?"

"No. I went the other way. And I didn't see much of anything, or anyone. It was quiet. A couple of cars passed me, but I didn't pay attention to who they were."

"So, there's no one who could vouch for your whereabouts between six-thirty and ten-thirty?"

"*Really*, Dale," said Leah indignantly, "are you accusing Kevin of something? Because I don't see—"

"I'm not accusing anyone of anything. Yet. I know a handful of things, so far. Rainey is missing, Kevin was one of the last people to see her before it happened, and you're Rainey's closest neighbors. At the moment I'm trying to figure out where *everyone* was, so I can try to narrow down when it happened. 'Some time between six-thirty last night and eight o'clock this morning' is not good enough."

Leah seemed somewhat mollified. "I understand. In any case, poor Rainey. Why would anyone want to kidnap her? She's so... harmless."

Dale frowned a little. Leah Torgeson still believed that her son had been lost in the woods. Even after what happened to Kathleen and Phil, and now Rainey, she was still not making the connection.

Or didn't want to.

He looked over at Kevin. His expression was perfect, exactly the right mixture of innocence, worry, and curiosity, with a little defiance as seasoning. Exactly what you'd expect from a teenager who had nothing to do with anything, was entirely blameless, but sensed that he was being subtly implicated in wrongdoing. If Tyler Vaughan was correct, though,

Kevin was in the middle of this, and was lying. But there was nothing in Kevin's manner that suggested anything other than his being as innocent as a newborn baby.

Either way, he wasn't getting anywhere questioning the kid.

"All right, then," he said. "Thanks. If you hear or see anything relevant, please let me know as soon as you can." There was a quick look of relief—but not on Kevin's face, on Leah's.

He frowned a little as they said goodbye and the door closed. Did she know more than she was letting on about her boy's wanderings? He walked down the sidewalk toward his car. Or was she simply thankful that with all the trouble Kevin had been involved in, here at least was one thing he had nothing to do with?

Two hours later, Dale was back in the station, with a clanger of a headache and no useful information whatsoever. None of the kids claimed to have any knowledge about Rainey's disappearance. In fact, when he had asked Phil Collette if he had any information about where Rainey Carrington might be, Phil looked him straight in the eye and said, "Who's that?"

Of the three, only Kevin admitted to having gone out the previous night. Kathleen said she'd been chatting online, talking with a girl who was going to be her dorm roommate at Willamette University in September. Her mother couldn't corroborate that.

She'd said, angrily, "I don't watch her every minute, Dale, and I don't need to."

Phil claimed to have spent the evening in the rec room playing video games. He said, and his parents agreed, that he had gone to bed at around nine o'clock.

The fact was, any or all of them could have slipped out unnoticed. All of them had first-floor bedrooms and could have climbed out of windows without any difficulty. Kathleen had a car and could easily have picked them up and driven up to Rainey's house in under ten minutes. Once again, assuming they *had* somehow been responsible for the kidnapping, there was no particular reason why they couldn't have accomplished the whole thing and been safely back in their respective homes in an hour or so. It was risky, especially in Phil's case—his absence would have been the most likely to raise eyebrows—but with a bit of luck, it wasn't impossible. And, of course, there was always the possibility of slipping out of after the parents were in bed, and the kids allegedly in bed and sound asleep.

He leaned back in his desk chair, and closed his eyes. For chrissake, he was actually believing that three kids, one of them ten years old, had kidnapped an adult and somehow hid her up in a cave in the Sisters, because of some alien guy without a face.

"I am losing my goddamn mind, that's what," he said under his breath.

Then, he frowned. That was the sticky part—the cave. Even if they did somehow grab Rainey, it was hard to believe they could somehow drag her up a three-mile hiking trail in the pitch dark, and then go home and act like nothing happened. Was that where she was really being held? A little unwillingly, his thoughts added, *If she's still alive.* If Tyler Vaughan was right about those kids, then they may have wanted to put Rainey out of the way. In which case Vaughan himself might be next.

He picked up his clipboard and looked at a phone number, then grabbed his phone and jabbed in the number with his index finger. After two rings, there was a click, and a female voice said, "Cascadia Zoological Research Station, Judy Kahn speaking."

"Hello, Doctor Kahn, this is Chief of Police Dale Blodgett. Is Tyler Vaughan there?"

"No," she said, her voice immediately becoming wary. "Tyler's out at the moment. Can I take a message?"

Tyler implied that Judy knew what was going on. More than likely there was no harm.

"Yes. Tell him I talked to all three children. No leads."

There was a moment's silence, and when she spoke, her voice was flat.

"They all denied knowing anything." It wasn't a question.

"Yes."

"We figured they would."

"There's still no proof that they were involved in Rainey Carrington's abduction."

"Tyler was under the impression that you believed him." Her voice gained a bit of an edge. The attack dog was baring her teeth a little.

"I'm not saying I don't. Only that there's no proof. No one saw any of them near Rainey's house last night. All of them have stories that are corroborated, as far as they can be, by their parents. There's nothing to go on, at the moment."

"You're giving up?"

He sighed with exasperation. "No, I'm not giving up. I'm saying that following that lead didn't give us anything. There's nothing to narrow down either when Rainey disappeared, nor where she currently might be. Tyler mentioned something about a cave."

"We're going up there as soon as Tyler gets back."

"I hope you're taking adequate precautions."

"Insofar as we can guard against something that's powerful enough to tear open, and melt, metal, yeah, we're being careful," she said dryly.

"It might be smart if I went with you."

"I don't think that will be necessary."

"I see. It's your call. You should realize, however, that now that Tyler has reported this to me, I have to follow up on it, which includes filing a Missing Persons Report for Rainey. This will eventually mean getting the state cops involved. There is clear evidence of kidnapping here, which there wasn't in the other cases, at least until now. So it's only a matter of time before some police investigator comes down and wants to know what's going on here."

"I'm no more eager to have that happen than you are, Officer Blodgett. The sooner we find Rainey, and put a stop to all of this, the better."

"Agreed."

There was a tiny pause, just enough to be noticeable. "I think that since Tyler and I know the area around the cave, it might be best if the two of us go up and check it out again."

She still didn't trust him.

"Like I said, your call. I'm only urging you to be careful until we know exactly what we're dealing with here. And you will keep me informed of whatever you find, right?"

"Of course."

"Good. I'll try to do the same."

"Officer Blodgett, I'm sorry if I came across as defensive," she said, a little more softly. "We're on the same side, I hope."

"I hope so, too."

"We'll be in touch later."

He hung up and massaged his temples. The two of them had something planned that they preferred he didn't see. Gotta hope they knew what they were doing.

Otherwise he'd probably find himself investigating two more missing persons this evening.

ten

. . .

Tyler walked into the research station at a little after noon, carrying a cardboard box. Judy, sitting at her desk, turned and looked at him.

"Got it?"

He nodded. "State of the art. I had to promise my left testicle in exchange if I damaged it in any way."

"Only the left one? You got off light."

He nodded again, set the box down on his desk, and opened it.

"Leon said this'll pick up a thermal signal if there's one there to be seen. It's the most sensitive portable thermal imaging camera there is." He lifted out a Styrofoam sleeve, and from that extracted a black box that looked a little like an overgrown video camera. "In fact, the problem is, it's so sensitive it picks up a lot of meaningless anomalies."

"Signal to noise again."

"Yup. But if there's anything behind that cave wall, this puppy will see it. They use these things to figure out if there are living people trapped in collapsed buildings after earthquakes."

"Excellent. Let's rock and roll."

The drive up to the trailhead proceeded for the most part in silence, punctuated only with thumps and creaks as the *Pigeon* struck potholes and ruts and still somehow managed not to have major jeep parts go flying off into the underbrush.

Finally, Judy said, "Hey, Tyler."

"Yeah?"

"You're really worried about Rainey, aren't you?"

"Of course."

"You can talk about it, if it would help."

"I don't see how talking helps. Doing helps. I hope."

She looked out the window. "Dale Blodgett called. He said he talked to all three kids. No tearful admissions of guilt. All three said they knew nothing and were innocent of every sin."

"I figured."

"You know, I think Blodgett's not a bad character. I thought he was a hick cop, when I first met him. Kind of a Deputy Cletus type. He's got more on the ball than I realized at first."

"That was my impression when I talked to him out at Rainey's this morning."

"I don't think he's got much in the way of imagination, though."

"Well, he acted like he believed me, anyhow. That's got to speak to some level of imagination."

"Yeah. And I think he does. Believe you, I mean. I don't think he wants to, but he does."

"I feel the same way myself."

He pulled over next to the trailhead. "Man," he said, as he was getting out, "I've visited this spot way too much, lately. I'm ready for some different scenery."

Packs on, and trudging up the trail, through the dark, damp trunks of Douglas fir, through thickets of salal and thimbleberry, and finally up out of the shadowy woods and into the alpine meadow that led down to the T-Three camera. They passed it, noting with raised eyebrows and a shrug that it was still sitting undamaged in its housing, its little glass eye pointing uphill toward the rock outcropping and the lava tube.

And then they stood in front of the dark mouth of the cave, dropping packs onto the ground, and trying to get past the shuddering horror that still permeated the area. They pulled out flashlights, and Tyler gently removed the camera and pressed a button on its side to turn it on.

"We ready?" Judy said.

"Yup. This is basically a thirty-thousand-dollar point-and-shoot. As soon as we get into the cave, I'll activate it. Highest sensitivity. We can shoot the entire wall. If there's any kind of heat source behind there, this'll see it." He switched on his flashlight and moved into the mouth of the cave. "However, if one of the images shows a tall, skinny silhouette with an oval face, I'm getting right the fuck outta here."

She chuckled, a little grimly, and turned on her own flashlight and followed him.

He led the way down the lava tube, and after about thirty feet, there was the cave wall, just as they had seen it before.

He studied the wall, shining his flashlight across its surface. "So, you really think there's something behind this?"

"I'll bet you a pint of beer at Dorrie's. Lava tubes don't end this way, with a flat rock wall. Call it a hunch, but I think Mister Faceless put this up to stop anyone who got past his little *Fear Factor* routine out at the cave mouth."

"Okay, then. Time to let the machine take a look." He swung out a little digital display panel, black for the moment except for a legend that said *READY*, and aimed the camera at the upper left-hand corner of the wall, and pressed the shutter button.

There was a click, and for five seconds, the digital display showed a kaleidoscopic smear of false color—the thermally-enhanced image of the segment of the rock wall that he had photographed. Then it went back to black, and the legend *READY* reappeared.

He shook his head. "Nothing but mush."

He aimed the camera a little to the right, and tried again. The second image was the same—nothing but a record of the microscopic differences in temperature across the rock wall.

As he moved farther to the right the rock wall gradually became a different color, signifying a slow warming.

"A little hotter over on the right."

"Angle of the sun warming the outside slope?"

"Could be." He worked his way downward. After another six images, he said, "No, it's not the sun. It gets warmer down toward the bottom."

"Geologic heat source?"

"Could be. This whole place is riddled with hot springs." He knelt, and aimed the camera at the floor of the cave, near where it intersected the end wall. The image popped out on the screen.

"No. The floor's cold. The only thing it's picking up is our heat traces left behind where we stood."

"Weird."

"Yeah." He once again aimed the camera at the wall, low down, and a little right of center.

The image came up. "I'll be damned."

"What?"

"There's something hot right over here."

"Let me see." She came and looked over his shoulder. He touched a couple of buttons on the camera's side to call back up the previous image. "What kind of temperature difference is that?"

"Looks like about a degree. A degree and a half, tops. Still, there's something that's warming that part of the wall, and the heat signature is leaking through on this side."

"Any idea what shape?"

He worked his way up the wall. "The signal starts to fade away about mid-wall. I'd say it couldn't be more than about three feet high."

"Guesses as to what it is?"

He didn't answer for a moment. "If this was the wall of a building, I'd think it was some kind of machine. An air conditioner, a computer, a photocopier, something like that. It looks short, squat, basically rectangular. If you're right, that this is some kind of relatively narrow rock wall, and assuming the floor of the cave continues fairly level on the other side, it's maybe three feet tall, four feet wide."

"Mechanical?"

"No way to tell. The signal's pretty uniform. That doesn't mean anything, though. You'd have a uniform signal if there was a sleeping bear leaning up against the wall."

"Bears aren't rectangular, Tyler."

He snorted. "I didn't say this *was* a bear. I'm just saying that the signal uniformity doesn't mean it's a mechanical source. But yeah, from the shape, it doesn't look like the blobby sorts of patterns you get from animals."

"Anything more?"

He shot a few more images of other areas of the wall. "Not that I can see. If there are other heat sources behind the wall, they're too weak or too far in to show up." He looked up at her. "But I guess I owe you a pint."

"Told you so."

"Yeah, yeah, I know. Score one for you."

"Yup. Can you think of anything we can do to get more information about what's back there?"

"I don't know, but I have to do one thing." He went up to the wall and shouted, "Rainey! If you can hear my voice, try to answer!"

He stopped and listened. Total silence.

"There's got to be a way to get past that wall." She reached out and brushed her hand over its rough surface.

He looked at her. "You still think there's some kind of button we could press, and a door will open, like in science fiction movies?"

"That'd make it easier."

"And then we could go down into the cave, and there'd be all this scientific gadgetry, and blue stuff boiling in beakers."

"Right. That's the idea."

"You've gotta stop watching the *Syfy Channel*. I think we should get out of here. My tolerance for this place is dwindling as we speak."

"I didn't like it in the first place." She led the way up out of the cave.

"You're the one who keeps suggesting coming back. I figured you were getting some kind of weird jollies from it."

"Hardly. But I think I might be getting used to it. However Slender Man is doing that to us, he may need to turn up the gain a little, because it's not really having the desired effect of keeping us out of his house."

They emerged into the sunlight, and he switched off the camera and flashlight and stowed both back in his pack.

"Okay," she said, as they hoisted backpacks and walked off down the hill, the sensations of chill diminishing as the cave mouth quickly dwindled to a darker splotch in the dark rock outcropping. "So, let's try to put the pieces together. Theorize."

"We don't have a lot to go on."

"No, but we have some data. The kids go missing, and return two to three days later. Rainey thought they were acting different, but we have only her word to go by."

"I think she was telling the truth." He wasn't quite shooting laser beams from his eyes, but it was close.

"Whoa, sport, I didn't say she was making stuff up. You're

a scientist. You know, replicability, peer review, all that sorta stuff is important. One person sees something, it didn't happen. Nothing personal, but it's an anecdote."

"I still believe her."

"For my part, I do too, and that's pretty amazing because I've never even met her. But anyway, we've got to look at the facts here. We know the kids disappeared, and then came back. Now Rainey herself is gone, and left a note that implicates the three kids in her disappearance. The 'PKK' thing—I don't see what else that could stand for."

"Me either."

"Then, we have the images of Slender Man, the breaking of the camera, the break-in at the lab, and the theft of your computer and the camera parts. And now we have some thermal images of something behind that rock wall."

"Yes."

"You know what strikes me?"

"What?"

"There's nothing to connect the two sets of data. They're entirely independent of each other."

"You think so? C'mon, Judy, what's the likelihood? Here's Slender Man, stalking around the Sisters and smashing cameras and breaking into the lab. I send his image to Rainey, and she vanishes. And at least one of the kids, when he came back, was discovered up in the Sisters. That's not a connection?"

"Not a very strong one. Listen, I know it's like, how could two sets of weird stuff be going on this close together, and not be connected? But Rainey's disappearance is adequately explained by the fact that she'd talked to the kids, and they thought she was onto them. It might have nothing to do with the pics you took of Slender Man."

"What about what I found online? Slender Man has been seen in the vicinity of child abductions in other places."

"Okay, there's that. But still. From the data we have, the

connection is kind of thin. Looking at this from a scientific standpoint, I'd definitely want to put that in the 'yet to be established conclusively' column."

"I guess." But he wasn't really convinced, and it came out in his voice.

"And it's also not been established where the kids were held while they were missing, and where Rainey's being held. It's only conjecture that it has anything to do with the cave."

"That's true."

"So the first priority is finding Rainey. Which will mean trying to figure out where she's being held."

"I have no idea how we could do that."

"Because, you do know… if she comes back…" She stopped, and looked over at him.

"I know. I said that to Blodgett. If she comes back, there's no guarantee she won't be changed, like the kids were."

She nodded. "Scary thought."

"Yeah." His voice was rough with anger.

She paused. "I think you're in love with her, Tyler Vaughan."

He cleared his throat. "I don't know. I don't think you can fall in love that quickly. I'm in serious *like* with her, that's for sure. She's just… she's sweet, and kind, and smart, and it really pisses me off that she's somewhere, scared and maybe hurt, and I can't help her."

"You *are* trying to help her."

"I've accomplished a hell of a lot thus far." He could almost taste the bitterness on his tongue.

She clapped him on the back. "We're working on it. We've got Blodgett on our side, and like I said, I think there's more to him that meets the eye. He's kind of got a lazy streak, I think. He doesn't like to be pushed into thinking, or acting. But once you get him going, I think he's got a good eye. He'll be a decent ally."

"At least he's not still investigating *us*. I wish I'd told him everything two days ago. Maybe I could have prevented Rainey from being kidnapped."

"Speculation, again. You can't fault yourself for what happened."

They hiked in silence for a while.

Finally he said, "I think this whole thing is going to lead to my getting fired."

"Why?"

"I'm hardly getting any of my own research done. I've got two papers in the works and have made zilch progress on either one of them since this whole thing started. If I don't have anything to show before long, Joe's going to tell me to get lost, and find another mammalogist who can actually produce grants."

She didn't respond.

"See? Don't have an answer to that, do you? But you know, I feel like I can't change course now. I can't say to hell with Rainey, I have my job to do. I love working at the lab, but this… this is more important."

"Then the decision should be clear."

"I guess it is. But I don't want to bring you down with me."

"You won't. I've got a paper in review right now, and another one that I should have done by mid-August or so. Joe's got nothing on me if I take a little break from the birdies and help you out."

"Just look out for yourself, okay?"

"Me?" She laughed. "You ever known me not to?"

"I guess not." They came down the slope, and the logging road appeared in front of them, with the *Pigeon* parked, squat and decrepit, in the pull-off.

She went over to the passenger side, and there was a clunk as she shucked her pack and stood it up against the jeep door.

He took off his own pack, and then glanced idly into the bed of the jeep. There was a sudden jolt of alarm, almost electric, but at first what he saw was so incongruous that he didn't recognize it. He thought, *No… what? That can't be…*

He spoke, controlling his voice with some effort. "Um, Judy? Come over here."

She came around the back of the jeep, and he pointed.

There, propped up against a box of survival gear, was his computer, the cord wrapped neatly around the base.

They were halfway back to the lab before either of them spoke.

"Well," Judy said, "that was pretty considerate of Slender Man, you have to admit."

"Jesus," Tyler said under his breath.

"Didn't return the pieces of the camera, I noticed."

"I don't even know how to think about this."

"It's definitely not what I thought was back there, when you said, 'Come over here,' in that voice that sounded like you were about to puke, faint, or wet your pants, or possibly all three simultaneously. I didn't even want to look. I was afraid of what I might see."

He shuddered. "I think this is almost worse."

Her eyebrows rose in surprise. "Why?"

"Because something horrible is what you'd *expect* to have happen. A warning. Like the scene in *The Godfather* where they put the horse's head in the guy's bed. Or maybe we'd find the jeep engine sabotaged, so that we'd be stuck up here overnight. *That* I would have expected." He swallowed. "Not my computer, all nicely tucked in, safe and sound. I'm surprised that there wasn't a card on it, with little flowers and bunnies, saying, 'Thank you so much for the use of your computer. It was so thoughtful of you to lend it to me. Love, Slender Man.'"

"At least you got it back." She considered. "But I see your

point. It may force a revision of our idea of what's going on, here."

"Of course, it all depends on what happens when get back to the lab and plug the computer in. If it blows up and kills me, then I'd say that our previous conception of Slender Man's motives might not change much."

"Always the optimist. That's why I love you, Tyler."

A half hour later, Tyler was sitting at his desk, his computer restored to its customary location. Then he sat there, staring at it with wide eyes.

"Go ahead, plug it in," Judy said.

"That's fine for you to say. You're standing on the other side of the room."

"Wuss."

He scowled at her, then plugged the computer into the power strip and touched the power button at the front of the hard drive.

There was a whirring noise as the computer started up, and then the lock screen came up. He typed out *tvaughan* and his password, and moments later, his desktop background—a photograph of an elk, staring at the camera—came up.

"Looks fine." He moved the cursor around, clicked on a file called *Images*, and went to a subfolder titled "T-Three."

It was empty.

"It looks like he wiped out anything from T-Three, but everything else looks untouched. Hard to tell for sure."

I wonder…

With a couple of mouse clicks he opened up his email software, and went to *Sent Messages*.

He scrolled down a short way. "Judy, come take a look."

She came over and peered over his shoulder.

"Notice something missing?"

"Tyler, how the hell am I gonna be able to see something that's not there?"

"All of the messages I sent to Rainey are there, *except* the one where I attached the photograph of Slender Man."

"Dude's thorough."

"So that means that the flash drive in my desk at home is the only remaining record of the pics we got from T-Three."

"I wouldn't say that too loud. Unless you want him ransacking your house."

"I wonder what Ahab would do if Slender Man suddenly showed up?"

"Probably try to incapacitate him with poisonous dog farts."

"Slender Man doesn't have a nose."

"Lucky him."

He clicked the mouse, opening up other files, looking in other locations on the computer. "Nope. Nothing else has been touched, as far as I can tell."

"Surgical precision."

"Yup."

She was quiet for a moment. "So, he definitely doesn't like it that you got pics of him. Otherwise, he's kind of going out of his way to be considerate."

"There's the kids. And Rainey being abducted. That's not really my definition of *considerate*."

"Allow me to remind you that we still haven't proven Slender Man was behind all that."

"He could have some ulterior motive for giving me back my computer. Maybe there's some kind of virus on it. Now that I'm connected to the server again, it'll proliferate and bring down major world governments, and it will all be my fault."

She stared at him. "You may be the most neurotic person I've ever met."

"Well, it's *possible*."

"I see now why you have such an objection to the woo-woos. You're a woo-woo yourself. You don't want the competition."

He turned to look at her, his brows drawing together with incredulity. "I am *not* a woo-woo."

"You are *too*. Okay, you're not into Bigfoot and psychics and crystals and pyramids and so on, but you're awfully good at making up wild stories and then worrying yourself sick that they might be true."

He gave her a sour look. "That's not the same thing."

"Oh, the hell it isn't. You're exactly like they are, building up a nice little pretend world to live in. The difference is, theirs makes them happy, and I don't think yours does."

"I'll be happy." His voice was mournful. "I'll be happy if we can figure out what the hell is going on around here. And get Rainey back. Especially that."

She patted him on the shoulder. "I know. We'll give it our best. But for now, try to stay optimistic. You're a lot stronger, smarter, and more capable than you give yourself credit for, sometimes."

He looked at her, eyebrows raised. "Judy, that may well be the nicest thing you've ever said about me."

"You didn't record it, did you?"

"No."

"Thank god. That means I can still deny I ever said it."

He gave her a rueful grin. "Yeah, yeah. You're all right, you know that, Kahn?"

"Don't start evil rumors like that. They get around."

He stood. "I gotta go. I told Leon if I finished with the camera, I'd get it back to him today. It's an hour down to Eugene, and he said he'd be in till five or so. If I speed, I'll just make it."

"See you tomorrow."

"Later."

"Oh, and Tyler?" Her face suddenly became serious.

"Yeah?"

"Lock your doors tonight, okay?"

eleven

. . .

Rainey opened her eyes in darkness so opaque that at first she wasn't sure she was actually conscious. Then she thought perhaps she had gone blind. After some minutes she decided, for no very good reason other than optimism, that it was simply dark, but the kind of blackness beyond experience. Total, palpable darkness, thick as tar.

She was lying on some sort of thinly cushioned surface, like a cot or camp bed. She reached down and touched it. It was a cloth-covered slab of what appeared to be foam rubber. Then she felt herself. She could tell by touch that she wasn't wearing the clothes she'd had on originally, a light cotton dress and sandals. The material she was clothed in now was so lightweight as to feel almost like nothing. It was a little slick, and felt synthetic. It made a faint swishing sound as it rubbed against itself when she moved. She was barefoot. Other than that, she was healthy and unhurt, except for a painful spot on her right hand, probably from a cut or a scrape.

She sat up. The place smelled damp and mildewy. She stayed motionless for a moment, dizzy and disoriented. How much of that was from suddenly finding herself in a strange space of unknown dimensions, in an unknown location, and how much was the residue of being somehow rendered unconscious, was impossible to determine. She forced her internal chatter to quiet and sat for a few minutes, listening. There was no sound. Wherever she was, either it was very well insulated from noise, or she was completely and utterly alone, or possibly both.

She stood, a little wobbly on her feet, and took a slow step forward. The surface underfoot felt like hard-packed earth, but was flat and smooth and easy to walk on. She took another step, then another, her hands out in front of her, one across her face to save her from colliding with low-hanging obstructions.

After ten steps, her outstretched hand touched the cold, rough surface of stone. She pressed her palms against it, trying not to think about what kind of centipedes, spiders, or insects her fingers might contact in such a wall. And, in fact, all they encountered were more stones, cool, slightly damp, rising above her head to an unknown height.

She decided to make a circuit of the place. Feeling forward with her feet, so as not to fall if there were any holes, pits, or uneven surfaces, and keeping her right hand in contact with the wall, she slowly made her way counterclockwise. The stone wall continued for about ten feet, then angled sharply to the left. About six feet farther along, her hand encountered a flat surface, made of some material other than rock. It felt like it could be wood, but it was impossible to be certain. There was a heavy metal ring set in the middle of it, and from this she deduced that it was probably a door.

She pulled on the ring. Nothing moved. If it was a door, it was locked or otherwise secured.

She let the ring drop, and it made a hollow *clunk* as it fell back into place, supporting her thought that the flat surface was wood, and that this was in fact a door. She felt the door from top to bottom. There was a narrow crack at the base and the top, which she could barely reach. The sides were delineated by thin, relatively straight gaps, but any hinges must be on the outside.

She followed the wall around, and soon came back to the bed. It seemed to be the only piece of furniture in the place. She did, however, find something pleasant—just before she reached the bed, her bare toe touched a cool, smooth surface resting on the floor, and she reached down and felt it.

It turned out to be a tray with a glass, a pitcher of water, and a plate with a sandwich. This discovery made her instantaneously aware of how hungry and thirsty she was. The next few minutes were absorbed in eating the sandwich, which turned out to be peanut butter and jelly, and drinking two glasses of water.

Her hunger and thirst sated for the moment, she sat down on the bed and pondered her situation. She was obviously captive, most likely after having been rendered unconscious by one or more of the Three Kids. She couldn't help capitalizing the words in her mind—they were beginning to seem almost mythically frightening, like the Three Witches or the Three Gorgons.

Where was this place?

She immediately thought of the cave Tyler and Judy had explored. This could certainly be a cave, although the door in the wall was an unusually human touch. Presumably, though, an alien who could melt a metal lockset could figure out a way to install hinges into an opening in a rock wall.

Her thoughts turned to Tyler. He would be beside himself by this time. She should have let him come and spend the night with her. Would the Three Kids have attacked if there had been two people there? It was too late to worry about that at this point. At least maybe Tyler would get her note and figure out what happened.

There was a faint creaking noise from overhead, the familiar sound of someone walking in a room one floor up.

She frowned. Okay, that was a footstep on a wooden floor. Not a cave, then?

She made her way back to the door in the wall. She stood for a moment, indecisive.

What did she have to lose? It wasn't like they didn't know she was down here.

She pounded on the door with her fist, shouting at the top of her voice, "Hey! Can anyone hear me? I've been kidnapped and I'm being held captive down here! Help!"

There was no sound but another thin *creak* from the floorboards over her head, and then silence.

She put her ear to the heavy wood planks of the door, hoping to catch even the tiniest hint of a noise. But either the thickness of the door defeated her, or else there was nothing there to be heard.

She retreated to the bed, and sat down again. No option other than to wait and see what happened. She had a moment's panicked thought of *What if they've left me down here to starve?* but she pushed it away. If they wanted her to starve, feeding her a peanut butter and jelly sandwich was a peculiar way to start. This was a cheering thought, and she lay back down on the bed, hands cupped behind her head, and dozed for a little.

It was perhaps twenty minutes later when there was the sound of a slide bolt being shot back, and the door swung open. She opened her eyes, and then winced at the glare, although the light coming in through the half-open doorway was actually quite dim. A tall, bulky figure blocked the opening for a moment, silhouetted, and then stepped inside. The person was so backlit it was impossible to see any facial features. No way to recognize who it was. She squinted painfully toward him? her? still standing just inside the door.

Try to get as much information as possible. She might have to rely on her memory to identify this person later.

"Good morning, Rainey," said a female voice.

I know that voice, she thought with some astonishment, and began desperately to try to figure out who it belonged to. "Hi. Why are you holding me captive?"

"I think you can figure that out for yourself, and honestly, I suspect you probably already have. I don't think it necessary to confirm what you already know."

"It's because you think I know more than I should."

"See, I told you that you already knew. I always had you figured for a smart girl."

"How long are you going to keep me here?"

"Here? Not very much longer, I shouldn't think. Captive? I think the best way to put it is, 'indefinitely.' I should get myself comfortable, dear. I believe the phrase is 'resign yourself to your fate.' You're not going home any time soon."

Her gaze moved toward the sliver of light alongside the door, where it had been left a little ajar.

The woman chuckled softly. "Feel free to try to beat me to the door. I can assure you that I am not only faster than you are, I am a good deal stronger. And even if, by some chance, you made it through the door and out, there really is nowhere for you to *go.*"

"I'll find a way to escape somehow."

"Well, you are entitled to your opinion, of course," the other woman said archly.

And suddenly she remembered a conversation in which she'd heard the same voice utter the same words... it seemed like ages ago, a discussion about Kevin Torgeson, in the Crooked Creek Post Office...

"Maureen?" Her eyes widened. "Maureen Sullivan?"

"Got it in one." Mrs. Sullivan laughed a little.

"What do you have to do with all of this?"

"I'm hardly going to discuss my role with *you.* But I thought it only reasonable that I at least tell you that your present uncomfortable quarters are only temporary. I regret their lack of amenities. There is a bathroom one floor up, but if you'd like to avail yourself of it, you will have to assure me that you won't try any of what the old police dramas used to call 'funny stuff.' Down here, you can scream your head off, and no one can hear you, so you may as well save the wear-and-tear on your vocal cords. Up a floor—well, it isn't likely, but still. If you try it, that will be your last visit to running water until we change venues. Are we quite clear on that account?"

"Yes." She had a sudden realization. "This is the basement of the Three Sisters Lodge, isn't it?"

"Excellent! Of course. A sub-basement, actually, and one that almost no one knows exists. My late husband's great-grandparents were rumrunners during Prohibition, and the sub-basement has a honeycomb of rooms such as this one that were used to store illicit booze. Phineas and Mary Sullivan were the subject of more than one investigation by the FBI. They thought correctly that the two of them were the leaders of the liquor racket in western Oregon, but despite being searched more than once, this little hidey-hole escaped all notice by the law." She paused for a moment. "I bring up ancient history only to reassure you that your discovery by any erstwhile rescuers is unlikely in the extreme. And that would include your intrepid young boyfriend, Tyler Vaughan."

She jumped a little at the mention of Tyler's name, but didn't respond.

"Oh, yes, dear, we know all about Tyler, and in fact at some point will probably have to deal with him, too. But he's well-connected enough that his disappearance would raise a lot more red flags than yours would. So, for now, we'll simply monitor his activities, and for his sake and yours we'll hope that he keeps on messing about with ear-tagging elk up in the Sisters, and leaves us alone."

She thought about a variety of responses to this. *Please don't hurt Tyler. You'd better leave him alone. Don't mess with him, he knows what you're up to.* None of them were prudent to say. None of the more threatening variants were even all that likely to be true. His image rose in her mind, vulnerable and earnest and trying his best to be brave. A pang of fear shot through her at the thought that anything could happen to him.

Had she fallen in love with him, then? Or was she just in Protect-the-Lost-Puppy mode?

In the end she said nothing, and this seemed to annoy Maureen. "In any case, we'll assume your cooperation, and it may be that there will be no need to do anything about Doctor Vaughan. In the meantime, do you need to use the facilities?"

She shook her head. "No, I'm fine." She tried to give her voice a confidence that she didn't feel.

"All right, then. I expect that you'll only need to be down here for a few more hours. There's an electric lantern set in a recess in the wall to the left of the door. It will give you a little light. I'm afraid that's all the comfort I can provide you for the time being, but it's better than sitting in the dark, wouldn't you say? You may avail yourself of it as soon as I've shut and re-bolted the door. I'd recommend that you remain seated where you are until the door is secure. That is purely for your safety, you understand."

Mrs. Sullivan retreated toward the door. The bright gap widened for a moment, then her bulky form was outlined in it. Then she stepped through, and the door closed. Complete darkness fell, followed by the sound of the bolt being shot home.

She stood and walked carefully in the direction of the door. She couldn't help herself, she had to try the door, but once again it wouldn't budge. After a few moments of feeling around, she found the electric lantern in a little cavity in the wall that her trailing hand must have missed on her earlier circuit of the room. She located the switch, and turned it on.

After a few more moments of squinting painfully in the brightness of the glowing fluorescent tubes, she held the lantern up, and looked around her little prison.

As soon as she looked at the wall, she realized that if she'd been able to see, she'd have known immediately that this was no cave. The stone wall was clearly not natural. It was built of rough-hewn blocks of rock, set together apparently without mortar, but so well-constructed that a knife couldn't have been inserted in the joints. The door was made of heavy wood planks, with a medieval-looking iron ring in the center as a door handle. The bed was an iron-framed cot with a thin and moldy-looking mattress, and a decrepit, yellowed pillow. The tray on which her sandwich and water pitcher had rested was the only incongruous touch of elegance. It was made of stainless steel, with brass handles, and had an elaborate engraving of flowers in the corners.

Of course. It was from the lodge. Maureen entertained rich guests. She had to have nice stuff.

She looked down at herself. The odd, lightweight cloth that had replaced her original clothes turned out to be a shimmery, gauzy material, colored an opaque silver. It looked like no cloth she'd ever seen before, but reminded her of the garb worn by astronauts in black-and-white science fiction movies from the 1950s.

She looked like she should be on a spaceship.

She giggled a little, rubbing the material between her fingers. It was oddly slick and unnatural, its surface reminding her of the greasy feel of Teflon.

She looked around again, her momentary amusement over her odd garments fading into melancholy.

No choice for the moment, of course. She couldn't go anywhere. She had to try to relax and think, and see if she could figure a way out of this. Which was not the same thing as resigning herself to her fate.

To hell with that.

With that not very tranquility-inducing thought in her mind, she went back to the bed, sat down, crossed her legs, and tried to meditate, clearing her mind of her fear and distractions and worry over Tyler.

What if this really is it? What if I'll never see my home again? My friends? My cat?

The idea seemed desperately sad. She pictured her little cottage, with its wild profusion of gardens, the quiet evenings reading a book, Bonkers curled up asleep in her lap. She tried to force it away, but the thought kept coming back. *And Tyler,* her mental voice added, as if not quite ready to abandon the elegiac train of thought it had embarked upon. She really wanted to see him again. Lots. The idea that she might never see him again struck her as so unfair. And then she realized, with some surprise, that she *was* falling in love with him, after all. Who'd have thought?

Some time later—it was impossible to know how long, in this dim, damp, rock-walled cell—there was a noise, and Rainey looked up from where she had been sitting, eyes closed, alternately meditating and trying not to nod off. There was the *clunk* of the bolt being thrown back, and the door opened with a creak. Maureen Sullivan came in, as usual looking like a warship sailing under full rigging. She was followed by Kathleen Standish, her freckled face alert and tense and unfriendly. They walked up to her, one on each side, and Mrs. Sullivan said, "Come with us. Please resist any temptation to shout out or try to escape."

She stood, and the two gripped her upper arms firmly. She was propelled out of her cell into a hallway, and then up a rickety set of wooden stairs between two rough-hewn stone walls. Kathleen opened the door at the top of the stairs, and Rainey found herself in an ordinary basement, surrounded by garden tools, coils of watering hose, and boxes marked *Linens* and *Kitchen Ware* and *China*. Mrs. Sullivan swung the door closed behind them.

She took a quick look over her shoulder. The outside of the door they'd just passed through was invisible. It evidently had slabs of stone affixed to its surface to hide its existence. She didn't wonder that the long-ago FBI investigators were never able to find the illicit distillery. It was brilliantly camouflaged.

"Keep moving." Kathleen gave her a little push.

"I *am*." She shot Kathleen an annoyed glance. "You really need to work on your attitude, you know that?"

Kathleen didn't respond, and she was escorted up to a second door, which was secured by a padlock. Mrs. Sullivan selected a key from a large ring in the pocket of her dress, unlocked it, and pulled it open. Kathleen and Mrs. Sullivan pushed her through the door into a room, only a little larger than the one she had just vacated, but wooden-floored, dry, with a few chairs, boxes, and other assorted oddments.

In the room were three people. Two sat in the chairs, one of them cross-legged on the floor. All wore the same gauzy silver material she did. She stared at the people in the room, and had to stop herself from giving a yelp of pure shock.

The three people were Kevin Torgeson, Phil Collette, and Kathleen Standish.

She frowned, craning her neck forward a little, and then looked back at the tall, blonde girl who stood in the doorway behind her, whose face wore an unpleasant smirk. Then she looked at the girl sitting in the plastic deck chair.

They were completely identical, down to the last freckle, the slant of the eyebrows, the way a stray lock of hair fell across their foreheads.

The Kathleen Standish in the doorway looked at her double, smiling in a superior fashion. The Kathleen in the chair winced and looked away. Rainey stepped forward, and looked at the two others. Phil Collette sat on the floor, looking small and lost, and his eyes were red-rimmed and puffy. Kevin Torgeson leaned back in his chair, legs stretched out in front of him, his pale, high-cheekboned face contorted with a combination of fury and fear.

The door behind her slammed shut, and there was the sound of the padlock being clicked closed.

"Rainey?" Kathleen's voice was hoarse. "They got you, too?"

She walked forward, and looked at Kathleen closely. If she'd needed any more proof, she saw it in the girl's face. The guarded, wary expression she'd noticed the first time she'd seen Kathleen after her return was absent. This girl looked scared, nervous, and exhausted, but there was no lingering doubt that she was the cheerful, outgoing eighteen-year-old that Rainey had seen around the village, and the other Kathleen was… who?

"Well, technically, the three of *you* got me. I was abducted by you three, last night."

"That's it, I knew it," Kevin said. "They've got duplicates of *all* of us."

"You didn't know?"

"We knew about me," Kathleen said. "Because we've seen her. But Sullivan won't tell us anything. Kevin guessed that they'd replaced all of us, and that probably no one was looking for us because no one realized we're still being held captive."

"There's the scars, too," Kevin said. "They took a bit of skin from each of us. DNA sample."

"Do you have a scar on your hand?" Kathleen said. She, and then Kevin and Phil, all held out their right hands, palm downward. Each of them had, on the back of the hand between the thumb and index finger, a small circular scab. She lifted her hand and examined it. The little painful spot she'd noticed when she'd awakened, and to which she had given no further attention, was caused by a wound in the same shape and location as the others'.

"So they're going to replace you, too," Kevin said.

"Do you have any idea what they're trying to accomplish?"

"No clue," Kathleen said. "They won't tell us anything. Only that we're being held here, indefinitely. They had each of us in separate rooms, down in some kind of cellar underneath here, but this morning they brought us up here. I don't know why."

"She mentioned to me something about that I wouldn't be here very much longer, and I got the impression she wasn't talking about just being in that the room down in the cellar. She sounded like she was talking about this building."

"Where are they going to take us?" Phil spoke up for the first time, his voice high and tremulous.

"I don't know," Rainey said. "I wish I did. I'm scared, too."

"So, no one knows we're here?" Kathleen said.

"Well, not here *specifically*, I think. But my friend, Tyler Vaughan—he's a scientist up at the research station in the Sisters—he's onto them. He accidentally took a photograph of something that they didn't want us to see, and sent it to me. Between that, and the fact that I went and talked to all of the duplicates, they decided I knew too much. But Tyler knows what's going on, and now that I've been kidnapped, he'll be trying to figure it all out. I left a note saying that I'd been abducted by the three of you. Well, not the *real* three of you, but you know what I mean. I'm not sure if he got it. They might have gone into my house afterwards and made sure there weren't any notes left behind, I don't know. But if he does find the note, he'll be putting the pieces together. He and the woman he works with, and also Dale Blodgett."

Kevin snorted. "Officer Blockhead? He couldn't find his

own ass if you gave him a map and allowed him to use both hands."

"I don't know if you're right about that, Kevin. I think he's smarter than you'd think. He's kind of lazy, but I think we'd finally gotten him to take this seriously. I hope that Dale keeps at it, because we need all the help we can get."

"But if there are people who are there, pretending to be us, no one will know we're missing." Phil hitched a sob, and then roughly wiped his sleeve across his eyes.

"Not no one, Phil," Kathleen said gently. "At least now we know that somebody else knows what's going on. Rainey's boyfriend is a scientist. He'll work on finding us."

Rainey started to say, *I didn't say Tyler was my boyfriend,* but then thought, *Oh, never mind, what the hell. If we get out of this, I bet he will be.* The thought made her smile. "That's right. We've got some smart people who are trying to find us now. They won't rest until they do."

"Or until they get caught, too." Kevin's voice was surly.

"Look, Kevin," Kathleen said, "you can give up if you want to. I'm not going to, and I bet Rainey won't, either."

"I'm not giving up," Kevin said. "If I had a chance to get at that Sullivan bitch, I'd wipe that smirk off her face pretty fast."

"I normally don't condone violence," Rainey said, "but I hope you get the opportunity."

"Once we saw my duplicate," Kathleen said, "and the scars on our hands, we thought about clones. But we talked about cloning in my AP Biology class last year, and I don't think you can make a clone in a few days. But however they did it, she looks enough like me that she's able to fool people. Even my mother, right? My mom doesn't know, does she?"

Rainey shook her head. "No. I saw your twin out working in the garden a couple of days ago. As far as I know, your mom doesn't suspect anything."

"Damn. So somehow, they not only created a physical

duplicate, they made a person who looks like she's my age, and has enough of my memories to act like me."

Rainey nodded.

"I don't think that's possible by anything human science can do."

Kevin snorted again. "Kathleen thinks Sullivan and the rest are aliens. It's because these silver things we're wearing look like spacesuits. And the fact that she spends too much time watching *Star Trek*."

"I think she's right," Rainey said. "The photograph that Tyler took—it was of something that looks pretty alien to me. We've been calling it Slender Man, but we don't know for sure what it really is, or where it comes from."

"You don't know," Kevin scoffed, "so you think it's an alien. You act like you have any idea what's impossible for human scientists. How do *you* two know what scientists can do? You're a kid and a herbal tea maker. What the hell do you know about it? Besides, it's not like the government ever tells anyone anything. There could be all kinds of weird shit going on in government labs and we wouldn't know anything about it."

Rainey shrugged. "Whoever is behind it, the fact is, the duplicates do act like you, convincingly enough that almost everyone was fooled."

"Almost everyone," Kathleen said. "But not you. You knew, somehow. And that's why they kidnapped you, right? Because you had figured it out. How did you know?"

"I'm not sure. Something seemed wrong about you. About the duplicates, I mean. There was something that was inauthentic. I recognized it right from the beginning, when I saw your duplicate, Kevin. The moment I saw him, it was like something in me said, 'Be careful, this isn't really Kevin.' And then, when he went into the house with your mom, he turned and gave me this look." She shuddered. "I could tell that he knew *I* knew. After that, it was simply a matter of putting the pieces together."

Kevin looked up at her, and his sullen façade softened for a moment, and he suddenly looked very young, and very scared. "My mom and dad… they're okay?"

She nodded. "I talked to your mom. I was going to say yesterday morning, but I'm not even sure what day it is. But she was fine. As far as I know, the four of us are the only ones who they've gone after. Tyler—my scientist friend—his lab has been broken into, but he's okay, or was as of the day I was abducted." She paused, and frowned. "Of course, I had no idea that Maureen Sullivan was one of them. Who knows who else they've replaced?"

"Well, *that's* a cheerful thought." Kevin's expression returned to its previous surly cast.

"Is there any way you can think of to get a message to your boyfriend? Or to Officer Blodgett?" Kathleen said.

"I can't think of anything. They're not nearly dumb enough to leave us with a cellphone."

"I had mine," Kevin said. "But they took it away when they took my clothes." His mouth twisted into a snarl. "Man, it skeeves me out to think of them stripping me naked while I was unconscious and dressing me in this tinfoil shit. They didn't even leave me my boxers."

"So there's nothing to connect the disappearances to Mrs. Sullivan?" Kathleen asked.

"No." Rainey tried to squelch the feeling of hopelessness that rose within her at the thought. "No one had the least idea that she had anything to do with it. I think I may have mentioned her name to Tyler once or twice, but only as a source of gossip and information. Now I wonder if she was looking for information herself when she talked to me, trying to find out how much I knew. Or suspected."

Phil's voice was mournful. "Mrs. Sullivan was one of my mom's first friends in Crooked Creek, when we moved here. I never thought she liked me very much, but I don't think she likes kids much at all. Now I wonder how long ago she was planning to kidnap me."

Rainey shrugged helplessly. "I don't know how anyone could link any of this to Maureen Sullivan. It would take a psychic even to see that there was a connection."

twelve

. . .

"Wensleydale, honey," Daisy Blodgett said, "I *really* think you need to find out what Maureen Sullivan is doing up there in the Three Sisters Lodge."

Dale sat at his desk in the station, looking up at his mother with a pained expression. "But why, Mom? Why in the hell should I investigate Maureen Sullivan? I don't have enough to do, with people disappearing right and left?"

"Well, that's what I *mean*, dear." Her voice was patronizing. "She's in the middle of it. All of it. All the disappearances, and... oh, *everything*."

Dale's expression deepened from pain, right through exasperation and out the other side, into helpless, incoherent bafflement. "But, Mom, Maureen has nothing to do with this! She's... she's a member of the Chamber of Commerce! She's... she's..." He paused, and swallowed. "Respectable!" Of course, that word would hardly carry any weight in Daisy's ears.

"*Respectable*." Daisy made a dismissive little gesture with her hand. "Huh. She's not respectable. She's a conniving, black-hearted, evil-minded—well, let me put it this way. Her aura is a disgusting muddy brown."

"Oh, okay, Mom." He rolled his eyes. "You shoulda told me that first. She's got a ugly-ass aura. I'll just run right out there to the Lodge and arrest her."

The sarcasm, as usual, went past Daisy without so much as ruffling her hair. "Well, I'm glad you're finally listening to me. It's *taken* long enough." She paused. "And you know how I know she's involved?"

"No, but I'll bet it has something to do with the I Ching or pyramids."

"No, dear, Tarot cards! The same way I knew about poor little Kathleen Standish!"

"Oh, of course." The headache that had never been far from him in the last few weeks reasserted itself with enthusiasm, and he rubbed his temples.

"So, I was doing a Tarot card spread for poor Rainey, and I think it's simply devastating that she's disappeared, I *told* you it wasn't only children disappearing and you shouldn't think it was some kind of nasty *pedophile* involved, that the answer lay in the Other Realms, but you wouldn't hear of it."

"I know, Mom, you were right as usual."

"So anyway, I was doing a spread for Rainey, and I turned over the card that covered her significator, and guess what it was? The Queen of Cups!"

Daisy waited for a moment for the significance of that to sink in.

He finally said, "Whoopee."

"But, *dear,* don't you see what that *means*?" The exasperation was clear in her voice.

He shrugged. "Gotta admit, I don't have any clue. But I'm sure you'll tell me all about it."

"I would have thought you'd have learned *something* while you were living at home." She sounded a little like Maureen, but telling her that probably wasn't the best idea. "The covering card stands for what's *blocking* you. What your *impediment* is. And she got the Queen of Cups!"

"So?"

"Wensleydale, don't you see? The Queen of Cups stands for an older woman, with light brown hair and blue eyes. Someone a little overweight, too." She said this last without any trace of irony. "Maureen could definitely stand to lose a few pounds."

"Mom, do you have any idea how many people around here that description would fit?"

"But darling, you're missing the main thing! Cups! As in wine cups!" Daisy mimed drinking a sip of wine, in case he had not taken her point sufficiently. "Think of all the parties and wedding receptions and so on they have up there! Our chapter of the Reformed Druids of North America meets up in the forest, right near the lodge, and one time I saw the dumpster being taken out, and it was *full* of wine bottles!"

He didn't respond for a moment. For one thing, as usual his mother's conversation had somehow disabled his ability to come up with a rational response. For another, he was forced into the recollection that the Reformed Druids of North America was a group who got together on the summer solstice to perform magic rituals, and preferred to work "sky-clad." "Skyclad" was druid-speak for bare-ass naked. Two summers ago, he had received a call from the lodge on the behalf of a frantic elderly German couple, who had been going for a nice stroll in the woods and had come upon a bunch of dumpy middle-aged naked people flinging leaves in the air, waving swords about, and chanting. Dale had been forced to cite his own mother for public indecency, an act he had yet to live down.

"But, Mom, if I'm gonna investigate someone, I have to have a reason—"

"I've given you several!"

"I need, um, more than reasons having to do with Tarot cards."

"Well, I was practicing my remote viewing last night, and I saw that Maureen was up to no good."

"Remote viewing?"

"You didn't even *give one look* at the book I got you for your birthday last year, did you?"

His cheeks warmed.

What the fuck? How does she always end up making me feel like I'm seven years old?

"No, Mom. I didn't. And as much as I appreciate all of the information, I have work to do. I'd love to talk to you more about this, but…"

"Maybe you could come over for dinner tonight," she said, hopefully. "Pasta primavera!"

"No, Mom, I got a date."

"With who?

"*Mom.*"

"That's what I thought. Well, remember what I said. Mark my words, that woman is behind all this."

"Yeah, yeah, okay. I'll investigate her as soon as I have time."

"I hope so. You never take anything I say seriously."

The phone rang. He gestured at it. "Gotta go, Mom. Phone call. You know, police business, like my *job*."

Again, the sarcasm missed its target by miles. "I understand, Wensleydale. Call me some time."

He nodded, and picked up the phone as Daisy walked out of the office.

"Blodgett, Crooked Creek Police Station."

"Dale, this is Sheila." He looked down, and saw that the light was blinking for the interoffice telephone line. "I've got a call from a Judy Kahn, up at the research station. She said she had news you'd want to hear, and she wanted to talk to you directly."

"Yeah, no problem, Sheila. Put her through." He pressed

on the button to disconnect, and a moment later it rang again, and he let up the button. "Blodgett."

"Officer Blodgett, this is Judy Kahn. You wanted us to let you know if anything more happened."

"Yeah?"

"Tyler got his computer back."

"How?"

"We told you we were heading back up to the cave…"

His eyes opened wide. "You found it up in the cave?"

"No, better than that. When we came back down, it was waiting for us in the jeep, with the cord tidily wrapped around the base."

"You are shittin' me."

"Nope."

He gave a low whistle. "Any idea what that means?"

"Slender Man is a considerate guy?"

"Sounds like it. And the computer was in good working order?"

"Yup. We checked it out when we got back to the lab. But every photograph of Slender Man had been erased from the hard drive, including the one linked in the email Tyler sent to Rainey."

"Clever."

"Yup."

"So the only copy left is the one Tyler has."

"Yes. The one on Rainey's flash drive."

"He should make more copies. Things have a way of disappearing, lately."

"Tyler's reluctant to do that. He thinks that his sending the photograph to Rainey is why she disappeared."

"There's no proof of that."

"I know that. And for my part, I don't think it's at all certain. But he doesn't want to put anyone else in danger." She paused. "Officer Blodgett, I'm worried about Tyler. I think he's going to try to pull the White Knight in Shining

Armor thing. He wants Rainey rescued, and he wants to do it himself."

"He told you that?"

"No. Only a hunch, but one borne of long experience with him. Tyler is one of the straightest arrows I know. He's also a really sweet guy. He sounds like a pessimist, to talk to him, but part of his pessimism is because he thinks that the world *should* work out to give everyone a happy ending. So he tries like mad to be the Valiant Hero, and gets his ass kicked, and then mopes around sounding like Eeyore. But it doesn't prevent him from doing it again the next time."

"I hope he realizes the danger."

"I think he does, but it doesn't matter. The only thing stopping him is that at present, he doesn't know where Rainey is. If he did, I think he'd go charging in without a moment's hesitation."

"And probably disappear himself."

"Yes. I thought you should keep an eye on him, if you can."

"Where does he live?"

"He lives in the little white trailer, on the left side of the road, on the road up to the lab. About halfway between the lab and the village."

"I know where you're talking about. I'll have someone swing by a couple of times this evening." He paused. How the hell he would explain to Bob McCloskey why he wanted Tyler Vaughan watched, he didn't know. Nor what they'd be watching for.

Hell. There goes my evening.

A little reluctantly, he said, "On second thought, I'll do it myself."

"I think that'd be a good idea. Maybe even stop in and talk to him and see how he's doing, let him know you're keeping an eye. I think he'd be less likely to run off and do something stupid if he knew you were keeping an eye him."

"Okay."

"Gotta warn you about his dog, though."

"He's got a vicious dog? He doesn't seem like the type."

"Not vicious. But you might want to bring a respirator. That dog's farts could melt plastic."

———

Dale left the station at around five-thirty, and went straight to Dorrie's Bar & Grill. His range of dinner choices at home at the moment were Canned Soup Heated Up or Canned Ravioli Heated Up, and neither one sounded very appealing, so he decided on a plate of Dorrie's Special Bar-B-Q Chicken Wings and a pint of Olympia instead.

At six-fifteen, he was sitting at the bar, gnawing on a wing, staring morosely at his half-empty pint and considering the fact that if he was going to go check on Tyler Vaughan later, he probably shouldn't have more than one more.

Dorrie came up and leaned on the bar. "So, how's my favorite cop this evening?"

"Jesus, Dorrie, it's been a day."

"You want me to keep your glass full, then?" She grinned at him.

He gave his pint glass a despondent look. "No, I can't. I gotta be able to drive. I'm keeping an eye on a guy who lives up near the Sisters, and I can't have Bob McCloskey pull me over and arrest me for drunk driving."

"Oh, surveillance, eh? Suspect in Rainey's kidnapping?"

"No, not a suspect. Possible next victim. He's Rainey's boyfriend."

"I see. You don't think he could have abducted her? You know, some kinky reason?"

"Nah. Not that type. If you'd seen him, you'd agree. He's kinda...." He looked for words. "He's kinda like the human version of a golden lab. Naïve, earnest, just wants to be friends."

"You gotta watch those overeager types," she said darkly.

"Nah, not this guy. He's okay. But I am worried that he'll be the next one to disappear. There's beginning to be a pattern, here."

"How does Rainey fit?"

"Lord, Dorrie, if I told you, you'd have me committed. But those kids, and Rainey—they're all pieces of the same puzzle." He emptied his glass, and within seconds, Dorrie had another one filled in front of him.

"Thanks. But that's gotta be my last. Seriously."

Dorrie leaned on the counter and gave it an ineffectual wipe with her dishrag. "You know, I was thinking about them kids, today. I think Maureen up at the Lodge musta felt bad about what happened to them, because she's given them jobs up there."

He choked on his swallow of beer, and for a moment wasn't able to get a word out. Finally he croaked, "What?"

"Yeah. I was surprised, myself. I thought Maureen hated kids. She never gives any of the local high schoolers summer jobs, far as I've ever heard, even doing simple stuff like grounds maintenance. This morning I was up there delivering two kegs of beer for a wedding reception, and I saw 'em. Kathleen, and that boy, you know, the one who was in trouble all the time."

"Kevin," he said, his voice still hoarse. "Kevin Torgeson."

"Yeah, him. She had them carrying in some boxes of stuff. I drove up there with Tim Lewis to bring the kegs. He helps me out whenever there's stuff that needs heavy lifting, I got a bad back and can't manage like I used to. And I was coming out of the lounge, and I heard Maureen say to that Kevin kid, 'Put them downstairs, with the others.' So she musta hired 'em for something, I guess."

He took another sip of beer, trying to stop the whirling in

his brain. Dear god, could his mom have been right? It was like that thing people always talk about, the monkeys pounding on typewriters long enough, and finally typing out something by fucking Shakespeare, or whatever.

"I guess so."

"Damn, Dale, you look like you seen a ghost. You think maybe Maureen Sullivan is up to something?"

"I don't know, Dorrie, god's honest truth. I don't know."

"I never thought Maureen cared about much but making money and passing judgment on everybody in the village." She chuckled. "You know what she said to me, once? I was up in the hardware store, and she pointed at the tattoos on my arm, and said, in this snooty voice, 'I cannot imagine why you would do that to your body. You do know it's permanent, don't you?' I said, 'So's being an opinionated bitch, apparently.' That shut her up. Temporarily, at least."

He laughed, a little hollowly. "Dorrie," he said, trying to make it sound offhand, "do you know what was in those boxes, the ones the kids were carrying into the lodge?"

She shrugged. "No idea. I figured probably designer toilet paper for the rich tourists to wipe their asses on." She gave him a conspiratorial grin. "You don't think she's a drug lord, or something? Maybe it was a shipment of heroin?"

"No. If she's up to something, it's not that."

And it might be worse. A lot worse.

Dale left Dorrie's a little before seven-thirty and drove off in the dusk up toward the shadowy bulk of the Three Sisters. By the time he got to Tyler's trailer, the light was fading fast. He pulled into the weed-overgrown gravel driveway and crunched to a stop behind Tyler's Civic and then sat there for a moment, looking at the light streaming out from inside.

A hand pushed aside curtains. Tyler's face appeared in the

window and then disappeared. A moment later, as Dale climbed out of his car, the front door opened and a wiry-haired mutt the size of a calf came bounding down the front steps and out into the yard. Two enormous paws were planted in the middle of his chest, and Dale, despite his weight, went over backwards like a bowling pin, right through the still-open car door, smacking the back of his head on the roof on the way down.

Tyler called frantically, "Goddammit, Ahab! Bad dog! You're not supposed to assault a police officer!"

The pressure on his chest suddenly lessened and he sat up, wiping the dog slobber off his face with one hand and rubbing the back of his head with the other. Tyler had Ahab by the collar and had dragged him a little way off.

Tyler was leaning over, yelling right into Ahab's face, "One of these days, you're really going to hurt someone! You are such a big oaf!" The dog was still wagging happily. "Now, *sit!*" Tyler yelled, and Ahab sat, his tail sweeping the ground with unabated good cheer.

"Jesus, Dale, I'm sorry." Tyler came over and helped him to his feet. "He's not dangerous, he's just dumb."

"No harm. I'll survive."

"What brings you here tonight?"

"I thought it might be smart to keep an eye on you, after what happened to Rainey. Judy Kahn told me you have the last copy of the photograph from your camera. I don't want you to disappear because of it."

Tyler patted the pocket of his jeans. "On a flash drive, right here. I'm not taking any chances."

"It's not smart to carry it around everywhere. If you disappear, so does it."

"I'm not going to disappear."

Suddenly, an eye-watering stink wafted by on the evening breeze.

"Oh, god, Ahab." Tyler winced and fanned his face.

Ahab, for his part, was still sitting obediently, his face wearing an innocent expression that said, *You think that was me? That wasn't me. Are you sure it wasn't you?*

"Wow," Dale said. "Judy warned me about that. Is he always that bad?"

"Yeah, he's kind of notorious. It's worse when he's inside. You can't escape." He paused, as the smell dissipated enough that they could breathe normally again. "So, you talked to Judy?"

"Yes. She called me this afternoon to tell me your computer had reappeared."

Tyler shook his head. "That was just bizarre. I still haven't figured that part out. Why would Slender Man return my computer?"

"I have no idea. Unless he was being considerate, it's hard to explain."

"So, is that why you came by to see me? Because if so, I have to tell you that don't know anything more now than I did this afternoon."

"No, it's not that." He gave Tyler a thoughtful look. "Judy told me she thought you were likely to go charging in and try to rescue Rainey."

"She told you that?"

"Yeah."

Tyler considered. "Honestly, I probably would, if I knew where to charge in to."

"That's what Judy said."

"I've been pondering all day if there's a way to figure out where she's being held. I don't have any clue."

"Good, and I plan on keeping it that way."

Tyler's eyebrows went up. "You have an idea about where she is?"

He scowled. "I am *not* gonna tell you."

"You *do* know!"

"How do you know that?"

"Well, otherwise, why would you have said that *you're* not gonna tell me where to go?"

"Look, Tyler," he said, in an exasperated tone of voice, "you sit tight here. Play with your dog, watch a movie, then go to bed. Put that flash drive somewhere safe. Don't forget to lock your doors. You're not gonna play detective, not on my watch."

"But Dale, Rainey's—"

Dale held up a hand. "No."

Tyler looked deflated. "All right. I'll chill."

Man, he IS like a golden lab.

After leaving Tyler's, Dale drove back down to the village and did a slow circuit of the streets. He deliberately drove past Kevin Torgeson's house, then Kathleen Standish's, then Phil Collette's. All of the houses were lit from within, but showed no particular sign of activity. At around nine-thirty he decided to make one more pass by Tyler's house, and as he drove up he was relieved to see the living room light still on.

Awesome. He was still unabducted. Time to check in with him, then maybe give a quick run up to the Three Sisters Lodge, although what the hell he'd say to Maureen if he saw her was uncertain. Then home and bed. Tyler would have to look after himself for the rest of the evening.

That was when he noticed that Tyler's car was gone.

He braked to a stop, his heart thudding in his chest.

No, c'mon, not another one.

He forced the thought from his mind, got out of his car, walked up the steps to the door, and knocked.

There were three deep-throated woofs from the other side, then silence.

No one answered the door, so he knocked again. This

elicited a prolonged volley of barking, but no human sounds at all.

Frowning, he reached down and twisted the door handle. It was unlocked. This time, he was ready for the canine assault, and he opened the door and quickly stepped aside. Ahab launched himself out, barking merrily, and ambled about the front yard for a while. He finally came up to Dale, sniffed his pant leg in an experimental fashion, and then wagged. Dale reached down and scratched him behind the ears.

"Tyler, you home?" he called, and then stepped inside.

There wasn't much to the trailer—a living room, disorderly and cluttered with books and papers, a little bedroom, and an even smaller kitchen, where the remnants of several previous meals still sat in the sink. Ahab walked up to the bin of dog food, and looked from it to Dale with hope in his eyes.

Dale ignored the attempted canine telepathy. He gave one more call.

"Tyler, you here?"

No one answered. Nothing in the trailer looked amiss, but Tyler Vaughan was gone.

thirteen

. . .

Tyler had gotten back home from Eugene at a little before seven o'clock, after successfully returning the camera. He'd consented, without much arm-twisting needed, to having a cheeseburger and a pint of beer with his colleague, Leon Zabowski, the one who had made him solemnly promise his left testicle in exchange if the camera was lost or damaged. They sat in the pub, surrounded by cheerful noise, talking shop for a while, and then Leon expressed curiosity as to why he had needed such a sensitive camera.

"You were pretty cagey when you picked it up," Leon said with a smile. "And you were on a mission, so I didn't want to slow you down. Now, you got a pint to drink and nowhere to go. Fess up. What are you up to, up there in the mountains?"

Fortunately, Tyler had anticipated that question, and had had an hour's drive to get his story straight.

"We were getting some anomalous shots down in a cave. Places out of convenient reach. We couldn't see what the hell was up there. It was a bad angle with flashlights, and we couldn't get enough of a signal using the thermal imaging equipment we've got. It was too far away. For a while, we weren't even sure whether it was animals or something else."

Leon took a sip of his beer. "And…?"

"Pikas. Honestly, that had been one of our guesses. There must be an egress to the outside, and they were nesting on projecting shelves in the upper parts of the cave. Pretty ingenious of the little bastards, frankly."

This satisfied Leon, and the conversation passed to other things, until Tyler finally consulted his watch, drained the last of his beer, and begged off. Leon gave him a smile and a farewell, and he headed out to his car to make the long drive home.

Now, pulling into his driveway, he pondered his course of action.

First duty was to go take care of Rainey's cat. She'd promised to look after Ahab, it was only right to return the favor. When she'd said that, he really thought he was the one in the most danger. He never thought he'd be doing this for her. And for how long?

But that only led his brain into melancholy places he didn't really want to go, and he pushed the thought aside.

After greeting and feeding Ahab, he headed for the door again, then turned and looked at the earnest, rather goofy face of his dog, who was sitting there wearing an expression that said, *You're not really going to leave me behind again, are you?*

"Hey, buddy, do you think you could be nice to a kitty?"

Ahab tilted his head to the side, which Tyler interpreted as a yes.

"If I'm gonna have any chance with this woman, you will need to be on your best behavior. She won't be happy if you fart in her house. Or eat her cat. *Especially* if you eat her cat."

Suitably lectured, Ahab comprehended that he was about to embark upon one of his favorite things, which was a car ride. Ten minutes later, after Tyler picked up the books scattered onto the floor, and had righted the floor lamp and swept up the remnants of the light bulbs that had formerly resided therein, they headed for the car, Ahab doing a ponderous dance of ecstasy around Tyler as he walked.

They drove down to Rainey's with Ahab's head hanging out of the passenger side window, his tongue flapping in the wind and liberally coating the back window with dog drool. They arrived as the sun was fading to crimson and sinking low in the sky. Tyler went around the side to feed the chickens, then let himself into the house with the key he'd taken from a peg in Rainey's kitchen the previous morning, after he'd discovered her disappearance.

The house was quiet and empty. He walked in, Ahab following docilely, his enthusiasm exchanged for a more restrained curiosity about this new, odd-smelling house. Bonkers the cat appeared from beneath a chair, meowing hungrily.

Ahab's ears perked up. Tyler reflexively grabbed his collar and stared right into his furry face.

"Be *nice*. We discussed this."

But Ahab, for his part, didn't bark or act aggressive. He cocked his head, and simply looked intrigued. Bonkers appeared to be entirely unafraid, and walked up, first rubbing against Tyler's leg, and then walking right between Ahab's front legs and around to the side.

Ahab registered the canine version of "What the hell just happened?" and peered back at the cat, who then came back, purring loudly. Ahab leaned downward to take a better look and give a sniff, and Bonkers smacked him solidly in the muzzle with the top of his head. Ahab recoiled a little, and then seemed to decide that it had been a gesture of affection, and resumed his visual and olfactory investigation of this new and peculiar life form.

"Okay. I'm going to feed Bonkers. You be nice, mutt."

He tentatively let go of Ahab's collar, and when the dog

gave no sign of an impending frontal assault, went in search of cat food. He located it in the laundry room, and put a scoop in the dish, gave Bonkers some fresh water, and then returned to the living room.

There, he saw a tableau that gave him a moment of pure, screaming panic.

Ahab had Bonkers pinned to the floor with one huge paw.

"Oh, my fucking god, Ahab, I *told* you not to eat the kitty!" he shouted, his normally baritone voice registering in the soprano range out of sheer hysteria.

It took only a second to realize—but it felt far longer—that Ahab wasn't, in fact, eating the kitty. Ahab was washing Bonkers' head, and the cat's black fur was silvery with canine slobber. Tyler registered, as he tried to return his heart rate to normal, that Bonkers was purring, and this must mean that he was somehow enjoying it.

Ahab looked up, his face expressing curiosity as to why his master had screamed at him. Tyler stared back at his dog, wide-eyed and open-mouthed. When no further shouts of alarm were forthcoming, Ahab returned to bathing the cat. Bonkers looked up at Ahab, eyes half shut, and nuzzled him under the chin.

"An inter-species romance. Between a guy dog and a guy cat." He thought about it for a moment, then shrugged. "Oh, well, I'm open-minded. But if you start humping him, dude, I'm putting a stop to it."

Ten minutes later, after watering Rainey's house plants, he decided with some reluctance that he had no further reason to stay in her house. He didn't want to leave. The house was permeated with her, and he wanted to stand there and absorb it. But he couldn't simply hang around. He had his long-neglected research to work on.

Not that he was likely to get anything done. He scowled at his own predicament as he dragged Ahab away from his unlikely lover and locked up the house. Who was he kidding? He couldn't concentrate, and it wasn't only because he was smitten with Rainey Carrington. He couldn't keep his mind off of all this stuff about Slender Man. And now that Rainey had been abducted, he felt compelled to figure out where she was being held and find a way to free her. Stop all of this craziness. Even if it cost him his job, an eventuality that was seeming more and more likely.

He returned to his house. It was run-down, smelly, and cramped compared to Rainey's sweet little cottage. Giving a heartfelt sigh, he unlocked the front door and went inside, relocking the door behind him.

It was only five minutes later that Dale Blodgett drove up, was tackled by Ahab, and delivered a stern adjuration that Tyler was to stay put. Afterwards, Tyler meekly returned into his house, feeling dejected and helpless.

"I am a complete wussie."

Ahab, sensing his master's dark mood, came up and rested his furry chin on Tyler's knee.

"What will I do if Rainey comes back, and she's all creepy and changed? I can't let that happen."

Ahab sighed.

"And how can I fight this when I don't know what I'm fighting? Or even who?" He reached down and absently skritched Ahab's ears. The dog's tail thwacked twice against the floor.

"It sucks. I'm a wussie, I'm going to be an unemployed wussie soon, I can't rescue the woman I've got a crush on, and my life sucks."

He sat there, his hand resting on the top of Ahab's woolly head, and suddenly the dog tensed up. Tyler looked down at him. Ahab raised his head slowly, and then turned and looked toward the front door of the trailer that opened off the little living room.

"Mule deer out there again? I am *not* letting you out to

chase them. Last time, you were gone for three hours and came back covered with mud."

Ahab didn't turn and look at him, but continued to stare at the door.

He stood, went into the living room, and flipped a light switch. The front yard was illuminated with a yellowish, unnatural glare.

"I don't see any deer out there, buddy, sorry."

The dog got up and went to the door. He stood on his hind legs, which made him almost as tall as Tyler, and peered out of the window.

"I told you. There's nothing out there, dimwit."

Ahab didn't bark or growl, but neither did he get down. He continued to stare out the window, looking toward the road, and beyond that into the dark line of woods. Tyler pressed his face to the glass, cupping his hands around his eyes.

And then something moved across the road, just past the reach of the fading edge of the floodlights. Something human-shaped, but too tall and too thin to be normal. There was only a moment's glance, and it was once again obscured by the shadowy tree trunks. His eyes widened and his heart galloped painfully.

"Oh, god. He's here. I'm fucked." He took the flash drive out of his pocket and looked frantically around for a place to hide it. He finally stuck it inside the tin of coffee beans on his kitchen counter, and slammed the lid shut, then returned to the front door window. There was no movement out there now, but he could feel the presence of *something*, out there just beyond where he could see. Something that was aware of him.

"Dammit. Dammit, dammit, dammit. What can I do?" He briefly considered making a run for his car, but realized that in every horror movie he'd ever seen, that was when the monster got you—when you decided on a frantic mad dash for car, house, somewhere safe.

But the problem was, running away was no good here. What would he do, get in his car and drive, keep driving? Go to Belize, like he'd threatened to do, forget about Rainey? That was the wussie speaking. What would a non-wussie do, here?

He reached over to his door, unlocked it, and slowly opened it. He expected Ahab to go plunging out into the front yard as he always did, but the dog stood there, pressed against his leg, a shudder vibrating its way through his frame.

"Hey," he shouted out into the night, his voice trembling a little. "I know you're out there. What do you want?"

For a moment, there was no sound but the rustle of the breeze in the trees. Then a voice spoke, and he immediately knew that he wasn't hearing it with his ears. The voice had no vibratory quality to it, no warmth, no breath. It was being created inside his brain, somehow, as if he had been turned into an antenna.

For now, I want you to listen.

"Why?" He tried to voice a defiance he didn't honestly feel he could back up. "Why should I listen to you?"

Because you will want to hear what I have to say to you.

"Where is Rainey? What have you done with her?"

That will be answered. Be patient.

"I'm not feeling patient!" he shouted, looking into the darkness for any sign of who he was speaking to.

You need not shout. I can hear you even if you whisper. But for now, you do not need to speak. Merely listen, and you will have answers to many of your questions.

"Why should I listen to you? Why shouldn't I tell my dog to attack you?"

There was a touch of amusement in the voice, as it rang inside his mind. *You are free not to listen, of course. But you are a scientist. Your life revolves around finding answers. I give you an opportunity to learn the answers to the questions you have been asking in recent days. I do not believe that you will turn away from them.* There was a pause. *And as for your dog, he does not seem to look upon me as worthy of attacking.*

He looked down at Ahab, and Ahab looked up to him with an expression that said, *Hell, no, I'm not going over there. You can go over there if you want, though.*

"You're no help at all."

Ahab gave an apologetic wag.

Tyler turned back to the figure in the woods. "How do I know you'll tell me the truth?"

You do not. That is for you to decide. You must use your brain to determine if my answers are truthful or not. Now simply listen, and then you will know.

He took a deep breath. "Okay, I'm listening."

I am the one you refer to as Slender Man.

"I already know that." He paused. "Sorry. I'm still listening."

It is not my name, but that is of no importance. I have been here for a long time. You measure time from the revolution of this planet around its star? It has been less than one of those. I lived in the cave up on the mountain, the one you went to with your friend.

"We know that, too."

The voice continued, flowing through his brain, steady, uninflected, nearly emotionless.

When I saw that you had a monitoring device pointed toward the cave, I destroyed it, thinking that you would believe an animal had done the damage, and not investigate further. It was a mistake. I did not know that the device could take images in the dark. Your technology is less primitive than I believed.

"It works on a motion sensor, and can take thermal images."

He looked across the street, and saw, faintly, the outline of a tall, thin, bipedal figure, a vague face shimmering in the dark. He shuddered.

My appearance frightens you. Why?

"You have no face."

I sense in other ways. Why does this frighten you?

"It isn't like us."

Not being like you does not mean evil.

"I know. But you abducted the children. And Rainey."

No. Not I. Another.

"Who?"

I will explain. When I knew that this Other was here, I came here to stop it. It is my work. It wishes to invade, replace, destroy. I repair and recreate.

"So, you're saying that you had nothing to do with the children being kidnapped?"

Not nothing. I come to where the Other is, to prevent it from doing more harm.

"That's why you're always seen near places where kids were abducted."

Yes.

"You've done this sort of thing in other places?"

Many other places.

"Why does the other one you're talking about keep doing this?"

You have not realized? It wishes to replace your people, to gain a foothold in your world. It is working toward conquest the way a parasite does, by taking your people and replacing them with ones like it.

"So, you're on our side, then," he said, a little tentatively. His brows drew together in disbelief at the calm in his voice. He was talking to an alien, and instead of the hard-headed skeptic taking charge, he acted as if it was the most ordinary thing in the world. Maybe Judy had been right. Maybe he *was* a closet woo-woo.

I am on the side of whoever is against the Other. It is my work.

"I thought you were evil. So do a lot of people. There's stuff out on the internet about you. It says you're hostile."

Most of that information is misleading and incomplete. Misleading and incomplete information does not hinder my work, so I have let it be.

"But you stole my computer and the camera."

I could not let images of me be broadcast by someone with your reputation as a scientist.

Tyler snorted. "If only you'd known what my reputation actually is, you probably wouldn't have bothered."

When I realized that you had images of me, and were sending them to a friend, I knew that you were jeopardizing my work and putting yourselves at risk. I took your information-storing device to prevent you from doing that. Once the images were removed, I had no need for the device and returned it to you. I trust you found it in correct working order?

"Yes. It's fine."

The strategy I have used was unsuccessful, for I had not counted on the curiosity of your species. I had thought that my working on your emotions as you neared the cave would be sufficient, but you kept coming back despite that.

"We thought it had something to do with the children. We thought you might have them captive up there. That's why we were trying to get in."

And I could not let you into the deep parts of the cave, where my living space and laboratory are. You know now, I believe, that the rock wall in the cave is artificial?

"Yes. We used a camera that can see heat signatures through walls. But we still don't know what's back there, or how you did that."

I can rearrange molecular structure as needed. The device whose heat traces you saw is a machine that keeps the appearance of the wall in place.

"But if you weren't keeping the kids back there, then where are they?"

I told you—there is another. Tonight, I will go to the Other and stop it. It has already replaced three of your people with duplicates, and it will soon replace the fourth. It must be stopped.

"Why didn't you do this sooner? I mean, before the kids were abducted. And Rainey. If you knew about this other alien thing, why didn't you stop it?"

I am powerful, but not omnipotent. I did not stop it for the simple reason that I did not know what form it had adopted, not until recently. It is a shapeshifter of remarkable skill. But now I have identified it and I will put an end to its activities here.

"Are Rainey and the real kids alive? Are they okay?"

I do not know. I hope that is so. But we must act tonight, as the Other has realized that I am here, and is making plans to take the four of them away.

"Away? Away where?"

You must know by now that we do not come from your planet.

"Yeah, I had kind of figured that out."

The Other has plans to take your people back to its home world. There, they will be used for experimental purposes.

Tyler felt a clench of nausea. "We've got to go! Now!"

We will. You have a task, which is to bring back any of the captive people to their homes. If there are any who have survived.

"But what about the duplicates?"

Leave that to me.

"Where are they?"

There is a place near here. It is a wooden structure, where people come and go frequently. The name of it is the Three Sisters Lodge. The one who owns it is the Other.

"Maureen Sullivan?" He couldn't keep the disbelief from his voice. "How on earth can Maureen Sullivan have anything to do with all this? She's just an obnoxious, gossipy middle-aged bitch."

You are mistaken. The person you knew of that name is dead. She was replaced by the Other shortly before I came here to this place. The Other can take many guises. It can walk among you, and you would never know.

"But how could it kill someone, and no one found out?"

It copied from her brain, learned her memories. Her knowledge became its knowledge. This is how the Other works. It takes, as a parasite takes, not caring if it harms or kills in the process. As for the real Maureen Sullivan… where her body is will probably never be known. It is most likely buried in some remote place up in the mountains, far away from where your people go.

"But if you succeed tonight, then she'll vanish again, and the police will find out."

All your people will know is that after tonight, she will be gone. They will think she disappeared, the way your friend and the three children did. The difference will be that she will not come back. And hers will be the last disappearance, until the Other finds a different place, and I have to begin the work again.

He swallowed and looked up into the clear night sky. He had come to a decision, although there had been no clear moment in his brain when it had occurred. "I will help in any way I can."

Then you believe what I have told you.

"Yes." He was surprised to hear how quickly the answer came. "I was trained as a scientist to accept the hypothesis that fits all the data best. This is the only one I've heard that makes sense. Despite the fact that it's exactly the sort of paranormal weird woo-woo stuff that I always thought was bullshit." He took a deep breath. "So there *was* a signal in amongst all the noise."

There is one other thing.

"What is it?"

There is, I think, one remaining image of me, on an information storage device in your house. It must be destroyed.

"Why?"

There is already enough information on my activities accessible to your people. If more becomes available, it will compromise the work. I cannot allow that to happen, for your people's sake.

"I'll delete it."

See that you do. I do not wish to damage the locking device on your door, but you know that I am capable of it.

"Yeah. I'd love to know how you did that."

It would not be safe for your people to have such power.

"You're probably right. We do enough damage with guns."

Then, shall we begin? You may take your transportation machine up to where the Other is, so that you can bring back your people if we find them. As for me, I will find my own way there.

"Okay."

You are still frightened, but not of me any longer.

"I'm terrified."

You have reason to be. The Other is very powerful, and has killed many times before now. But we must hope for success.

"I'm hoping."

As am I.

Tyler drove up toward the Three Sisters Lodge in the dark, his mind in a whirl.

He felt a little disembodied. One part of him knew he was scared out of his mind. Another, however, was numb, felt completely unable to connect to the terror clamoring for his attention.

A third, the rational part of his brain, was aghast that he was actually doing something based on the fact that a faceless alien dude told him a local bed-and-breakfast owner was actually an alien, too, who had been replacing local kids with clones so she could take over the world.

The upshot of it all was that either the world was way different than he thought it was, or he'd lost his marbles completely.

Maybe both.

And now, Slender Man was gonna go stop the evil bed-

and-breakfast owner, and rescue Rainey and the kids, and he wanted Tyler to delete his photograph from Rainey's flash drive so that it didn't interfere with him the next time she appeared and started abducting kids, maybe this time in the guise of the local Avon Lady.

He rolled his eyes.

Yup. I'm losing my mind.

But he continued to drive.

The Three Sisters Lodge was an old, timber-framed building, its roof covered with moss-encrusted cedar shakes, sitting on a rugged hill surrounded by huge Douglas firs. The interior was the height of elegance, and its clientele largely made up of the wealthy—tourists from Europe and Japan who wanted to see the wilderness but not *too* close, thank you very much, and people from nearer by who were willing to splurge on the sky-high rental fee for wedding receptions, fiftieth birthday parties, and golden anniversaries. Wandering in and around the lodge left you understanding how there could be a place whose description required the use of the words "rustic" and "upscale" in the same sentence.

Tyler pulled into the parking lot, and shut the engine off. The lodge sat, serene in the moonlight, welcoming and friendly. The wide windows of the dining room cast a yellow glow out into the tastefully maintained border gardens. He squinted through the windshield. There were only a handful of people still eating dinner. He looked at his watch. It stood at 8:34.

He pulled out his cellphone and dialed Judy Kahn's number. It rang four times, and then he heard, "You've reached Judy Kahn. I can't get to the phone right now, but if you'd like to leave a message, please do. If you don't want to leave a message, why'd you call in the first place?" Then there was a beep.

"Hi, Judy. It sucks that you're out. I was hoping to talk to you. I guess you were right about me wanting to be the knight in shining armor, or whatever. I'm up at the Three Sisters Lodge, and am going to try to rescue Rainey. But you should know that we were wrong about Slender Man. He's on our side. It's Maureen Sullivan who is the one that's behind it all. I know that sounds like I've lost my marbles, but you've got to believe that I'm convinced. I'm not calling you to come try to help. In fact, it would be better if you didn't. If I get kidnapped, or killed, tonight, you're the last one left who knows the whole story, and then it'll be up to you and Dale. But I wanted to say thanks for helping me with all this. You're the best."

He disconnected, shut off his cellphone, and slipped it back in his pocket. Then he looked back up at the lodge.

What to do now? Go up and knock on the door, demand to see Maureen, and tell her that the jig is up, he knows she's an evil superpowerful alien shapeshifter? Or wait here for Slender Man to show up and start kicking ass? Slender Man hadn't said that he had to get involved with any fighting, which was just as well, because the year of karate lessons he'd had in high school was kind of a long time ago.

He got out of his car and closed the door as quietly as he could. The night was clear, cool, and still. He looked around. There was no sign of anyone, including Slender Man.

Slowly, he edged up the sidewalk toward the lodge, heart thudding in his ribcage.

Was Slender Man right? Were Rainey and the kids really being held here? How could something like that be going on right under the noses of everyone—Dale, the staff of the lodge, the guests staying here?

He reached the top of the sidewalk, where the stairs led up to the front door. He stepped off into the shadows, trying not to trip over clumps of plants hidden in the darkness at the foot of the building. He crept along the wall until he reached the beginning of the dining room window, and then peeked in.

There were four or five couples seated at the tables, lingering over glasses of wine. Wait staff glided through the room, picking up empty plates and used cloth napkins, finishing up the work for that evening's dinner. At the far end of the room was the entrance to the kitchen, lit brightly with fluorescents. He didn't see Maureen, but as the owner, there was no particular reason she'd hang around the dining room in the evening.

A tall young woman with blonde hair and freckles came out of the kitchen, walking toward the right. She was not dressed like wait staff—a guest, perhaps? She had a serious, almost grim expression, and her stride was purposeful. Not the look of someone on a relaxing vacation.

And then, just as she vanished from view, she turned and looked right toward him.

He gasped and flattened himself against the wall. Who was that? Kathleen Standish? He'd never seen her before, but hadn't Rainey mentioned something about her being tall and blonde? More importantly, had she seen him? As bright as it is in there, all she probably could see were reflections of the dining room.

He stood there for some moments, waiting for the front door to open, but nothing happened. Gradually his heart rate returned, if not to normal, at least to the staccato baseline it had achieved as he drove up, and not the painful hammering of the last few seconds.

He crouched and continued to make his way along the wall, underneath the window. His thought, for no particularly good reason, was to make his way around the back of the lodge. Nefarious doings presumably wouldn't be going on in front, right in full view from the dining room. May as well see what's happening around the back.

The corner of the lodge had a prickly stand of juniper, and he edged gingerly through it, trying not to get too caught on the spiny branches. He came to the end of the wall, and stepped around it.

He found himself face to face with a thin, pale-skinned teenage boy with overlong brown hair and a nasty smirk.

Tyler said, "Oh, *shit!*" and turned, but the boy grabbed his upper arm with more strength than would have seemed possible for someone of his stature. Tyler twisted around and ran face-first into the juniper, which blocked his escape as effectively as a wall would have.

"Who are you and why are you sneaking around here?" The boy pulled him free from the juniper bush.

"I'm one… I'm one of the guests," he said, breathlessly. "I was wandering around outside for some fresh air."

"You lie poorly. Not that I expected the truth. Come with me." He turned and dragged Tyler off toward the back of the lodge. He struggled, but in that viselike grip there was no possibility of getting free.

He looked over at his captor. "I know what you're up to."

"Oh?" the boy said, amusement in his voice. "How satisfying for your curiosity."

"Yes. You're the duplicate of Kevin Torgeson."

The boy didn't turn. "And I believe you're Tyler Vaughan, the nosy biologist and aspiring future lover of Rainey Carrington. Am I correct?"

They rounded the back corner of the lodge. "You won't get away with this."

"Is it a requirement that the good guys always say this to the bad guys when they're captured?"

"Well, you won't." He winced at how lame that sounded.

"Not even curious as to how I knew who you were, eh? In any case, you're not in any particular position to stop us."

"Where are you holding the real Kevin, and Kathleen, and Phil? I know you're all duplicates."

"That's fine. I'm suitably impressed that you know all about us. In the end, though, it's irrelevant that you do, because you can't do anything about it. As for where they're being held, you'll find that out soon enough."

Kevin dragged him up a set of back stairs toward what appeared to be a utility entrance and opened the door. Light flooded outward.

I can't go in there. If I go in there, I'll never be seen again.

He leaned back, pulling against the force Kevin was exerting. Kevin let go of the door and turned, his face twisted in a snarl. Then Tyler braced his feet on the edge of the top step and flung himself backwards.

The duplicate Kevin was strong, much stronger than would be possible for a sixteen-year-old boy, but he had no more weight than the original Kevin had—140 pounds, tops. Tyler was four inches taller, and outweighed him by thirty pounds. Kevin gave a roar of anger. He apparently realized a moment too late that if he hung onto Tyler's arm he would be pulled over himself. He reached backwards for the door handle to save himself, but missed it by inches. Kevin fell forward against Tyler, and the two of them rolled backwards down the stairs into a heap at the bottom.

Ignoring the pain from scrapes along his back and a dull ache from where his head had hit the sidewalk, Tyler scrambled to his feet and dazedly ran along the back of the lodge, past a set of stairs that came down from a verandah, and then downhill toward a garden whose plantings looked like a surreal, colorless charcoal sketch in the moonlight. Footsteps pounded the ground behind him, but he ignored them, concentrating on pure speed. He turned the corner, and with a rush of exhilaration, saw the parking lot with his car in the distance.

Where the hell was Slender Man? He'd said he was going

to come here and save the day. A lot of good that would do if Tyler was already a prisoner.

The sidewalk angled around the edge of the building and he followed it, trying to ignore the ache in his side, and ran right into the tall blonde girl he'd seen earlier.

She reeled backwards a couple of steps, but caught Tyler's left arm, and a moment later, he felt his right one pinioned behind him. He struggled, and screamed, "Help! Someone help me!" But this time he was caught like an animal in a trap. A hand clapped over his mouth. The fingers gripping him tightened painfully, and finally he stopped moving, breath coming in ragged whimpers.

Suddenly, the light from the front floodlights of the lodge were blocked as someone stepped in front of the three of them. Tyler looked up, squinting at the dark silhouette, and then Maureen Sullivan spoke, her voice full of high good humor.

"Mr. Vaughan. We've been expecting you. Welcome to the Three Sisters Lodge. We'll do everything we can to make your stay a memorable one."

fourteen

. . .

"Do you think it's possible," Rainey said, "that the next time only one of them comes in, that between the four of us we might be able to overpower them?"

"We both tried it," Kathleen said. "Before you and Phil came. When we were still being held in the cells down in the basement. I heard someone coming, and I hid behind the door. When the door opened, I jumped on the person. It was my duplicate, with food for me. She held me off with one hand." She frowned. "They didn't give me any food that day, as a punishment. Kevin tried to fight her, too. She's incredibly strong. I'm guessing all of them are."

"But against all four of us?"

"I'd try it again," Kevin said. "I don't know what they're planning on doing with us, but I'm sure it's not anything good. I don't want to sit around and wait. Sooner or later they're going to decide that they don't want to worry about feeding us and guarding us, and then we'll be dead. I'd rather get killed fighting them than wait around for them to execute us."

"Me too," Phil said. "I don't think I'll be much help, but I can try."

"I'm guessing that even if we can catch them when the door to this room is unlocked, and somehow disable them, there will be other locked doors to get through. Maureen doesn't strike me as the type to leave us an easy escape route."

"What do you think they're trying to do, by doing all this?" Kathleen said. "By kidnapping us, and replacing us. I mean, the three of us, we're just kids. What can that possibly accomplish?"

"I've always thought that terrorists tend to go about things the wrong way," Rainey said. "If you *really* wanted to scare people—demoralize them, make them feel like there's no point in fighting—don't go after big, high-visibility targets. Hit a small, obscure town, somewhere where everyone feels safe and complacent. That'd be the way to strike at the heart." She shook her head. "It's terrible to think about, I know. But suppose Maureen and her cronies *are* aliens, all under the direction of the creature that Tyler got a photograph of."

"What did it look like?" Kathleen asked.

"Thin. Kind of stretched-out looking. And it had no face."

Kevin snorted. "Like the Headless Horseman, or something?"

"No. Not no head, no face. No facial features. No eyes, nose, or mouth."

Kathleen shuddered. "What was it you called it?"

"Slender Man. Tyler found out it's been seen other places there have been abductions."

"And you think it's somehow in league with Maureen and the duplicates?"

"Yes. And maybe they're planning on... I don't know, taking over. Starting a war on humans. The best place to start would be in a small town. Somewhere where people weren't used to thinking that they were unsafe."

"Like Crooked Creek."

"If you could make inroads into a place like that, it

wouldn't take much to convince people that nowhere is safe. And when you've destroyed people's confidence, you're halfway to winning the war."

"You still don't have any proof that any of this is true," Kevin said. "Mrs. Sullivan could still be some kind of creepy pedophile lady, or something."

"Who can make clones in a day or two from a piece of your skin," Kathleen interjected.

"That doesn't mean she's an *alien*," Kevin said.

There was the noise of someone descending stairs, and a tread approaching the door, followed by the click of the padlock being unlocked. Rainey tensed, looking from face to face, seeing her tension reflected there.

Is this it? Am I about to be in the first physical fight I've ever been in?

Then the door opened, and a person was flung through it, stumbled, and fell in a heap on the floor.

It was Tyler.

She rushed to him as the door closed, and there was the click of the padlock being refastened. He struggled to his feet, and she helped him up. His face was scratched and bruised, and his shirt torn. Blood seeped through the cloth on his back.

"Oh, my god, Tyler." She put both hands on the side of his face and looked into his eyes. "Are you hurt?"

He shook his head, but when he spoke, his voice was unsteady. "All superficial. I walloped my head a good one." He touched the back of his scalp, and winced. "And I took some skin off my back when I fell down the stairs."

"Turn around."

He did, and she pulled up his t-shirt. Along his spine were a series of parallel scrapes.

He shook his head. "It's no big deal."

She let go of his shirt. "How did they catch you?"

"I came out here to try and free you. Slender Man told me this is where you were being held captive."

"*Slender Man* told you? And you *believed* him?"

Kevin snickered. "Some scientist."

Tyler looked around, as if seeing the other three for the first time. "Are these…"

"The real Kevin, Kathleen, and Phil."

"But Maureen is really behind all this…" Tyler frowned in confusion. "Slender Man told me that. And he was right. I saw her tonight, and she was in charge. She told the duplicate kids to lock me up with the others."

"The easiest way to lie is to tell part of the truth."

"So Slender Man was trying to get me to come out here, so that he and Maureen and the duplicates could get rid of me, too."

"That's what it looks like."

"We're going to try to attack them," Kathleen said. "The next time one of them comes in here alone."

Tyler nodded, and touched the scrapes on his face. "I'm not much of a fighter, but count me in. I owe them a bruise or two."

"I'm not sure how much hope to have," Rainey said. "They're well prepared. They're not going to make escaping easy."

"I wish Dale knew more about what was going on. I only found out about Maureen after he talked to me." He brightened. "I did leave a voicemail for Judy, though. I told her I was coming up here. When they find out that I've been abducted, I'm sure Judy will tell Dale about the connection to Maureen."

"Who's Judy?" asked Kathleen.

"The woman I work with."

"What good does that do?" Kevin said. "She'll get caught, too."

"You don't know Judy. A fight between Judy and a rhino, I'm putting my money on Judy."

"Do you have any idea why they're doing all of this?"

Rainey said. "Have you found out anything more since I was kidnapped?"

Tyler shook his head "I know they're trying to replace more and more people. And the real ones..." He stopped, and looked apprehensive.

"What about us?" Kevin said.

"They're planning on taking us all away. Away, off the Earth."

"Slender Man told you this, too, I suppose." Kevin's tone was scornful.

"Yeah. It *sounded* plausible at the time."

"Some scientist," Kevin said again.

Again there came the noise of the lock being unfastened, and the door opened. This time it was the duplicate Phil Collette, carrying on his outstretched arm a silvery folded piece of cloth, and a shiny metal device that looked like a large hypodermic syringe. The real Phil, eyes wide, gave an involuntary whimper.

The duplicate went up to Tyler.

"Strip. And put these on." He handed Tyler the cloth.

"Here?"

"I'm not concerned about your modesty." The duplicate Phil smirked.

"And the syringe is for if I don't cooperate?"

"No. We need a little tissue sample. You can cooperate, or I can always return with two or three helpers. Would you rather be seen naked for a few moments, and reclothe yourself quickly, or be forcibly stripped and dressed while you struggle? It's entirely up to you."

Tyler looked at him, and then reached for the clothes.

The duplicate Phil handed them to Tyler, and his smirk widened. "Good. Maybe you learned something from trying to fight with us earlier."

Tyler took the clothes, and then flung them against the wall.

"Fuck you, kid." He gave a quick glance at Rainey and Kathleen.

Simultaneously, the three flung themselves on the duplicate Phil. Kevin and the real Phil joined in. The duplicate fought like a cornered animal, and even five against one, it was uncertain they would succeed. Finally they pinned him to the floor, where he lay, struggling and snarling up at them, his voice not sounding in the least human.

Now what? They couldn't stay here, trying to hold him down, until one of the others arrived...

"Hold him!" Kevin shouted, and ran toward the corner of the room and picked up a chunk of cinder block that lay there, behind some boxes marked *Christmas Ornaments*. Kevin ran toward them, and swung the block aloft, his face twisted in a horrific grimace.

Instinctively, Rainey shouted, "Kevin, don't!" An incongruous thought crossed her mind, that perhaps only another child do this. The instinct in adults to protect children is too strong, even given the knowledge that the Phil Collette they had pinned wasn't the real Phil, might not even be a real child at all. But Kevin had no such reservations. He swung the cinder block around in a vicious arc, and there was a sickening crunch as the block struck the duplicate Phil's face.

A spasm, like the cracking of a whip, lifted the duplicate's body off the ground. The cinder block rolled aside.

Rainey turned away, unwilling to look at the crushed face that she still could not help thinking of as human. She collided with Tyler, and they instinctively held each other. Kathleen was sobbing, Kevin panting, his face still pinched into a snarl.

And then the real Phil, half in triumph and half in terror, ran up to the body of the body of the dead duplicate, and kicked it repeatedly, shouting, "That'll show you! You aren't me! I hate you! I hate you!"

Rainey let go of Tyler, and grabbed the struggling Phil, whose thin, pale face was twisted and desperate.

"No!" She held him until he stopped struggling. "No, Phil." She kept her voice calm with an effort. "It's okay. It's gone. You're you, and it wasn't you. Don't hate. It makes you like them." She took his tear-stained face in both hands, and turned it away from the duplicate's body until he was looking into her eyes. "We're here, Phil. We're real, and we care about you, and we're going to get you home safely to your mom and dad."

"But they…" Phil turned his eyes unwillingly back toward the duplicate. "My mom and dad, they thought… *that* was me."

"They wanted to believe you were back home and safe so badly that it was easy for them to be fooled, because they love you." She made her words steady and strong. "But we're not fooled. We know who you are. And you know who you are. We'll get you home. Do you believe me? Are you okay now?"

Phil looked back at her. Something relaxed in him. He nodded. "I'll be okay." After a moment, he turned out of her grasp, and went over to look at the body of his dead duplicate one more time, but his face was calm now.

"Phil, you really shouldn't…"

Phil shook his head. "No. I want to look at him again. I need to. One last time."

Kevin cleared his throat. "Hey, guys? Can we save the therapy session until we get the fuck out of here?"

"He's right," Tyler said. "Before the others come to investigate."

"With all the noise, I'm surprised they aren't rushing in here already," Kevin said as they walked out into the dimly-lit passageway.

Kathleen took a deep, hitching breath. "I think this place is pretty well sound-insulated. They wouldn't put us anywhere that the guests could hear us if we screamed."

As they exited the room where they had been confined, behind them was a stone wall where the hidden door to the sub-basement lay. Ahead, a set of wooden stairs led upwards. Tyler led the way, followed by Kevin and Kathleen, and then Rainey and Phil. Phil took Rainey's hand and held it tightly.

She looked down at him, and a wave of sadness swept over her. That child was going to need years of counseling after this experience.

Of course, they probably all would.

They walked single-file up the stairs, which creaked alarmingly. Tyler reached the top first, and twisted the doorknob.

It was locked.

"Shit!" he said, in a hissing half-whisper. "We're locked in."

"Hey, I think this might help." It was Phil—and in his hand, he had a keyring. "The fake me had it in his pocket. It came out part way when I kicked him."

Rainey looked at him in amazement.

"Kid, I don't know you, but you're awesome." Tyler took the ring, which had about a dozen keys of different sizes and shapes. The third one turned, and there was a click as the lock opened.

Tyler turned the doorknob, and opened the door slowly. He peered out. "I think the coast is clear."

Tyler went out, followed by Kevin and Kathleen, and finally Rainey and Phil. Rainey looked around. They appeared to be in a back hallway, one with no guests' rooms. A sign on one door said *Laundry Room*, and another said *Utility Closet*. Farther along, a larger sign, protruding from the wall above a door, said *Office*. Past the office door was what they were looking for—a sign with large letters that read, *EXIT*.

Tyler pointed, Rainey nodded, and they quietly moved

toward the exit. They had gotten halfway down the hall when there came the dreaded sound of voices.

A strident female voice was saying, "Where is Phil? He should be back by now. We have to get the rest of the preparations ready tonight, or there'll be hell to pay."

With that, Kathleen's double came around the corner, and for a moment stopped in her tracks, her mouth open. Just behind her, the duplicate Kevin came out into the hall and nearly collided with her. Kathleen sprinted toward them, and Kevin started to follow, but Kathleen called out, "No! I'll take care of them. Go get Sullivan! Now!"

Rainey looked around for somewhere to run. The hallway behind them ended in several closed doors, one of which led down to the basement prison they'd escaped. Kathleen ran toward them, a fierce expression on her face. Rainey had the sudden realization that considering the trouble they'd had with Phil's double, there was no way they could take down Kathleen's.

Time. They needed time.

Next to them a door led to something called the Tillamook Room. Rainey flung it open and shoved Tyler inside so hard he almost fell, and then grabbed the real Kathleen's arm and yelled, "Inside!"

Kevin followed with no urging. But then Phil, his eyes huge, gave an inarticulate scream and bolted down the hall toward the exit.

"Phil!" She ran after him. "Phil, wait!"

He reached the door, and grabbed for the handle. There was a momentary glimpse of the dark night sky, a breath of cool air. Then Kathleen's powerful arm looped around Rainey's neck, and she was pulled backwards.

"Stop." Kathleen's voice wasn't loud, but was powerful enough that Phil froze and turned back toward them, eyes huge. Rainey clutched at Kathleen's arm, trying to loosen her grip, but it was like trying to bend a steel bar.

"Phil, don't take another step. If you do, I will snap her neck like a twig." Kathleen's grip tightened. "You know I can do it. And you know I will."

"Please." Phil's voice trembled. "Please don't hurt her."

"I won't. Not if you close the door."

The metallic click as the door latched was the most despairing sound Rainey had ever heard.

fifteen

. . .

Dale Blodgett returned home feeling distinctly uneasy.

He'd gone up to the Three Sisters Lodge and done a slow circuit around the place. Nothing looked out of order. He'd debated momentarily whether he should go in and have a chat with Maureen, but his common sense rebelled.

He turned the nose of his car toward home. What would he have told her, anyway? That he was investigating her because a bartender and his mother's Tarot cards suggested that she was up to something?

As for Vaughan, it was a safe bet he wouldn't stay put. He was probably up at his secret cave again. If he got attacked by a bear, or fell off a cliff in the dark, it wouldn't be Dale's fault. It wasn't like Vaughan hadn't been warned.

So he pulled into his driveway, but still had the nagging feeling he'd missed something.

This whole thing doesn't add up, he thought as he got out of his car and walked up the dark sidewalk to his front door. How could those kids have been held up in a cave? And why would Slender Man return Vaughan's computer?

He shook his head. There was something he wasn't seeing, here. Some vital piece of the puzzle that would make the rest of it make sense. But that piece was proving to be pretty damned elusive.

His telephone was ringing when he opened the door, and muttering under his breath, he jogged over to it, lifted the receiver, and said, "Hello?" in an irritable voice.

"Officer Blodgett, this is Judy Kahn. I'm sorry to call you at home, but I had no choice."

"What's happened? Do you know where Tyler is?"

"You already know he's disappeared?"

There was something about Judy that always succeeded at putting Dale on the defensive. "Yeah. I went up earlier, and told him to stay put, like you said. But when I checked on him later, he was gone. I think he's been abducted."

"No. He hasn't been abducted. Not yet, at least. Tyler's doing the Knight in Shining Armor thing. He's gone up to the Three Sisters Lodge."

He dropped into his armchair, feeling like he'd been punched in the solar plexus.

"The Lodge? What the fuck is it with the Lodge all of a sudden?" He swallowed. "Pardon my French."

"Tyler left a message on my voicemail saying Maureen Sullivan was behind all of the disappearances, and he was going to go up to the Lodge and rescue Rainey and the kids. We've got to stop him. Or help him. One or the other."

"I... I was just up at the Lodge. It all looked quiet."

There was a pause. "Look, Officer Blodgett. You can come along if you want. If you don't, I'm going by myself. I know, I'm doing what I told Tyler not to do. I don't care. I'm not going to stand by and let him get hurt. And I'm going *now*. So you can sit there and argue if you want, but I'm going to hang up on you and head for my car."

"Wait!" He gave a quick, irritated wave of his hand, not that she could see it. "Okay, okay. You're not going up there alone. Where do you live?"

"I'm at 505 Stone Quarry Road. Second house on the left after you turn off the highway."

"It's on the way. I'll meet you there in five minutes."

"After six minutes, I'll be in my own car, and you'll have to catch up." She hung up.

He swore under his breath, dropped the phone onto his end table, and ran back out of the front door, slamming it shut without locking it.

"You must have broken every speed limit there was," Judy commented with a wry smile, as she jumped into the passenger seat of Dale's car. "That was four and a half minutes flat."

"One of the perks of being a policeman." He accelerated down the road and back toward the highway that led up toward the Lodge. He looked over at her. "Maureen Freakin' *Sullivan* is behind all this?"

"That's what Tyler said, in his message." She gave him a wry glance. "On the other hand, he also said that Slender Man was a good guy."

"Jesus." He frowned and shook his head. "You don't think... maybe, that he was being forced to say all that? To lure us up there?"

She looked out of the window, at the tree trunks slipping past, darker columns against a dark background. "That occurred to me. All I can say is, his voicemail didn't *sound* forced. Tyler's kind of an emotional guy. If he was being threatened, or had a gun to his head or something, I think I could tell." She paused. "He didn't sound scared. He sounded sad. And resigned. Like he figured he was about to die, and was going ahead and trying to be brave anyway."

He shook his head. "Yeah, but Maureen? Why Maureen?"

"Why not?"

"She's not my idea of a criminal mastermind." He shrugged. "But I'm outnumbered. My mom and Dorrie Keene both think she's involved."

"Dorrie, as in Dorrie the bartender?" She sounded incredulous.

"Yeah. My mom told me she was suspicious of her just today." He hoped furiously that Judy wouldn't ask how she knew, and luck was on his side this time. "And then I stopped by Dorrie's for a beer after work, and Dorrie said she noticed that Kevin Torgeson and Kathleen Standish were working up at the Lodge. Dorrie thought it was a weird coincidence."

"I don't. Not anymore."

"I guess I don't, either. But hell, can't you trust nobody? I've known Maureen Sullivan all my life. Disliked her for most of it, but still, I never thought she was some kind of alien spy, or whatever." He winced. "God, it sounds stupid as hell when you say it that way."

She shrugged. "I guess we'll find out one way or the other if they were right," she said as they pulled into the parking lot below the lodge.

He got out of his car and looked around. Everything seemed calm. The lights from the Lodge dining room, and the exterior floodlights, cast a golden glow over the tastefully maintained landscaping. He moved toward the front steps, feeling distinctly foolish. What would he say to Maureen when she appeared at the front door, asking why he was here? "You're under arrest on suspicion of being an evil alien mastermind?"

Next thing, he'd be the one who was being locked up. In the loony bin.

Suddenly, his head rocked back, as if he'd been struck. He looked over at Judy, dazed, and saw that she was standing there, wide-eyed, and in her next step she stumbled and almost fell. He felt the way he had when, as a child, a firecracker had gone off next to his ear, but here, there was no sound at all, and the silence somehow blanked out all the other, ordinary noises for a moment. It was as if, for less than a second, both of them had gone completely, utterly deaf.

"What the hell was that?" she whispered.

"No clue. It felt like my ears popped."

"I've never had my ears pop like that. It was like a sonic boom. Only silent. I know that sounds ridiculous."

"What could cause something like that?"

"I don't know."

Then there was a sudden, and unmistakable noise—a crash, and a shout, from around the side of the Lodge. Dale ran toward it, reflexively drawing his gun, Judy's footsteps slapping the pavement immediately behind him.

As he rounded the corner, he saw something that at first was as baffling as the soundless shock wave—so baffling that for a moment, he couldn't figure out what he was looking at.

That's a weird-looking window… there never was a window there before…

Then he realized it wasn't a window. There was a large hole in the outside wall. The wood, stone, and drywall that had made up that part of the lodge wall had simply ceased to be. There was no rubble, no pieces of broken siding. The edges were as smooth as if they'd been cut.

And through that hole, a tall, skeletally thin figure stood with his back to them.

Slender Man.

Dale ran to the hole in the wall, and as part of him was thinking, *This is the stupidest thing you've ever done in your life,* he climbed across the vaporized edge of the Lodge wall and into the brightly lit interior of what looked like a meeting room. Judy scrambled up behind him, and then he stood there, blinking in the glare of the fluorescent fixtures, trying to see where he was.

There was a long table in the center, such as might be used for a business meeting, or to hold hors d'oeuvres for a party.

Along the wall were overstuffed armchairs, and near the window was a table with magazines, a lamp, and a bookshelf with an assortment of little ceramic statues, all sitting on lace doilies.

Tyler Vaughan stood in one corner with Kevin Torgeson and Kathleen Standish. Kathleen looked like she was in shock. Kevin, for once, had lost all pretense of being a badass, and had a look of abject terror on his face.

Near the hole in the wall, and still as a statue, stood Slender Man, surveying the room with a most seeing look on his eyeless face.

And near the splintered wreckage of a door in the far wall—which looked as if it had been unsuccessfully barricaded with a sofa, before being battered inwards hard enough to split its paneling into tinder—stood two people. One of them was Maureen Sullivan, looking as angry as Dale had ever seen anyone. The other one was... Kevin Torgeson?

Dale turned his gun from one Kevin to the other, and then toward Slender Man, his mouth hanging open a little.

No one moved.

"Jesus Christ, what the actual fuck is going *on* here?"

"Dale!" Tyler shouted desperately. "Don't shoot Slender Man! He's on our side!"

The duplicate Kevin's face showed sudden terror, and he pointed at the real Kevin, standing next to Tyler. "Officer Blodgett, you've got to help me! He's the duplicate! He tried to kill me! And that's the duplicate Kathleen, too!"

Dale turned toward them, frowning.

The fear on the real Kevin's face suddenly vanished in a sardonic sneer. "C'mon, Officer Blockhead, even *you're* not stupid enough to believe *that.*"

Dale said, "Well, that was easier than I thought it would be," and swiveled his gun back toward the duplicate Kevin.

The duplicate launched himself at Dale, lips pulled back in

a rictus of fury that looked almost inhuman. His fingers, splayed like talons, reached toward Dale's throat.

There was a gunshot, and the duplicate Kevin did a face-plant onto the floor. He flopped like a beach fish, ending on his back. His mouth opened and closed soundlessly. Then his backbone arched so that only the back of his head and his heels were touching the floor, and he shuddered. A little bit of blood bubbled from his mouth, and he died, his eyes still wide with fury.

Dale swallowed, and then looked up toward Maureen Sullivan, and his gun swiveled in her direction. She turned toward Slender Man, and a look of freezing hatred passed across her chubby face.

"You can't stop us," she breathed.

And a voice, spoken without speaking, rang in all of their heads. *Oh, but I can.*

She looked at Slender Man's expressionless, featureless face, and then at Dale, still holding his gun pointing at her midsection, and then turned and fled through the broken door.

"Where's Rainey?" Dale asked a little breathlessly, trying to keep his eyes from the body of the boy he had killed. *Not really Kevin,* his mind repeated. *The real Kevin is over there. I didn't just shoot an unarmed teenager. I hope.*

"We don't know." Tyler's voice sounded hopeless, on the verge of tears. "She got separated from us. She and Phil. We think Kathleen has them. The fake Kathleen."

They are nearby.

Dale's eyes popped open, and he whirled to face him. "How can you talk with no mouth?"

Slender Man's voice sounded mildly amused. *There will perhaps be time to discuss that later. For now, we must see about rescuing the woman and the boy. They are in a room nearby.* He turned his smooth face toward Tyler. *You will wish to come.*

It wasn't a question.

Tyler swallowed. "Of course."

"Like hell you're going alone," Judy said. "I mean, no disrespect to you, Mister, um, Mister Man, but I'm here to keep Tyler from doing anything stupid. Lately it's been a full-time occupation."

As you wish. Slender Man turned to Dale. *You must take these two children, and get them safely out of here. I will see to the others. You, I believe, are a law enforcement officer?*

Dale nodded. "Yeah."

You will no doubt be called upon to investigate what has happened here?

"Yeah. Probably."

I recommend waiting until tomorrow morning to take action. You will very likely be contacted by the lodge's staff, reporting that Maureen Sullivan is missing. It might be prudent to pretend surprise.

He nodded again.

"But... the damage to the lodge..." He couldn't help stammering a little. "What happens when I get called by someone who works at the Lodge, and I have to write a report about what happened here? I mean, with dead bodies lying all over, and everything?"

As for the damage the Other did here, and anything left behind by its activities— here he gestured at the body of the duplicate Kevin *—leave that to me. If we are successful tonight, then there will be no trace of what happened here, except for the fact that Maureen Sullivan will never be seen again. If we are not successful, then you will be the only one left who knows the truth, and you must look to protecting your own people.*

Dale nodded, and heard himself say, "I understand." But part of him thought, *I don't really understand. I don't think I'll ever understand what happened tonight.*

He gestured for Kevin and Kathleen to go outside through the hole in the wall, and he followed them. Kevin gave one last, wide-eyed look at the staring, bloodstained body of his duplicate as he passed.

"Good luck, Tyler, Judy," Dale said.

They looked over toward him. Their expressions looked those of soldiers about to go into battle, and who are fully expecting to die.

"Thanks, Dale," Judy said. "You've been awesome. Sorry I was such a bitch to you."

As he jumped through the hole and onto the grassy lawn that surrounded the Lodge, he looked back through the opening.

About a ten percent chance, he thought, that he'd ever see any of them alive again.

He debated briefly turning and running back into the Lodge to try to help, but an odd thought came to him, seeming to come from outside.

All shall be well. For now, get the children back to their parents, and you will have done what you needed to do.

He put his hands on Kevin and Kathleen's shoulders. "My car is right over there. I'm going to get you back home."

sixteen

. . .

Slender Man turned and walked noiselessly across the Tillamook Room, and Tyler and Judy followed him out of the broken doorway and into the hall of the Lodge.

"Is Rainey safe?" Tyler asked, despite himself.

For now.

Judy squeezed his shoulder gently.

They went past the utility rooms, and the laundry, and the door that opened onto the staircase down to the basement. Then the hall turned a corner, and there were several doors with numbers that were probably guest lodging. Slender Man came to room number 14, whose door was slightly ajar.

He reached out his pale, long-fingered hand, and pushed the door open.

They were facing into an elegantly decorated room, with a king-sized bed covered with a colorful quilt, an old-fashioned wooden writing desk, and a loveseat with paisley upholstery. The wall had tasteful watercolor paintings of wildflowers. Near the door a little three-legged table supported a goofy-looking wooden statue of a bear with a toothy grin, standing on its hind legs, with a carved base that said, *Welcome to Oregon. I'm Pleased To Eat You.*

The overhead lights were off. The only illumination came from a lamp on a table near the bed, and it cast eerie shadows on the faces of the three figures who sat on the edge of the bed, posed as if for a photograph.

Kathleen Standish sat in the middle, arms locked around the necks of Rainey and Phil. Her face was frozen, her eyes like steel, and she turned to face Slender Man. "Not one step further, or they both die."

That would be a regrettable action.

"Let me go," Kathleen said, "and I'll release them."

So you realize that your leader has betrayed you?

Her face twisted into a snarl. "She lied to me. She said if you found out about us, she'd make sure I was safe."

It has no need for its tools once they have served their purpose. It will not take any risks to save you now that it sees that it cannot win here.

Kathleen's arms tightened, and Rainey gave a little gasp. "You leave, and let me go. I don't care about Sullivan. But I'm not going to let you get your hands on me. I'll kill them both, I swear I will. I'm not going to wait forever."

Then we are at an impasse, as I will not leave until these two are safe.

She gave a peal of harsh laughter. "I can afford to wait longer than you can, because you have nothing to bargain with, and I can kill them one at a time. Slowly." She looked over at Tyler. "I think I'll start with this one." She gave Rainey a little shake. "Would you like to watch your lover die, Tyler Vaughan?"

Rainey's eyes grew wide, and she clutched at Kathleen's arm as it tightened across her throat.

Tyler turned, and with a quick, almost reflexive motion, grabbed the statue of the smiling bear, and shouting, "I am *so* fucking sick of you people!" he flung the statue at the duplicate Kathleen Standish. It struck her a glancing blow on the forehead and her head rocked backwards.

Howling, she staggered back, and lost her grip on Rainey and Phil. Rainey jumped up and ran forward into Tyler's arms, but Phil stumbled and fell, and Kathleen was on him in a second.

Judy ran and caught the boy's shoulders, pulling him away from Kathleen's clutching fingers, and the boy scrambled on all fours to a spot behind Slender Man, his breath whining in his throat.

Kathleen turned on Judy in fury. Effortlessly, she put one hand in the middle of Judy's chest and flung her through the air like a ragdoll, and she struck the wall with a sickening crunch and collapsed in a heap. Kathleen made a desperate bolt for the door, but in one stride, Slender Man reached the duplicate and picked her up by her throat one-handed, his long fingers squeezing, her feet dangling a foot from the ground. Her eyes bulged, and her cheeks turned red. Her mouth moved soundlessly. Her hands grasped ineffectually at Slender Man's thin, impossibly strong arm. Then, just as before, there was a sudden shudder that ran through her body, like the cracking of whip, and Slender Man dropped the duplicate's body onto the floor with a thump.

Tyler held Rainey, rocking her slightly, and looked up at Slender Man who was watching them—if that was the right word—with the familiar curious tilt of the head that Tyler had first seen on a camera image, what felt like a decade ago. Phil sat in a corner, leaning against the wall, his eyes wide and unseeing. He looked like he was in shock.

There was a groan from the side of the room, and Tyler looked over at where Judy had fallen. She lay on the floor, her right leg twisted awkwardly underneath her. Her face was chalky white in the artificial glare of the lamp.

He stared at her for a moment, his brain shouting recriminations at him. *God, I'm such an asshole! She looks like she's dying! I was so relieved that Rainey was okay that I almost forgot about Judy!* He pulled out his cellphone, and said, "We've got to get an ambulance up here!"

Wait.

Slender Man walked over and crouched down by Judy. She turned a terrified face toward him as he leaned over her, looking like a spectral scarecrow, his featureless face shining slightly. He reached out, and lifted her broken leg. Judy screamed and writhed as his fingers first straightened out her leg, and then tightened over the injury.

Then her breath caught in a whistling gasp, and she shuddered.

"What did you do?"She looked up at him, her voice weak. She sat up, and flexed her leg carefully.

Slender Man reached down with one long, spidery hand, and helped her to her feet.

It is better to heal than to destroy. I have had to do both tonight. I much prefer the former.

"Thank you." Judy went over to where Tyler and Rainey stood.

And there is other healing to do. Physical hurts are often not the worst. He went over to Phil and knelt, his long, spidery limbs folding as he crouched, making him look more inhuman than ever. He touched Phil's face with one thin finger.

Child. You know that you are safe now?

Phil looked up at him, his eyes still blank, but tears streaming down his face. "Yes." His voice was high, thin.

This will be a difficult time for you. Your task will be to forget what has happened here. The ones who wished to harm you are gone. They will not return. You have nothing more to fear.

"But, they…" And finally Phil's voice hitched a sob, but he controlled it with an effort. "They could come back. They could kidnap me again. Make another… another me, like they did before."

They will not do so. I will be watching.

"You'll protect me?"

It is my work. You have my word. And these others —he gestured toward Tyler and Rainey— *they have risked much to help you. They are your friends, and they will not abandon you, either. If you need to talk to them, in the coming days, when you find yourself frightened again, you will go to them. They will understand, and help you. And with time, your fear will become less.*

Phil nodded.

They will bring you home now. Slender Man paused. *You have nothing more to fear.*

He stood, straightening his thin legs. He offered his hand to Phil, and Phil unhesitatingly put his small hand into Slender Man's pale, long-fingered one. They walked over to the others, and Slender Man placed Phil's hand in Rainey's.

You should leave now. I will deal with what has happened here. I am certain by now that the Other has fled. It does not remain behind to contemplate its defeat. You see how it left its own comrades to their fate.

"I can't believe that all this noise hasn't had guests and staff swarming the place," Tyler said.

The Other has ways of keeping curious eyes from prying, as I did, up at the cave. You may be certain that no one has had the slightest desire to come down this hallway this evening. I am guessing that the guests all felt oddly sleepy tonight, and have retired to their rooms early, and that no one has seen or heard anything unusual.

"So now, we just… go home?" Tyler said.

Yes. I will manage this. You take care of your own needs, and find your way home. What has happened here is over.

Judy looked back at Slender Man, and then walked out into the hall, still stepping a little gingerly on her right leg.

"C'mon, then," she said, and Tyler put his arm around Rainey's waist, and they followed her, Phil with his hand still tightly clasped in Rainey's. They went down the hallway toward the exit, meeting no one. A lone young man sat at the front desk, and he gave them a nod and a smile as they left, as if nothing out of the ordinary had happened that evening, as if they were guests who had every right to be there.

They were crossing the parking lot when there was another explosion of soundless sound, and Tyler knew that the space where the hole had been was now filled up with timbers, showing not so much as a crack or a scar.

"I wish I could do that," Judy said.

"I'd be just as happy never to see anything of the kind again." Tyler tightened his arm around Rainey's waist, and they walked back toward the parking lot, and the waiting car that would bring them back to their homes and lives.

epilogue

. . .

Rainey Carrington stood at the stove in her bathrobe, stirring a pot of oatmeal. She added a couple of shakes from the cinnamon bottle, and then a dollop of honey, smiling at the waves of fragrance that came up with the steam. She walked to the table and set the pot down on a hot pad, then went to the fridge to get orange juice.

Tyler came into the kitchen, yawning, his chestnut-brown hair in disarray, clad only in a pair of old sweat pants. He came up behind her, slipped his arm around her waist, and rested his head on her shoulder.

"Hi," she said. "You didn't want to wake up, this morning."

He kissed her on the ear, and she smiled and carried the pitcher of orange juice to the table.

"Breakfast is ready. You need to eat. You have an interview today, remember?"

"I know." He stretched, his spine cracking pleasantly, and

then sat down at the table. "I'm still not sure what to make of it."

"You'll find out when you get there." She spooned oatmeal into his bowl, and filled his glass with juice.

"No harm in checking it out, I guess."

"Exactly." She rested her elbow on the table, and her chin in her hand. "Do you still miss working at the lab?"

"Sometimes. I was lucky that Mason Cleary gave me a job at the hardware store right here in the village, after I got fired. I think that was Dale's doing. He's a decent guy, Dale."

She nodded. "But you miss the lab."

He nodded. "Mostly, I miss actually doing science. It was what I was trained for, and I still feel like it's what I should be doing. Plus, I miss working with Judy. She's awesome."

"We have her over for dinner all the time."

"I know. But it's different than being colleagues."

"I'm sure."

He sighed. "Plus, I think I still feel kind of humiliated that I got fired."

"You suspected it was coming."

"I know. But it was painful even so." He shook his head. "Joe felt bad. You could tell he didn't want to do it. But he saw the handwriting on the wall. I was a liability. Funding in science is so competitive, he couldn't afford having a drag on the market."

"Well, you're not a drag on *my* market," she said lightly, and touched his shoulder.

He looked up and smiled.

"I don't know if this is the direction for me. This job, I mean," he added hurriedly. "Not *you*."

"Like I said, there's only one way to find out. All it's costing you is some time and a drive to Portland."

He looked out of the window. "It's cold and miserable out today."

"There won't be any snow once you get to Eugene. After

that, just drizzle. And I'll have a fire going, and me and Bonkers and Ahab will be here waiting for you when you get home."

He looked at her, and smiled. "That sounds awesome. Whatever happens with the job."

Tyler pulled over at a roadside rest stop along I-5 for lunch and a brief catnap at a little after noon. He'd packed a peanut butter and jelly sandwich, an apple, and a thermos of coffee, and after these were duly consumed he tilted his seat back and settled in. The interview wasn't until three o'clock, and he was making good time, despite the drizzle and fog that was a constant companion during winter in the Pacific Northwest.

Before he dozed off, he pulled the scrap of paper out of his pocket, and looked at it again. He'd torn it from the "Help Wanted" section of the *Portland Tribune* the previous week. It said:

Wanted: Zoologist, to lead expeditions to exotic lands. Must be comfortable in wilderness situations. Experience with cryptozoology helpful. Call to schedule an interview. Euphoric Esotericists Travel Agency, Inc., 330 West Helmetsie Avenue, Portland, OR. (503) 237-7088.

"Euphoric Esotericists." He chuckled. "Just the name would have had me running for my life, six months ago. Now, I might be working for 'em." Then drowsiness overtook him, and he slept.

And dreamed.

In his dream, Slender Man was talking to him, from right outside the car, leaning over, his pale, featureless face close to the window, rainwater trickling down the smooth surfaces where eyes, nose, and mouth should have been.

You are about to step forward, Tyler Vaughan. His unmistakable voice struck like a bell on the inside of Tyler's skull.

"What does that mean?" His voice was muzzy with sleep.

Your work. I have my work, you have yours. Yours is about to carry you far away.

"I don't want to be far away. I want to be with Rainey."

She will be part of it. The two of you cannot be separated that easily. But you must be brave. You have always feared the unknown.

"I'm not a brave person."

People are not brave. Acts are brave. When you stood up against the Other and its minions, to save the woman you loved, that was a brave act. Today will require a different kind of bravery—the courage to let yourself not understand, at first. The courage not to know.

"Rainey once told me that I didn't like not knowing all of the answers. That I was a scientist because it fooled me into thinking that there are always answers to be found."

There is nothing wrong with seeking answers. But in order to find them, you have to be willing to let yourself be ignorant, and not to fear your own lack of understanding. It will be hard for you, but you are capable of it.

"Why did you come to tell me this?"

I owed you that much for your help with the Other. It was not easy for you, I know. And you have lost your livelihood because of it.

"Not only because of that. Also because I opened up my big, fat mouth on *Good Morning America*."

And all of those acts led to your saving three innocent children's lives, and the life of Rainey Carrington, and it also led to your finding love. I would not call that an unfair trade.

"Me either. But is this interview going to be that scary?"

Simply do not question what happens. Understand it with your heart, not your mind. It will only frighten you if you try to explain it with the part of your brain that is convinced that it knows everything.

"I'll try."

You trusted me once, and you saw the results. Trust me now.

"But this is a dream. You're not really here."

Once, I affected your emotions at a distance. Why do you think I could not also speak to you at a distance, while you sleep?

"It's pretty hard to believe all this."

You are still trying to understand. Do not worry about understanding everything right away. Here, it is only necessary to listen to your heart. Trust that understanding will follow.

"I'll try," Tyler said again, a little more indistinctly, and turned his head against the seat headrest, and fell deeper into sleep, into a place where no dreams could follow.

Tyler looked up at the building in front of him, and checked the address on the torn scrap of paper for a third time. 330 West Helmetsie Avenue. Yes, that was right. But the store-front he stood in front of was about as far from his concept of a travel agency as he could imagine. It was, in fact, a garish, and rather run-down, Chinese trinket shop. The sign over the door was in Chinese characters, with no English transla-tion. An oversized gilt foo dog sat in the window, giving him a toothy grin. Brass incense burners, faux-jade ornaments, and draperies of gaudy silk sat on shelves and hung from racks.

He looked at the other shops on the street. There were only two close by—a rather skeevy looking dim sum place, and an herbal medicine store. Neither looked promising, so he walked forward, with some trepidation.

As he opened the door, a bell jingled. A wizened old Chinese woman sitting behind the counter looked up as he entered.

The woman said, "Welcome to *Te Gao Jia Fei Wu Dian*," in a voice that sounded like an unoiled gate.

"I..." He stopped and swallowed. "I thought this was a travel agency. I'm here about a job."

"Oh. Travel agency," she said, acting not at all surprised. "Okay, come with me." She got up and motioned for him to follow her. They walked through a door behind the counter, and then up a rickety set of wooden stairs.

The woman opened the door at the top. "Down there, on right. First door." She raised one eyebrow, and gave him a cryptic smile. "My name is Patty." She thwacked him on the shoulder. "I like you. I'll tell Jared that. You won't have any problems."

The left wall had several windows that overlooked a disreputable back yard. The first door on the right had a sign that said, *Euphoric Esotericists Travel Agency, est. 1984.* He pushed the door open.

A battered IKEA desk stood inside, covered with papers. There was a chair with a gouge in the seat, and an end table that looked like it was on the verge of collapse from the weight of three magazines, two *National Geographics* and a *Time* that was six weeks out of date. Otherwise, the room was empty. Then an inner door opened, and a tall, thin man emerged, dark blond wavy hair pulled back into a ponytail. His movements radiated an intense, chaotic energy, as if he was driven by an engine that was always on the verge of overwhelming the mechanism it powered. His body was all points—sharp elbows, a prominent Adam's apple, angular cheekbones and chin. His skin was tanned, with crow's feet around eyes of startlingly different color. One bright blue, one golden brown.

"I'm Jared Alvey." He clasped Tyler's hand. "You must be Tyler Vaughan. You called about the job, I think. Zoologist, right? Come in, come in."

He followed Jared, already puzzling over how differently

this interview had gone than any other he'd ever had. Even for summer jobs as a teenager, he'd had to step forward, identify himself, and act professional. Jared, however, seemed not to care anything for professionalism. Tyler had the impression that he could have showed up in his sweat pants, and Jared would have neither noticed nor cared.

"Sit." Jared gestured at a chair that was about the only surface in the room that didn't have something on it. A variety of bizarre items stood on tables, in corners, hung on the walls—masks, maps, skins, skulls, leather-bound books, a huge tribal drum, and a rather deadly-looking metal-bladed spear standing in the corner.

He looked around him in wonder.

"So." Jared fixed his odd, bicolored gaze on his face. "When can you start?"

"Start?" he sputtered, and realized that was the first word he'd said since he'd walked into the office. "But you haven't even interviewed me!"

"Oh, yes. I suppose we should do that, shouldn't we? Observe the niceties and ceremonies and rituals, and all that sort of my-word-what-a-lovely-place-you-have, here-have-a-cup-of-coffee kind of stuff. Rituals are important, you know." He raised an eyebrow. "*Very* important." His voice dropped a little as if to emphasize the significance of what he'd said.

Tyler stared at him, a bewildered expression on his face.

"Not what you expected, I'm sure," Jared said.

"I didn't think you'd be upstairs from a Chinese gift shop."

Jared laughed. "Oh, that's really part of the operation. It's a front. Did Patty give you her usual greeting?"

"What?"

"Welcome to *Te Gao Jia Fei Wu Dian*."

"Yeah, she said something like that."

"She does that to all of the white people who come in."

"What does it mean?"

"It means 'Overpriced Crap Store.' It's her little joke."

"So Patty is an—"

"Don't call her an employee," Jared said hurriedly. "At least not in her hearing. You want her on your side. *Employee* sounds subservient. She's a member of the permanent staff. She'll help to train you once you officially start work here."

"But… don't you want to know my qualifications?"

Jared pawed through a few papers on his desk, and finally selected one. "Let's see. Tyler Vaughan. B.S. in biology from the University of Arizona. M.S. same, specialty in mammalogy. I believe your thesis on dominance hierarchies in ungulates was very well received?" He looked up and smiled.

Tyler goggled at him.

"Ph.D. from the University of Oregon, three years ago. Hired virtually immediately afterwards at the Cascadia Zoological Research Station. Stellar performance until a little problem, oh, what was it? Last summer some time, I believe. Hardly your fault, from what it appears. Narrow-minded educational middle management and foolish priorities by funding agencies. Trust me that we won't hold *that* against you."

"How…" Tyler choked a little on the word. "How did you find all that out?"

Jared patted a laptop, one of the only concessions to modern technology in the room. "The internet is a wonderful invention, don't you think? I could have also looked up names of friends and former lovers, but I thought that was inappropriate. We don't want to pry, after all."

"And so… you think…"

"I think you'll be ideal. Usually, you have to run the gauntlet with my secretary, Armas, and my coworkers Miles and Conrad. Conrad is my son, but please don't hold that against him." He laughed at his own joke. "Conrad is off on expedition currently, Miles is on his week's vacation visiting family in Bucharest, and Armas… well, Armas is… away. I really shouldn't say more. But suffices to say we're short-handed at present. I recently hired a personal assistant named Helen, but we could use the technical expertise of a scientist like yourself." He looked down at an appointment calendar on his desk, and flipped a few pages. "We have an expedition leaving for Indonesia in"—he counted rapidly, jabbing the calendar with a bony forefinger—"sixteen days. It should be enough time for you to familiarize yourself with the fauna, crypto and otherwise, that we're likely to find there. Two-month expedition. More excitement than you should be legally allowed to have." He smiled engagingly, odd eyes glittering.

"And you're going there looking for what, exactly?"

"You have heard of *Homo floresiensis*?"

"Um, yes. That's the little extinct hominid that lived some-where in south Asia, up till twelve thousand or so years ago. Coexisted with modern humans for thousands of years, they think. I read a paper about it a while back."

"You have many of the particulars correct, with the excep-tion of the word *extinct* and your use of the past tense."

Tyler stared at him. "They're still alive?"

"Yes. They are only one of many species that are known, in colloquial speech, as 'Yetis' or 'Bigfoots.'"

He took a deep breath. All of the phrases he'd saved up since the ill-fated *Good Morning America* interview rushed through his mind, and he forced them back, with some difficulty.

"Bigfoots?" was all he said.

"That's what they're commonly called, of course. Not what they call *themselves*." Jared gave him a canny look. "Some of the more primitive species are probably allied to the lineage we now know as australopithecines. Others are more advanced. *Homo floresiensis* is of uncertain intelligence and advancement levels, as they have never been intensely stud-ied, until now. We are going there to make first contact."

"So, you believe they actually exist?" Tyler said, before he could stop himself.

Jared stared at him for a moment, and then burst into guffaws. "I shouldn't think we'd be likely to fund an expedition chasing something that doesn't exist, do you?"

"I guess not."

"So, can we count you in?"

Tyler took a deep breath. "I'm not a primatologist."

"I know that," Jared said, patiently. "Can we count you in?"

"I don't have the money for a plane ticket."

"All expenses paid, of course."

"I, um. I'd have to discuss it with my girlfriend. I mean, we live together and all, so I can't just…"

"Bring her along."

"What?" He shook his head, attempting to clear away the confusion.

"Bring her along." Jared spoke slowly and with exaggerated clarity. "Your love interest. Your sweetheart. Your *petite chou*. She's very welcome to come along. We have to keep our staff in good spirits, you know, and having you pining away missing your girlfriend for eight weeks isn't exactly a recipe for keeping you working happily."

He had the sudden feeling of swimming in a fast-flowing river, and being dragged along faster and faster, despite his desperate attempts to fight the current.

"We have pets," he said, a little breathlessly.

"Patty loves animals," Jared said confidently. "You can trust them to her while you're away. She'll relate to them on quite their own level, trust me. And you'll return to find them fat and happy, and probably highly reluctant to return home."

"But…" He tried furiously to think of another reason to argue. "Passports? Visas?"

"Taken care of."

"How?"

"We have connections." Jared wiggled his eyebrows again. "Channels. Strings to pull. There won't be any difficulty."

"What about safety? Danger? You know?" Tyler heard himself speak, and thought, *Geez, you just sounded like the biggest weenie in the world.*

Jared apparently didn't notice the increasingly desperate tone in his voice. "Oh, of course there's danger. That's nothing new to you, having worked with animals as you have. And, you know, we're quite reassured on that account by your… your recent activities."

"But…"

Jared waved a dismissive hand. "No need to bring up that unpleasantness again. A terrifying episode in your life, I'm quite sure. But it all ended happily, and that's what counts. Your role was really quite heroic, you know. Quite heroic. And heroism of that sort never remains secret." He patted his laptop affectionately again. "Nor should it, in my opinion."

"I need time to think about this." He looked around frantically, and felt a sudden desire to run away.

"Starting salary is sixty thousand dollars a year. Plus expenses incurred on expedition, of course. And we even throw in free transportation of your body home, and burial costs, in case of… shall we say, unfortunate occurrences."

And in his head, a solemn, bell-like voice intoned the words, *Trust me now… do not question what happens. Understand it with your heart, not your mind. It will only frighten you if you try to explain it with the part of your brain that is convinced that it knows everything.*

His heart was pounding, and it was with a kind of disbelief that he heard himself say, "Okay, sold. I'll need to return home for a few days to get my things in order. I'll… we'll… be back early next week."

Jared reached across the desk, and Tyler found his hand enveloped in Jared's strong bony one. "Excellent. I think you're in for the adventure of a lifetime."

a request

Please do us a favor to help other readers find Gordon and his books.

On social media: likes, comments, and shares go a LONG way. Links are in the next section.

Follows and reviews are critical: If you liked this book, please tell the world! It just takes a moment of your time and will really help us out. Amazon, BookBub (https://www.bookbub.com/authors/gordon-bonnet), and Goodreads (https://www.goodreads.com/author/show/4779649.Gordon_Bonnet) are the best places to start.

And anywhere else you search for or buy books.

Thanks! - GB and CB, the Little Bustards

about the author

Gordon Bonnet has been writing fiction for decades. Encouraged when his story "Crazy Bird Bends His Beak" won critical acclaim in Mrs. Moore's 1st grade class at Central Elementary School in St. Albans, West Virginia, he embarked on a long love affair with the written word.

His interest in the paranormal goes back almost that far. Introduced to speculative, fantasy, and science fiction by such giants in the tradition as Madeleine L'Engle, Lloyd Alexander, Isaac Asimov, C. S. Lewis, and J. R. R. Tolkien, he was captivated by those writers' abilities to take the reader to a fictional world and make it seem tangible, to breathe life and passion and personality into characters who were (sometimes) not even human. He made journeys into darker realms upon meeting the works of Edgar Allen Poe and H. P. Lovecraft during his teenage years, and those authors still influence his imagination and his writing to this day.

This fascination with the paranormal, however, has always been tempered by Gordon's scientific training. This has led to a strange duality: his work as a teacher, skeptic and debunker on the popular blog *Skeptophilia,* while simultaneously writing paranormal and speculative novels, novellas, and short stories. Gordon explains this, with a smile: "Well, I do know it's fiction, after all."

He blogs daily, and is never without a piece of fiction in progress—driven to continue (as he puts it) "because I want to find out how the story ends." From historical fiction (*Kári the Lucky*), to murder mysteries (the Parsifal Snowe Mysteries, beginning with *Poison the Well*), to paranormal fiction with a humorous twist (*Periphery* and *Lock & Key*) to the truly terrifying (*Gears* and *Descent into Ulthoa*), Gordon's fiction has something for all tastes!

Find him conversing with his dogs (and perhaps his wife) in Trumansburg, NY, or the following platforms:
- Website *http://www.gordonbonnet.com*
- YouTube *https://youtube.com/@skeptophilia1509*
- Skeptophilia blog *http://www.skeptophilia.com/*
- Twitter *@TalesOfWhoa*
- TikTok *@LittleBustardBooks* and *@gordonbonnetauthor*
- Instagram *@skygazer227*

Or, ya know, the Google.

also by gordon bonnet

In the Midst of Lions (Book One of Arc of the Oracles)

The Scattering Winds (Book Two of Arc of the Oracles)

The Chains of Orion (Book Three of Arc of the Oracles)

The Communion of Shadows

Behind the Frame

Gears

Sephirot

Descent into Ulthoa

Lock & Key

The Shambles

Kári the Lucky

Kill Switch

The Fifth Day

Snowe Mysteries *(beginning re-releases 2023)*

Book 1: Poison the Well

Book 2: Dead Letter Office

Book 3: Face Value

Snowe Mysteries *(available now)*

Book 4: Past Imperfect

Book 5: Room for Wrath

Book 6: The Obituary Collector

Book 7: Slings and Arrows

The Boundary Solution Series (stay tuned for re-releases)

Sign up for Gordon's Little Bustard Books Newsletter and Obscure Weird Tidbits at his website: http://www.gordonbonnet.com

excerpt from "the shambles"

. . .

At a little after two a.m., Officer Khalil Mansour passed the cell where Cyprian Grove was being held. Rosa Lamperez had told Mansour about the shoplifter's odd outfit —"He looks like he got dressed in the dark from inside a dumpster"—and Mansour, who had just gotten off shift and was ready to clock out, was curious enough to take a look.

Grove was in the middle of the cell, on all fours, head down.

Was he puking?

But the guy didn't seem to be sick. He was moving his hand along the floor, backing up a little at a time, his nose inches from the cement, frowning in intense concentration. Between his fingers he held a piece of chalk. He was drawing a line on the floor, every so often turning his head to sight down it, checking it for straightness.

With his face nearly resting on the dirty cement, he met Mansour's eyes and gave him an impish grin.

"Got to make sure it's as straight as I can manage." Grove's tone was conversational tone, although his words were a little muffled because he was still in the odd position with his cheek near the cold concrete surface and his skinny butt in the air. "Hope you don't mind my drawing on the floor, though. I'm not usually a graffiti artist."

"You need to stop," Mansour said. "Give the chalk to me."

"Nope." Grove looked up with an amiable smile. "When they frisked me and emptied my pockets, they missed this. Fortunately. I always carry it in case of an emergency."

"An emergency?"

Why was he letting this guy draw him into a conversation? Rosa had been right. He was a wacko. It was time to just go in there and take the chalk.

A card key allowed any on-duty officer to get in the cell quickly in case of an emergency. Mansour reached out to swipe the key in the reader, and Grove chuckled.

"Oh, no, you don't. Getting tackled once in a night is enough." He continued his line on the floor all the way to the back wall, stood and looked Mansour right in the eyes. "Hope it's straight enough. It'll have to do."

The light on the lock turned green. Mansour pulled the cell door open. At the same moment Grove, wearing a goofy grin, wiggled his fingers. "Ta-ta, now, Officer. Give my regards to the muscle-bound guy who arrested me, and the cutie who took my fingerprints."

Then Cyprian Grove stomped on the chalk line with the foot wearing the dress shoe. It made a resounding smack.

Mansour ran through the door. "What the..." He stopped, looking around the cell as if he expected Grove to reappear like a stage magician, sitting cross-legged on the bed, holding a white rabbit in one hand.

The cell was empty.

Police Captain Sarah Persinger leaned back in her chair, and gave the three cops who were seated in her office a pissed-off glare.

"Okay, Mansour, you're telling me Cyprian Grove vanished. Stomped his foot, and went through the floor like jail cells come equipped with some kind of fucking trap door."

"Captain, you saw the CCTV camera footage..." Mansour began.

"What I *saw* was that as soon as you opened the cell door, he dropped down on all fours, and after that mostly what I saw was your backside."

"That's because he was gone."

Her eyes narrowed. "Don't give me that bullshit. People can't go through cement floors, but they *can* crawl. And the only way he got out of that cell is past you."

"Then where did he go, Captain?" Lamperez said. "If he got out past Mansour, or behind him or whatever, the guy would still have to get through the locked door at the end of the hallway. The CCTV down there doesn't show anything."

Persinger gave her a sour look. "I wasn't the one who was there. I also wasn't the one who opened the cell door immediately before a prisoner escaped."

"He was drawing a line on the floor with a piece of chalk," Mansour said.

"I don't care if he was writing out one of Shakespeare's fucking sonnets. You had no reason to open the cell door."

"Grove didn't get out through the door, Captain." Mansour thrust his chin out.

"Well, I can tell you he didn't turn himself sideways and go through a chalk line on the floor." Persinger turned toward Williamson, who had been sitting in silence the entire time, his eyes distant. "What about you, Williamson? What can you tell us about our magical disappearing man?"

Williamson shook his head. "There's something wrong

with him. Wrong in the head, you know? He was shoplifting all of this food, looking me right in the face as he did it. When I took him down, he laughed, like it was no big deal." He met Persinger's eyes steadily. "Like he knew he didn't have anything to worry about. Like he knew he could get away if he needed to."

Persinger snorted. "So you believe Mansour's story, that this man fell through a crack in the jail cell floor?"

No one spoke.

She shoved the paper away. "We need to find this guy and get him back into custody. Because right now, all four of us are looking like incompetents who can't even keep an unarmed shoplifter locked up for the night. I'm gonna have to file a report on this, and when the Chief of Police sees it, which he will, it's gonna make the whole lot of us look like the Keystone Cops. Internal Affairs is gonna investigate this thing from top to bottom no matter what, but we need to do whatever we can to stop this from blowing up in our faces. I want Grove found." She moved her glare to Mansour., and then to Lamperez. "I want him brought back in, and I want it done before the Chief of Police hands me my ass on a platter. Understood?"

"Yes, ma'am," all three said.

As they were leaving, Williamson turned to Mansour. "I believe you, Khalil. There was something weird about that guy. He wasn't no ordinary shoplifter, that's for damn sure."

Mansour shook his head. "I saw it, Dean. I saw it with my own eyes. He was drawing a line on the floor with this little stub of chalk. And he said something about always carrying it with him, because it could come in handy in an emergency. Then he stepped on the line, and went right through it." He held out one hand, palm upward. "I can't explain it any better than you can. But I'm as sure of it as I am that I'm standing here right now. Persinger can threaten me all she wants, but I'm not going to lie."

"So maybe she's right about one thing. Maybe we need to find Cyprian Grove and see if we can figure out what the hell is going on here." His expression was grim. "But if we do catch that crazy sumbitch again, I'm gonna check his pockets for chalk."

From "The Shambles" by Gordon Bonnet. Look for the re-release in April 2024 from Little Bustard Books.

www.ingramcontent.com/pod-product-compliance
Lightning Source LLC
Chambersburg PA
CBHW032028310726
48972CB00002B/570